Earth's Greatest Hero Is Missing!

But Who's the New Guy?

It's a crisis on some Earth or other when a lab experiment gone wrong hurtles young physicist Matt Dawson through the dimensions. He winds up on a world much like our own except costumed super-heroes with scientifically impossible abilities actually exist there.

Meanwhile, the greatest hero of them all has mysteriously disappeared, and his long-time arch-enemy is losing no time setting an enormous criminal master-plan into motion.

It's not Matt's world or his fight — but should he get involved anyway? Especially since he has super-powers himself?

But forces bigger than he knows are stirring... and in the end he may not even have a choice.

Astroman
Book One

The Secret Citadel

Dwight R. Decker

Vesper Press
Northlake, IL

Cover and facing title page illustration by Alan Fletcher Bradford
"Broken Symmetry" illustration by Sam Kujava

Interior illustrations are original or in the public domain.

Some indirect references to commercial properties and fictional characters are made for purposes of parody. Names of actual celebrities and properties are used for purposes of verisimilitude, without endorsement or authorization by their respective owners. No effect or claim on trademark or ownership status is intended or should be inferred. All characters are fictitious and bear no relation or resemblance to anyone with the same or similar names.

*V*Vesper Press

Northlake, Illinois

Dedication

In Memory of Otto Binder
1911 – 1974

As a writer, he had an irrepressible sense of humor that made science fiction and comic books fun and joyous, even despite the tragedies of his life. He also invented many of the concepts that this book… er, pays homage to.

Contents

Part One

Broken Symmetry

SAM
KUJAVA

Chapter One: **When Worlds Intersect**

Couldn't this crisis wait until morning? Matt Dawson thought with a yawn as he drove through the warm spring night and passed under the "Broken Symmetry" sculpture spanning the road at the entrance to the Fermilab grounds.

The sculpture was actually three metal partial arches not quite meeting each other overhead, supposedly representing the symmetry of a perfect universe that was broken by the Big Bang, when the purity of absolute nothing was disrupted by the violent addition of something.

As his well-aged, third-hand car headed along the road towards the brilliant shining column of lights ahead in the darkness, Matt ruefully reflected on how for him, the purity of nothing had been a wonderfully refreshing dreamless sleep, violently disrupted by his phone going off. He had spent a week of days and nights on this project, grabbing an hour's nap here and half an hour's doze there, until Dr. Farber found him nodding over his laptop and ordered him to go back to his apartment and get in some real sleeping time. That would have been fine, except Dr. Farber then called him two hours later and told him to get back to the lab at once.

That was Fermilab, the Fermi National Accelerator Laboratory, named after pioneering physicist Enrico Fermi, a scientific research institution on the prairie south of Chicago where particle beams were generated and accelerated in a huge underground ring some two miles in circumference. Nearby was an even larger ring six miles around, but now no longer used.

Matt turned into the parking lot near the main building and pulled the car into the first available space. He jumped out and trotted across the pavement with a relaxed, easy grace that belied the fact that he was several hours short of sleep. He was a twenty-four year-old grad student who had always tried to stay in shape, with short, dark hair and a closely-trimmed mustache and beard combination. Even though he looked more like a young athlete than a scientist, he wouldn't have been here if he hadn't shown academic promise.

But even so... he glanced overhead, saw stars twinkling in the velvety black sky, and briefly thought of the road not taken. Astronomy was where his heart was — but not very many job openings, and physics had seemed the safer bet for a solid career. Sometimes he wondered if perhaps he should have followed his heart after all.

Ahead towered an oasis of light in the surrounding darkness. It could have been a resort hotel, a free-standing monolith sixteen stories high rising in splendid isolation out of the Illinois farmland. Beyond were the regularly spaced lights of a vast circle that resembled a racetrack, marking the ring of the particle accelerator that lay buried beneath the prairie.

Matt pushed through the front doors and came into the vast entrance hall. The building was actually two narrow office buildings standing side by side, with the space between them glassed in as a colossal atrium. Though the interior design was late 20th Century modern, the architect had reportedly been inspired by a medieval French cathedral in the layout of the enormous enclosed space. Overhead, the atrium walls were rowed with balconies all the way to the roof sixteen floors up, while in front of Matt, the center was landscaped with a large plot of grass and small trees.

The atrium may have been nearly deserted at that hour, but the corridors in the office section bustled with activity as scientists, grad students, and technicians hurried in both directions. Yet the noise was strangely subdued, with only occasional muffled muttering and no laughter. Something had gone very wrong, Matt knew. A former director of Fermilab had once described science in action as "drinking champagne out of styrofoam glasses at one in the morning because somebody did something right." If the experiment had been successful, everyone would have been laughing and talking and toasting each other, but there was none of that tonight.

Matt spotted someone he knew in the crowd, a fellow grad student named Winkler, and stopped him as he tried to rush past.

"I just got here," Matt told him. "What's going on?"

Winkler, a somewhat overweight young man with a short beard and no mustache, was out of breath and gave every impression that he really had to be somewhere else, but paused for a moment to snap, "The experiment failed."

"But how did it fail?" Matt asked. "What happened?"

Winkler was obviously trying to get away and leave it at that, but decided to elaborate at least a little. "That's just it. Nothing happened."

"What do you mean, nothing happened?" Matt pressed. "When you accelerate a proton beam to nearly light-speed, something has to happen!" A beam with an energy of 120 billion electron volts and over a megawatt of sheer power doesn't just waft away with the wind.

"If we knew why, we'd be halfway to fixing the problem, wouldn't we? But no, we simply lost beam, like we were pouring all that energy into a hole in space and nothing came back out. Patel thinks one of the magnets in the Main Injector went down and that may have something to do with it, so the tech guys are checking it out now." Winkler then broke away, blurting, "Go see Dr. Farber in the control room — he'll know something if anybody does!" He raced off, leaving Matt almost as puzzled as before.

This was extraordinary. The experiment was supposed to have been routine, not even breaking new ground but a test to confirm some odd results from a previous run, and to train some of the newer grad students and technicians in leading-edge neutrino research. It was so routine that Matt didn't even have to be present for the actual event.

He stopped in the control room where worried-looking young men and women sat at long desktops along the walls and pored over banks of glowing screens mounted in front of them. No one looked very happy here, either, nor did they have any more time to answer Matt's questions than Winkler had. Only the boss could tell him what he needed to know.

As Matt came up, Dr. Farber, a short, portly man of about forty-five in a sport shirt, sat staring at a large screen on a desk and swore.

"It's still not right!" The project's principal investigator took a moment to wipe sweat off the glistening bald spot on top of his head, and glowered at the placidly glowing screen as though sheer force of will could change the numbers it was insistently displaying.

Matt stepped to Dr. Farber's side and took a look at the screen himself, though it didn't tell him a whole lot. "I came as fast as I could."

Dr. Farber barely glanced up to acknowledge him and typed a few lines on the keyboard in front of the screen. "Sorry to get you out of bed, Dawson, but we've got a problem here."

"Winkler told me a little," Matt said.

Dr. Farber frowned. "A little would be overstating the case. We don't know anything except that we're pouring energy in and getting nothing back. If I didn't know better, I'd say everything was working perfectly."

"What do you want me to do?" Matt asked.

"You'll be my gopher," Dr. Farber told him. "I can't be everywhere at once and everybody else is busy, so…"

In other words, as the lowest ranking grad student on the team, Matt would be the one to do the non-critical drudge work. Oh well, it was what they had hired him for. If he wanted to put a positive spin on it, it was all part of his education and training.

Dr. Farber was interrupted by the phone in his shirt pocket. He pulled it out and answered. After listening for a few moments, he looked back at Matt. "It may not be anything but at least it's the slightest hint of something that may lead to something that has a suggestion of a possible clue. Carhart says they aren't just getting anomalous readings from one of the magnets out on the ring, there's something else going on. As in, 'You've gotta see *this*!' He wouldn't tell me what I so urgently have to see, just that I have to see it for myself to believe it. So who knows what's happening out there. Take a cart and go check on it, then get back to me if it's something worth following up."

Not much later, Matt was wearing a hardhat and driving one of the facility's electric golf carts down the narrow access tunnel that followed the accelerator ring all two miles around. Along one wall was the ring itself, an endless band of tubes, box-like containers for the ultra-powerful magnets, and thick swathes of cabling connecting everything, overhead were regularly spaced fluorescent lights that shone with stark white light, and on the other side was blank concrete. Ahead was only a bleak and dreary vista of endless tunnel.

The questionable magnet was about half a mile in. When Matt reached it, he found a couple of parked carts along the wall and a trio of hardhat-wearing technicians examining the tubing and wiring with various handheld diagnostic devices with illuminated displays and readouts. He knew one of the techs as a casual acquaintance and afterhours drinking buddy — not that Matt drank much or even had time for that particular hobby — a young man named Carhart who was about the same age he was. The tech was another example of the road not taken. If Matt had just gone to the technical school that advertised a lot during cheap TV time instead of spending the best years of his life going for an advanced degree... As a technician, Carhart probably already made more money than Matt ever would.

"How's it going?" Matt asked, climbing out of the cart.

Carhart glanced at him. "Big guy too busy to come himself? Then he'll just have to miss the next fireworks show, but maybe you can convince him I'm not seeing things." He looked back at the EMF detector he was holding. "Something's way off here. I can't find anything wrong with the magnet, but the meter's showing some kind of stray pulse every five minutes."

"It's that regular?"

"You could set your watch by it," Carhart said. "Anything with a period like that has got to be artificial. We're obviously picking up interference from somewhere."

"But from where — and from what?" After all, they were underground and miles from any possible source.

"If I knew that," Carhart replied, "they'd be paying me a lot more. Maybe somebody ought to check topside and see if some kid's running his RC race car up there."

"Do you think it's related to Dr. Farber's problem with the missing proton beam?"

Carhart shrugged. "Beats me. All I know is we're checking out everything that's the slightest bit suspicious, and so far this is the only thing we've got. Oh, that isn't even the weird part. There's also a flash of light like a giant spark in mid-air when the interference peaks. I mean it's *huge*, and we can't figure out where it's coming from. All I know is that they never said anything about it at DeVry."

Or at CalTech, Matt thought. Before he could think of a question to follow up, Carhart cut him off.

"You're just in time. There should be another pulse coming along in about ten seconds. I want to see if I can get a fix on it." Carhart bent over his detector and checked the numbers showing on the display.

Matt stepped back to give the technician a little more room.

"Here it comes," Carhart said, watching the glowing readout.

Almost instinctively, Matt took another step back.

"Holy Christ!" Carhart exclaimed. "This is the biggest one yet! What's that kid running up there, an RC semi-truck?"

Suddenly, floating between Matt and the massive tubing, a lividly white-glowing sphere of energy flashed into instantaneous existence from out of nowhere, starting from the size of a golf ball and expanding to that of a basketball, sparks crackling around it. Even a few feet away from it, Matt could feel the heat.

Some kind of artificial ball lightning? I'd better get a picture of this. He started to take his phone out of his pocket— and the energy ball exploded in a blinding curtain of light. Matt was knocked backwards. There should have been a wall to stop him, but there was nothing, only a black void suddenly all around him. He yelled but nothing came out. Carhart was gone, the world was gone, and he fell through nothingness.

It must be a wormhole! shot through his mind after the first momentary terror faded. He was astonished that a routine test of the accelerator could have created such an exotic byproduct, but it was more like a rabbit hole, the one that Alice fell into. His ears roared, he spun end over end into the infinite blackness...

A moment later, he stopped spinning and dropped gently to rest on what felt like a tilted slab of smooth concrete. The roaring in his ears faded out and his eyes focused again. *Where the heck am I?* was his first thought as he glanced around. He had dropped his phone somewhere in the middle of the transition and his hardhat had gone whirling off into oblivion, but losing them was the least of his problems.

He wasn't in Wonderland and there wasn't any white rabbit. He was in what seemed to be a laboratory that had just been wrecked in an explosion. The room was filled with smashed and ruined machinery, and acrid smoke from several small fires. Some of the overhead fluorescent lights were on, others were burned out or broken. Swathes and loops of thick cables dangled limply from the ceiling, torn out of their brackets. Matt was sitting on a section of a wall that had been blown in and toppled on its side. Nearby, an unidentifiable machine that looked something like an old-fashioned stock ticker sizzled, smoked, and threw off sparks.

Maybe he had hit his head. Maybe Carhart had carried him up to one of the workrooms in the main building, maybe the problems with the accelerator had led to an accident, and maybe he had just now come to...

But the details were wrong. Even before it was wrecked, the lab had hardly been the gleaming, high-tech model of efficiency he knew from Fermilab. The equipment had the bulky look of vacuum tubes reluctantly giving way to transistors, of hand wiring instead of printed circuit boards, of machined metal instead of molded plastic.

The thought of time travel crossed Matt's mind. He briefly considered the possibility that he had fallen through a wormhole to emerge in the laboratory of some would-be inventor circa 1955 who had accidentally created a miracle with World War II surplus. If that was the case, he could probably only get back to his own time the hard way, by living long enough.

There was no obvious indication of what had caused the explosion. Matt had a passing thought that the proton beam had to go somewhere and it had a lot of power behind it. But the beam had been lost nearly an hour before and this had apparently just happened, unless time was skewed in some way, too. What the sputtering stock ticker exactly did wasn't evident, either, but Matt noticed that the number-display dials on its face had been set to 5:0:0 min. Carhart had mentioned that the energy manifestation had been surging at five-minute intervals—

A man shouted in an adjoining room, beyond a smoke-filled doorway in the wall on the opposite side of the lab. "Get out of here! This is Dr. MacTavish's private laboratory! Don't touch that cabinet! You don't have any right—" A gunshot cut him off and Matt heard him gurgle and fall to the floor.

What have I gotten myself into? Matt wondered in horror, and glanced hurriedly around for a way out.

A bulky figure appeared in the doorway, wearing what looked like a fireman's protective suit with hood and goggles, and carrying a pistol in a gloved hand.

"There's another one in here," the apparition said in a voice muffled by a respirator, and without a pause, pointed the pistol at Matt and fired.

Matt was too shocked by the cold brutality of it to react. He was being murdered without a second thought, without a chance to defend himself, and then the bullet slammed into his chest.

The impact knocked him back a little, more because he was expecting it than actually feeling a blow. He looked down at his shirt, but instead of a spreading bloodstain, he saw a splotch of smashed lead. The bullet hadn't even penetrated the cloth of his shirt.

Several thoughts crossed Matt's mind. If this was an actual robbery, wouldn't the perpetrators use real bullets? Had he somehow stumbled onto a movie set? But if it was a movie, where were the cameras? Or was it an elaborate prank? He had been the evil genius behind a couple of those himself during his undergrad days at CalTech, but this didn't feel like a practical joke.

Matt stood up and started for the doorway. The hooded man fired several more shots at him, only adding to the lead smears on his shirt.

Matt barely felt them. One thing was clear, however. Prank or movie set or whatever, the hooded man was not getting the results he wanted.

"Boss!" Matt heard him exclaim, desperation coming through loud and clear despite the muffled voice. "We got trouble! I think it's Astro-man, only he ain't wearin' his suit!"

Matt then heard the reply, distant and tinny, apparently coming over an earphone inside the hood. "What th—? Astroman!? But we— Never mind! Abort the operation! Now!"

The hooded man threw his now empty gun at Matt's head, then whirled and ducked back into the other room. Matt dodged the gun out of instinct — if bullets couldn't hurt him, that certainly wouldn't — and followed.

He stepped into the room just as two men in protective suits and hoods ran out through a door in the far wall. This room was an office, filled with smoke and ransacked, with filing cabinet drawers standing open and files and papers scattered across a desk and the floor. A feebly moving young man in a lab coat lay sprawled on the worn and shabby carpet in a spreading crimson pool of his own blood. He wore a necktie under the coat, one more indication that this definitely wasn't Fermilab or even the 21st Century.

Matt wanted to chase after the hooded men and find out what was going on, but the man on the floor took priority. All thoughts of pranks and movie sets faded from his mind. This was serious, though he couldn't understand why the bullets fired at him had been so ineffectual but other bullets had badly wounded the man here.

As Matt bent over him to see if there was anything he could do, the victim moaned and muttered something nearly lost in a gurgle as blood oozed from his mouth. For a moment, Matt ignored what the man had said, assuming it had been too faint and garbled to understand. Then he realized he had heard it and he had understood it.

"Don't let... Bolton... get the... transuranics..."

Understanding the words was one thing, but understanding what they *meant* was another. Matt looked into the young man's face. This was a complete stranger but his heart went out to him. The man was too young to be a scientist or professor, and was probably a grad student who had come to grief doing some professor's dirty work. Matt could only sympathize.

And that was all he could do. Matt wished he had taken the first aid course at the YMCA he had once considered, but he hadn't, and now it looked only too likely that the stranger would bleed to death while he watched helplessly.

Suddenly, Matt sensed someone approaching. How, he wasn't sure. It was as though he could hear footsteps he couldn't possibly hear, walking slowly across the floor in the next room, beyond the door the hooded men had used for their exit. Matt looked up at the doorway just as a uniformed security guard with a drawn pistol cautiously stepped through.

"Do you know first aid?" Matt demanded before the guard could say anything. "This man's dying!" Without waiting for an answer, he stood up and started towards the doorway.

"Hey, wait—!" the guard exclaimed with a threatening wave of the gun, but Matt was past him and out the door.

For a moment, Matt half-expected a bullet in his back, but as he had hoped, the guard had decided helping the dying grad student was more important than stopping him. Besides, the fact that Matt wore civilian clothes rather one of those hazmat suits probably made the guard think he was one of the staff rather than a hostile intruder.

Now Matt was in a long corridor, trotting past open doorways that led to offices and workrooms. *Just where am I?* he had to wonder again. Fermilab had been the leading edge of architectural and interior design, but this building looked like a decrepit old high school turned only half-convincingly into a research institute.

Matt broke into a run, thinking that if he could catch up with the hooded men, he might be able to get some answers. Then his feet left the floor, then his whole body, and he shot down the hall in lateral flight, like a human torpedo. The shock of realizing what he was doing occupied his attention for moment — *How am I doing this?* — then he saw the wall at the end of the corridor coming up fast.

It was a solid, blank wall, and he didn't have time to figure out how to stop. Matt tensed, clenching his teeth, and waited for the inevitable. He slammed into the wall at full speed—

—And broke through. The plaster and bricks crumbled into powder when he hit, and he barely felt the impact as he bored through the wall and out the other side.

But there had been just enough resistance to tip him off balance. He landed on a grassy lawn and somersaulted several times. Most undignified, it seemed to him. As he came up, he fleetingly hoped no pretty young women had been watching. Saying "I meant to do that" probably wouldn't convince them.

It was night here, too, and stars twinkled in a clear black sky overhead. The building Matt had just left the hard way really did look like a high school long due for demolition. It was three stories high and Matt had punched a hole through a wall on the first floor. Lights were on in most windows, and flames were shooting out of at least a few. In the distance, Matt could hear approaching sirens.

Even though it was a moonless night and the grounds were lit only by scattered, ineffectual streetlamps, Matt found he could make out a remarkable amount of detail as he looked around. It was as though he could suddenly squeeze more information out of a low level of light than any human being really should. The building was set on a wide lawn, with other, similar buildings nearby connected by narrow lanes and sidewalks. It wasn't so much a high school but more like the campus of a small private college. The terrain was flat and could have been former Illinois prairie, but it certainly wasn't Fermilab.

That much Matt took in within seconds as he got to his feet. He also heard an engine starting up and rotor blades turning from around the corner of the building he had just exited. He took off running, taking care this time to stay on the ground, and rounded the corner. As he had guessed, the hooded men were making their escape in a small helicopter, just now rising off the grass of the front lawn.

It had already risen a few feet when he reached it. He leaped, hoping to jump on the landing skids. He miscalculated and shot straight up, right through the spinning rotor blades. He felt the impact as a light tap, but the blades snapped with a loud crack and the debris went sailing in all directions. The helicopter dropped back to the ground, landing heavily. It wouldn't have been fatal for the men inside, but they were probably badly jolted.

Matt hovered in mid-air, not the least bit hurt but thoroughly at a loss as to what had happened to him. He had already smashed through a brick wall, and bullets had flattened against his skin. The thought came to him that perhaps the nuclear accident at Fermilab had somehow changed the structure of his body, given him powers of some kind.

He worked his way back down to the ground, and work may have been the right word. If it took an expenditure of energy and physical effort to climb that high into the air, it took an equal amount of energy and effort to climb back down. He wasn't even sure how to get down at first. It wasn't graceful, but imagining an invisible staircase and walking down turned out to be an effective psychological trick.

People were waiting for Matt. Flanked by two armed and uniformed security guards was a tall, thin, white-haired man of about seventy in a lab coat and tie. He came forward with an outstretched hand as Matt stepped down from an imaginary stair to the grass.

"Thank you, Astroman!" the man exclaimed in a Scottish accent that sounded almost too exaggerated to be real, as though he was simply playing a comic Scotsman and his actual accent was something else.

Even so, he somehow came across as perfectly sincere in how he spoke. He had a neatly trimmed goatee and wore startlingly thick wire-rimmed glasses. "If it hadn't been for you, those goons would have gotten away!" Then, as he got a better look at Matt's face, he gasped, "Wait a minute! You're not Astroman!"

Matt glanced in the direction of the wreckage of the helicopter. Several other security guards had come up and were rather roughly hauling some stunned and badly shaken men out of it.

Matt turned to the old man. "Look," he said a little desperately, "I don't know what this is all about and I don't know what's going on. My name is Matt Dawson and I'm just a grad student working at Fermilab. I don't know where I am or how I got here."

The old man blinked. "I think we'd better talk," he said after a moment's thought. "Come with me." He gave his lieutenants some instructions in regard to dealing with the police, whose arrival was now imminent, then led Matt down a sidewalk to another building.

"Just what did I come in on, anyway?" Matt asked along the way.

"You broke up an attempted robbery," the old man said. "We make some extremely valuable products here and certain criminals will stop at nothing to steal them. We'll never be able to prove it, of course, but I'm sure Garth Bolton was behind tonight's work."

Bolton... the badly wounded young man had spoken that name. "Er... Garth Bolton?"

"Aye!" the old man said, mistaking Matt's puzzlement for a polite acknowledgement. "Who else has the organization to pull off an operation like this? Who else would even need what we make here? He never would have dared try it before tonight, but with Astroman missing... well, the master criminals are beginning to crawl out from under their rocks."

Matt shook his head. So far, he had understood precisely none of it. All that he knew was that he was no longer at Fermilab. "Broken Symmetry" was right. Whatever symmetry kept one universe from overlapping another had been briefly disrupted. Matt had fallen through a wormhole and come out somewhere else. He didn't even want to think about where that somewhere else might be.

Chapter Two: **Stranger in a Strange Universe**

The old man was Dr. Angus MacTavish, late of Edinburgh and proprietor of MacTavish Laboratories near Weston, Illinois. The problem was that Matt had never heard of MacTavish Laboratories and Weston was a town that had voted itself out of existence so Fermilab could be built on the land where it had stood. Worse yet, Dr. MacTavish had never heard of Fermilab.

When he took Matt to his office and showed him a wall map of DuPage County, it was at once obvious that a basic principle of physics was being violated. Two objects — in this case, laboratories — were occupying the same space simultaneously. There was no sign of the huge expanse of land that should have been differently colored and labeled "Fermi National Accelerator Laboratory Area" just east of Batavia. In its place, the town of Weston was still on the map, and it had long disappeared from any contemporary maps Matt had ever seen.

The office reminded Matt of the principal's office at his old high school, a dreary, dingy room with a light fixture overhead that was just a lightbulb inside a white glass bowl with some dead insects silhouetted at the bottom. Dr. MacTavish sat down at his desk, a battered old wooden affair whose top was somewhere beneath a vast clutter of loose papers. Protruding from the sea of paper were an old-looking telephone with a rotary dial and a metal box with pushbuttons that was possibly an intercom. Hanging on the wood-paneled wall behind the desk were several framed diplomas and a painting of a castle that may have been the one in Edinburgh. The rest of the office was filled with a filing cabinet, a couple of crammed bookcases, a manual typewriter on a stand next to the desk, and some unidentifiable pieces of machinery in various states of repair and assembly.

There were no computers, no signs of any higher tech than vacuum tubes and electromechanical components. If it hadn't been for the calendar for some electrical equipment supply company on the wall that read

July, 1967, Matt would have thought he had been sent back in time to 1948. But 1967 didn't really relate to what he saw around him, either. If what had happened to him was time travel, he had apparently gone sideways as well as backwards. He had also shifted from late May to midsummer.

He wearily sat down on a wooden straightback chair in front of the desk, his lack of sleep for the past week catching up with him. He had forgotten about his changed relationship to physical objects, and a moment later he found himself sitting on the floor with pieces of the chair around him.

"Don't worry about it," Dr. MacTavish said, not quite as unconcerned as he tried to sound. "It was an old chair anyway. Try the metal one in the corner."

Matt brought that chair in front of the desk and gingerly lowered himself onto its seat. This one held up better. As long as he was careful, it seemed, he could handle objects normally.

MacTavish eyed Matt critically. "You don't look like Astroman. Not a bit. You're much too young. But you're hyper. How?"

"Look," Matt replied in some exasperation, "if I'm hyper, it's because I don't understand a thing about what's going on. I've never even heard of anybody named Astroman!"

"I don't think we're quite speaking the same language," MacTavish said. "'Hyper' means beyond the norm. Someone who is more powerful than the average human being is what we might term a 'hyperman.' It's a translation of Nietzsche's *Übermensch*, though I've also seen it rendered less commonly as 'superman' or 'overman,' such as in philosophical texts specifically discussing the Nietzschean concept. The name 'Astroman' was applied to a man who came from another planet as a wee bairn and acquired all manner of remarkable hyperpowers in Earth's environment. He can fly, see through walls, and lift great weights. He's also impervious to bullets, and if you weren't, we wouldn't be having this conversation now. Myself, I've always been dubious about the coming from another planet bit because Astroman looks too human to be the product of even parallel evolution, but that was his story and he did have those powers. I suppose calling himself Hyperman would have been rather too Nietzschean, rubbing in his presumed superiority as a man beyond men, and Astroman sounded friendlier as just someone from the stars. Or perhaps the name was simply already taken or too similar to something else. I always suspected there was more to the story than Astroman ever revealed, but could hardly even guess what it might be. You're not Astroman, obviously, yet you have the same powers. Where do *you* come from?"

At first, Matt's reason rebelled against even trying to deal with the question. An inner conviction told him that what was happening couldn't be happening. Even though it was happening. The words "cognitive dissonance" flashed across his mind.

Especially that business about somebody called Astroman. It sounded like a character he had once read about in a comic book as a kid, before he had outgrown such childish nonsense and taken to reading serious, hard-core science fiction, and then actual science books after that. Once he was proud of having given up comic books and reading *real* books instead, but now he was starting to wish he had read more comic books after all. They would have been more useful as a guide for orientating himself to the skewed reality he was now facing than any number of science-fiction novels written by knowledgeable authors conscientious about scientific accuracy. Unfortunately, he couldn't remember enough about the comic books he had read to be of any use in the present situation.

Even if the conscious part of Matt's brain resisted the overload of inarguable facts challenging his concept of the real world, he couldn't shut his thinking down completely. An answer slowly took shape in his mind. It was not something he was comfortable with, but it was the only one that seemed to fit...

Suddenly, he felt dizzy, almost sick, and he found himself gulping for air like a carp stranded on the beach.

MacTavish looked alarmed. "Is something wrong, laddie?"

"I - I'm not sure," Matt stumbled. He had been too occupied up to now with everything else to notice it before, but something was wrong with the air he was breathing. While it seemed normal otherwise and he could breathe well enough, it was as though he couldn't get all the oxygen he needed out of it. "It's the air, I think. It feels too thin, like I'm five miles up."

Dr. MacTavish took a breath, then exhaled. "It seems fine to me," he said after a moment. "But if you just got here, it may take some time to get used to things. If it's any consolation, Astroman was able to breathe and eat like we do, so it might just be a matter of adjustment."

"I hope so..." Matt croaked. The dizziness was already ebbing, however, and to his relief he did seem to be adjusting. "Anyway," he went on, "I'd guess I'm from a parallel world. Or is that idea too crazy?"

"I'll entertain any theory long enough to consider it," Dr. MacTavish said. "You're here, but you're obviously not *from* here. So how did you cross from your world to ours?"

Matt explained as best he could, though there was some difficulty in that while science on both worlds was generally the same, just half a century behind on this one, the vocabularies were somewhat different. So were areas of emphasis.

"So what does your research consist of?" Dr. MacTavish had asked.

"For the project I'm involved with," Matt replied, "we accelerate proton beams to the speed of light and then have them collide with carbon atoms."

Dr. MacTavish didn't seem to quite follow. "What does that get you? Some wonderfully exotic form of matter with fabulous properties?"

"Well, neutrinos, actually." Remembering he wasn't on the same world, Matt quickly added, "I mean, uncharged particles without any mass—"

"The word is the same here," Dr. MacTavish said in an apparent attempt to head off a Physics 101 lecture that he of all people certainly didn't need. "But... that's *all*? You're spending millions of dollars to make *neutrinos*? What's the point of that? If you feel as though you really have to find out what makes the dreary little things tick, I suppose no scientific endeavour is ever truly a complete waste, but I'd prefer to spend my resources on more promising areas of study."

Matt shrugged. "We look at it as exploring the bedrock of the universe."

"If that's all the further you've gotten," Dr. MacTavish replied, not sounding very impressed, "then your bedrock doesn't go down very deep. But perhaps our universes really are different."

He then launched in his own version of Physics 101, and it sounded like his theoretical understanding of subatomic particles was somewhat different from Matt's, though it seemed to work about as well for explaining most phenomena. For all Matt knew, the old Scotsman's theory might even be the better one. But it still didn't leave Matt any closer to going home.

"Interesting," Dr. MacTavish mused at the end of it. "On your world, you run a multi-billion-dollar machine to smash atoms. On this world, Garth Bolton's men break in on a dangerous atomic process at a critical moment and the experiment goes gang aft a gley. Somehow, this combination of the two happening at the same time seems to have opened a crack between universes, and you were unfortunate enough to fall into it."

"But can you repeat the process?" Matt asked. "Can you send me back?"

MacTavish spread his hands in a helpless gesture. "I honestly don't know." Seeing the look on Matt's face, he quickly explained. "Theoretically, it should be possible, of course. After all, you came here from there, so you should be able to go from here back to there. It's just that what brought you here was an accident I'm not sure we can duplicate. I appreciate your situation, but there isn't much I can do about it right now. We don't even understand the theory behind what happened, let alone possess the technology to locate your world in space and time and send you there safely."

Matt felt bleak. If he had wanted to move across town, let alone to another universe, he would have planned for it, and packed clothes and other necessities to take along. As it was, the transition had been sudden and unexpected, and all he had brought with him were the clothes he happened to be wearing at the time. Besides a credit card that was now so much inert plastic, his money was limited to about thirty dollars in his wallet. He probably couldn't spend even that without being arrested for counterfeiting, since most of the dates on the bills and coins would be 21st Century, to say nothing of possibly different Presidents. Thirty dollars wouldn't go very far anyway, even in 1967.

His last girlfriend had objected to the hours he was putting in at Fermilab and finally took her affection elsewhere, so he wouldn't be pining for the lost love he had left behind. It was bad enough to realize that he would never see his family and friends again. For their part, they would think he was simply missing, but eventually they would realize he wasn't coming back from wherever he had gone and give him up for dead. Somebody would clean out his apartment, and maybe his parents would figure out who was entitled to what little there was in his checking account. As far as his world was concerned, he might as well be dead, though no one realized how accurate the old cliché about going to "the next world" actually was in his case. He wished he could have said goodbye, but if he'd had that much warning, he would have done his best not to make the trip at all.

Wishing wouldn't change things. Matt realized that he was stuck on this world for the foreseeable future. Even if a way could be found to go home again, it might take years to develop. In the meantime, life went on. Maybe he could adapt to this world of half a century before his own time. It might not even be so bad. If 1967 wasn't exactly a Golden Age, perhaps it would qualify as at least a Silver Age.

"On the other hand," MacTavish continued, "since it seems likely you'll be here for a while, you'll need lodgings and employment. Would you be willing to work for me?"

The idea caught Matt by surprise, as he hadn't even started thinking about more immediate practical concerns. Since he had no place to go and no prospects of even his next meal otherwise, his options weren't very plentiful.

"Sure," he said, a little surprised that his most pressing problems had been solved so quickly.

"I may need a new assistant if poor Rusty doesn't pull through," MacTavish went on. "Plus, you're scientifically trained as well as hyper-powered. You'd be a good man to have around, and I'd like to study you anyway. Why not spend the night here and we can talk about the terms and arrangements tomorrow?"

Matt nodded in agreement, since a bed was starting to sound like an especially attractive offer about now, and stifled a yawn.

MacTavish pressed a button on the intercom on his desk. "Edmond — would you come into my office, please?" He released the button and looked back at Matt. "Edmond's my right-hand man, the most promising young student I've seen in years. I'm going to be frightfully busy trying to clean up the mess from tonight's nasty bit of business, so I'll have him set you up in one of our dormitory rooms. He can answer your questions—"

"How much can I tell him about me and where I come from?" Matt asked.

MacTavish seemed surprised by the question. "Why, anything you like. I have no secrets from him. I trust him like my own son. Maybe more," he added thoughtfully. "Milt took a little too much after his mother... In any event, I'm even hoping Edmond will find out everything there is to know about you so he can tell me!"

The door opened and a thin, tall young man in a lab coat strode into the office. He had thick glasses, a pale face, and short black hair. His face was a frozen mask of grim rectitude, and Matt suspected that the joke hadn't been told that would bend all that seriousness into a smile. Edmond assumed a position in front of the desk, more or less ignoring Matt, and stood virtually at attention. Matt had the distinct impression that Edmond's only complaint about protocol was that he wasn't allowed to salute.

"You called, sir?" Edmond barked, more a statement than a question. His accent was English and Matt wondered briefly if a better name for him might be Jeeves.

MacTavish's eyes rolled toward the ceiling for a moment. "Oh, for heaven's sake, Edmond! Relax!" To Matt he said, "Our Edmond takes his duties a wee bit too much to heart."

"Only trying to do my job, sir!" Edmond declared, still standing rigidly in front of the desk.

"And I appreciate it," MacTavish assured him, "but this isn't Sandhurst. At ease!"

Edmond somewhat reluctantly relaxed and MacTavish continued.

"This is Matt Dawson. He's the mysterious hyper-powered visitor from another world who saved our skins tonight. He'll be staying with us for a while, so see that he's settled into one of the vacant dorm rooms. Answer his questions and find out all you can from him."

Edmond's eyes went wide for a moment, as though the new development was both a surprise and unwelcome, but he recovered quickly and replied smoothly, even a little unctuously, "Very well, sir. I'll do my best."

MacTavish stood up, smiled broadly, and extended his hand to Matt across the desk. "Welcome to our world, laddie! I hope your stay is a pleasant one."

Matt stood up and took the old scientist's hand very carefully in his and shook gently. "Thanks. But pleasant or not, I just hope my stay here isn't a permanent one."

"I'll work on that," MacTavish promised. "Oh, one more thing. Although I certainly can't complain about your facial adornment, given my own — that rakish Van Dyke suits you rather well, I think — the sad fact of the matter is that beards and mustaches are only sported by men of my age and are quite out of style for young men today, except among the artier sort of Bohemians. I would strongly advise the clean-shaven look when you venture into public, if only to avoid attracting undue attention."

Matt rubbed his beard. He'd miss it, but he also had to wonder if he even *could* shave, or if his hair was "hyper" like the rest of him. "What about the hair on my head?" he asked. "Does that have to be short?"

"Short hair is indeed the current mode for young men, and yours is about right."

"Then the Beatles haven't happened here?"

"The who?"

Different group, Matt was tempted to say but didn't. It definitely was an alternate world. If long hair for men was still on the taboo list here, Matt was just glad that he had never gotten around to having his earlobe pierced so he could wear an earring.

Even out of the office and in the hall, Edmond retained his formal bearing, "Walk this way, please," he said and started down the corridor.

Tired and disoriented and sick at heart as he was, Matt was sorely tempted to take him at his word and *walk that way*. Say, by parodying Edmond's rather stiff stride as a goosestep. But common sense and mainly exhaustion won out over humor and he walked normally at Edmond's side.

"You look rather human for claiming not to be from this world," Edmond observed diffidently. "Are you from Helionn, like Astroman?"

Is Helionn the name of the planet this Astroman came from? Matt was too tired to pursue it and left it at explaining briefly about alternate worlds and the wormhole.

"Fascinating..." Edmond murmured. "A duplicate Earth where human beings identical to us speak colloquial English..."

A hint of sarcasm in Edmond's tone annoyed Matt. Perhaps if their positions had been reversed, he wouldn't have believed it, either, but at least he would have been polite about it. At that point, they came to the end of the hall and a pair of doors leading outside. Matt reached them first and pushed on through, just tired and irritated enough not to think about where he was and what he was doing, or what doing what he did meant when he did it where he was.

With a screech of hinges tearing out of the frames, the double doors flew out into the darkness and sailed across the lawn.

"Oh my God..." Edmond choked. He stopped for a moment to inspect the damage while Matt looked on in embarrassment. "I'd better have someone attend to this right away... as if we hadn't had enough damage to the place already tonight!" Edmond turned and glared at Matt. "Just be careful from now on, will you? Well, let's get you situated..."

Edmond led Matt along the sidewalk between buildings. Over on the next avenue, a police car went by with a single flashing red dome light on its roof, and in the distance, a clutch of police cars and emergency vehicles surrounded the spotlighted wreckage of the helicopter Matt had downed. It looked as though the official investigation of tonight's incident was already in progress, and Matt was grateful to Dr. MacTavish for slipping him away from the authorities and sparing him hours of questions he probably couldn't have answered very well.

For most of the walk across the campus, Edmond was grimly silent, apparently thinking hard. At first Matt wondered if he was put out with him about the door.

As they approached the dormitory, Edmond suddenly spoke up. "I'm Dr. MacTavish's right-hand man, you know. He's a very busy man and can't be bothered with mundane trivia. If he wants something done, I'm the one he has do it. So if you need anything, ask me first. I can speak for him and make decisions when it comes to administrative matters."

Oh, Matt thought. It wasn't the doors at all. He had to smile as Edmond went on in that vein, emphasizing his importance in the scheme of things around here. Matt had seen it before on his own world. Edmond was trying to protect his turf from the newcomer and ensure his dominance in the pecking order. Matt was a scientifically trained grad student from another world, with superhuman abilities to boot, and someone certain to excite Dr. MacTavish's interest and curiosity. Edmond must have sensed a possible threat to his own position.

As far as Matt was concerned, Edmond could go on being Dr. MacTavish's first mate. Matt may have needed a job, but let it be something more interesting than placing orders for Bunsen burners or making sure the cook in the dining hall wasn't taking choice cuts of meat home with him, or whatever Edmond did. At the moment, all Matt really wanted was a place to sleep.

Edmond took him into the dormitory, a run-down brick building that had probably seen occupants wearing raccoon coats, assigned him a tiny room with a bed and not much else, and gave him a bundle of sheets, towels, and a pillow from a supply closet.

"Remember," Edmond told Matt as he was leaving the room, "I report directly to Dr. MacTavish. If you follow the rules and do what I tell you, we'll get along fine. If you cause me any trouble, I can cause you a lot more. Good night."

Matt was too polite and too tired to tell him to perform a physiologically impossible act on himself, but his thoughts ran in that direction. He breathed a sigh of relief as soon as Edmond closed the door behind him.

"The fly in the ointment..." he muttered, and began unfolding the sheets.

Chapter Three: **A Sound Scientific Basis**

Matt's exhaustion caught up with him and he slept until ten the next morning. He opened his eyes and for a moment couldn't understand why he wasn't in his own apartment. Then he remembered and his heart sank.

At least he hadn't smashed anything rolling around in his sleep. It was hard enough being careful when he was awake, with everything seeming so fragile and paper-thin here.

A note taped to the door announced that Dr. MacTavish would be occupied for most of the day trying to sort out the mess from last night's attack, but Matt was welcome to eat in the dining hall and wander around the grounds. The note had been signed by Edmond.

Great, Matt thought. He was burning with several hundred questions that he hadn't been thinking clearly enough last night to ask, but the doc and the eager-beaver deputy were telling him to just stay out of the way. Maybe he could figure some things out on his own about powers and this world in general.

Matt went down the hall and found the shower room. Whether taking a shower was worth the trouble was another matter. Locally acquired dirt washed off easily enough, but removing his own body products, like sweat and hair oil, were the real problem, since the water merely beaded on his skin without much effect. With some experimentation, he discovered that hard scrubbing did seem to get acceptable results. When he came out of the shower, the water fell away and he was almost instantly dry without needing to use a towel.

The next item was shaving, since besides his beard he now had a noticeable stubble on his cheeks. He had nothing to shave with, however, since no one had thought to supply him with basic necessities like a razor or even a toothbrush. He would have to forego shaving until later. Then he wondered how much later. Would he be able to shave on this world at all, or would his facial hair be too tough for even the sharpest razor blades? Having to pluck his beard and mustache hairs one by one was hardly a cheering prospect.

He went back to his room and dressed, then looked for and found the dining hall. He hadn't eaten since a quick supper the night before, so he was seriously hungry. Parallel world or not, he was still human. His metabolism wasn't based on chlorophyll and he wasn't going to get his energy from sunlight.

Lunch and dinner may have been cafeteria-style hot meals prepared by a cook or two, but breakfast was just a buffet with a last few pastries and some boxes of cereal that were brands he recognized. *Hey, they even have Cheerios here!* It and Kellogg's Corn Flakes probably dated back to before any major divergence between the worlds.

The food was good enough for what it was and he ate his fill. It seemed pointless to worry about whether the local nutrients were too different for his body to handle since there wasn't anything else available that he could eat. Besides, this evidently very similar Astroman had managed to live on this world without starving to death.

After the late breakfast, Matt strolled around the complex. It was a bright and sunny day in mid-summer with some scattered clouds in the sky. The sun was warm and should have felt pleasant. Instead, his extended perception seemed to be jamming his sensory inputs. His brain was receiving too much information and refusing to deal with it. If anything, he felt a little numb, slightly removed from the world around him. He could objectively feel every nuance of the sunlight on his face if he concentrated on it, but it didn't seem quite real and he couldn't enjoy the sensation.

Seen by daylight, MacTavish Laboratories reminded Matt more than ever of a small college campus. In particular, the one seen in an old Disney movie called *The Absent-Minded Professor* (the original Fred Mac-Murray version, not the later Robin Williams remake). That early '60s or before time period seemed to fit for what he was seeing, too. *It's an old-school school*, he thought. Old brick buildings with ivy-covered walls were set back on wide lawns and looked out on avenues lined with tall maples. Not all of the buildings were in use, and through the windows appeared empty inside, while others had been remade into makeshift laboratories and workshops. The shrubbery was largely untrimmed and groundskeeping was apparently kept to a minimum of cutting the grass once in a while. It looked as though Dr. MacTavish had bought a defunct college. Perhaps its location, somewhere out in the countryside with only farmers' fields spreading into the distance all around and not very close to any towns, had been part of the appeal, both for privacy and for minimizing the damage if some experiment went wrong.

Meanwhile, Matt's brunch was resting heavily on his stomach and suddenly he didn't feel very well. It was some kind of gastric upset, as though he had eaten a great deal of perfectly good food but for some reason his digestive system was having trouble getting anything useful out of it. He made a quick dash back to the dorm, then spent an hour or so lying on his bed and waiting for his churning insides to subside.

After that, he felt fine, even a little hungry again, but... *I hope it doesn't take too long to get used to the food here!*

Matt went back outside and resumed his walking tour of the grounds. Soon he came to the scene of last night's adventure. A repair crew was already patching the hole he had made in the building wall while several men in suits were examining the burned-out wreckage of the helicopter. Something told Matt they were plainclothes cops or detectives, perhaps even FBI agents, and it might be a good idea to stay away from them for a while until he'd had a chance to talk things over with Dr. MacTavish at greater length. He had no idea how much of his actual story the authorities here would accept, or what kind of trouble he might be in for if he babbled too freely.

Matt turned away and walked up another street. This one dead-ended at a high chain-link fence topped with barbed wire. Beyond stretched flat Illinois farmland lush with green fields of mid-summer corn stalks. Matt stopped at the fence and started to turn back, then remembered fences here didn't mean what they did on his world, A leap of ten feet was just a hop compared to his more than twenty feet the night before.

He jumped, intending to merely clear the fence, only to discover that gravity didn't mean the same thing, either. He could have stopped at ten feet. He could also continue rising. The controlling factors seemed to be a conscious decision and simply thrusting himself into the direction he wanted to go. This completely defied physics as he understood it — what was propelling him? — but so many other physical relationships between him and this world were wrong that there was little point in arguing with himself about what he should be able to do. If the screwy physics here worked in his favor, he might as well take advantage of it where he could. He went on rising, curious to see how high he could go.

As high as he wanted, apparently. Beneath him, the MacTavish Laboratories complex shrank to a square of building roofs, green lawns, and avenues set in a patchwork of farmers' fields and country roads, with the gridwork of streets of a small town that was probably Weston a mile or so distant.

Climbing like this bothered Matt at first. Every instinct programmed into him from millions of years of evolution as a ground-dwelling species screamed at him that this wasn't natural. Being this high off the ground without any visible means of support meant he was about to fall and be killed when he hit the dirt. But he didn't fall, and gradually his subconscious mind accepted the fact that gravity was no longer all-powerful.

Matt needed a moment to place where he was. This was an aerial view of DuPage and Kane Counties and Chicago's southwestern suburbs as they might have looked about 1948 on his world, before the urban sprawl had swallowed the open spaces and farmland between the smaller cities and towns. Batavia, Wheaton, Naperville, and Aurora were less than half the size they should have been. On Matt's Earth, they were growing explosively, Naperville in particular spurred by the corridor of high-tech companies along I-88, but here those cities had remained sleepy little farming towns. For that matter, there wasn't even any sign of I-88. Four-lane highways simply didn't exist this far out of Chicago.

As Matt rose higher into the sky, the enormous city spreading along the lakefront to the east came into view. Wanting a better look, he experimented to see if he could angle his trajectory into lateral flight. He put his arms out and tensed his body in the direction he wanted to go. That was all it took. His body followed the direction he was pointing and his flightpath curved from the vertical to the horizontal. Exactly *what* was propelling him, he had no idea, but the more he tensed forward, the faster he flew. If there were any limits on how fast he could fly, they were probably the result of increasing air resistance at higher speeds. As it was, he estimated that he could easily cruise at sixty to a hundred miles per hour relative to the ground. It should have been exhilarating, but...

He had daydreamed about flying when he was a child, imagining how it would feel to soar through the sky with the wind against his face and blowing through his hair. Now he was actually doing it, but the feeling was strangely muted and flat, as though he was one step removed from the process. While the view was spectacular, it was like being up in an airplane even if the airplane was missing. There was nothing between him and the ground a thousand or so feet below except air, but the landscape seemed not quite real, like seeing it through an airplane window.

As he approached, he saw that Chicago was smaller than he remembered. Even from this altitude, he could see that many of the newer buildings had not been built yet and the skyline seemed lower, even shrunken, like in old photographs. While this was supposedly 1967, half a century before Matt's time, it somehow looked older still.

When he reached the city, he flew north along the Lake Michigan shoreline, with the lakefront buildings to the left and the lake to his right. He followed Lake Shore Drive, still unsure of his limits and wanting to stick to familiar landmarks before venturing into the unknown. He passed over the north side of Chicago and the beaches and apartment buildings lining the shore, past where Lake Shore Drive abruptly turned inland and ended at Sheridan Road, into Evanston, and flew on towards the north. He spotted the campus of Northwestern University where it should have been, and the North Shore Canal emptying into the lake, but there was no sign of the Bahai Temple even though its mosque-like architecture would have been obvious.

A little further north, a sudden screeching noise slammed into his ears. It was an ultra-high pitch probably far beyond the limits of normal human hearing, but to him achingly loud and disorienting. It nearly knocked him backwards when he hit it, like an almost physical barrier. Looking down, all he saw were the grid-like streets of the normal northern suburbs, except, somewhat to the west, what seemed to be a large circular lake the size of several city blocks, with unnaturally blue water. The sound was coming from there.

As he looked more closely, he realized that it wasn't a lake at all but a huge flattened dome about a quarter of a mile in diameter and maybe a couple of hundred feet high at the center, It had an utterly smooth and seamless mirror-like surface, and the blue was simply reflected sky. It didn't seem to be solid and Matt noticed some distortion and wavering, as though it was some sort of energy projection. He couldn't see through it no matter how intently he stared at it, and what was underneath would have to remain a mystery. Judging by the traffic passing it on nearby streets, no one seemed to regard it with particular concern, probably considering it a familiar feature of the scenery. Matt had a very distinct feeling that it would be bad for *him* if he approached it any more closely, and he took a wide looping detour out over the lake to give it a wide berth.

He would have to ask Dr. MacTavish about the dome, since it seemed wildly advanced even for a funhouse mirror version of 1967. If this was something threatening even to a hyperman and he wasn't really as invulnerable as all that, he had better find out about it before he spent too much more time in this world.

He went on north past Wilmette and over Waukegan, and the urban sprawl faded out into detached suburbs, then smaller towns, then farms, fields, and woodlots. From the air, generic countryside should have looked about the same as it did on Matt's world, but there were differences even so. He looked for the Great America amusement park, which ought to have been a conspicuous feature just off I-94 to the northwest of Waukegan, but he only saw a large dairy farm where he expected roller coasters and water slides. There wasn't an I-94, either. He could see a road running from south to north about where the interstate between Chicago and Milwaukee should have been, but it looked like an ordinary highway with frequent intersections.

No '50s Interstate Highway project?

He noticed something ahead in the distance, a moving spot that seemed to be coming towards him. It was too big to be a bird, and its flight was too fast, its trajectory too steady, to be flying by flapping wings. Perhaps, Matt thought, he was about to meet this Astroman fellow in person. Astroman was about the only thing he could think of that matched the profile of the approaching object.

As he looked more intently at it, his extended perception focused, and an image took shape. It wasn't a hyperman, it was a hyper*dog*. A flying dog with golden brown fur, it was of no breed Matt could identify but maybe what you would get if your female Labrador retriever had a brief affair with a passing German shepherd. As the dog came closer, Matt saw that it even had a silly little cape with a stylized "A" emblem sewn on it attached to its collar. Was this Astroman's pet dog? Matt wondered if he had other pets — cats, gerbils, goldfish — and if they all had little capes, too.

The dog slowed up as it came nearer. At first, it had a playful, eagerly expectant air, but that faded when it got a closer look at Matt. How intelligent the dog was, Matt didn't know, but flying towards him, it wouldn't have been able to smell him, and it might have assumed that any flying man it saw in the distance had to be Astroman and didn't examine him with its extended vision. The dog regarded Matt puzzledly, then suspiciously.

Matt tried to make friends. "C'mere, boy," he said, and held out his hand to signal an offer to pat the dog's head if it came within reach.

The dog stopped in mid-air some feet away, reared back, and snarled.

"Er... nice doggie?" Matt ventured.

The dog barked angrily at Matt, then turned and flew away, heading out across the lake in the direction of Michigan.

Matt could only conclude that if the dog felt that way about it, there was no use trying to improve the relationship. He didn't follow the dog, but watched it until it vanished in the distance.

Well, that was strange... One more mystery among the many piling up.

He flew on north along the lakefront and into Wisconsin, but since he didn't want to get lost, he soon decided to turn back. Returning was easy enough. Fly south to Chicago, then make a right and head straight out to the western suburbs. Finding the MacTavish Laboratories complex from the air was a little harder, since Matt hadn't memorized its exact location in the altered landscape, but his extended perception proved useful. To his astonishment, he discovered he could read street signs from a mile up. He merely had to focus on a distant object, and the longer he looked at it, the more clearly he could see it. It wasn't so much telescopic vision as a continuously sharpening focus. Again, he had no idea how it worked or why this world was so different in that respect.

Once he found MacTavish's lab, Matt landed behind a building, trying not to be seen by any police investigators on the grounds. Discretion still seemed to be the best policy. Also, the landing had been a little rougher than he had intended, and he hoped nobody had seen the somersault he made across the grass. Flying was the easy part, landing he'd have to practice.

Coming around the building, he stopped a passing lab technician on the sidewalk and asked where Dr. MacTavish was. The technician referred him to the office, where he said the boss was still trying to straighten out the legal and insurance ramifications of last night's raid.

Before long, Matt came into the front office and interrupted the receptionist, a rather austere-looking woman in her forties, as she was busy typing invoices on a manual typewriter, and asked to see Dr. MacTavish.

"Oh, I'm sorry," she said in some irritation. "He's very busy with Edmond right now. Edmond left explicit instructions that they weren't to be disturbed."

It occurred to Matt that this was the first female employee he had seen in MacTavish's organization since he got here. Otherwise, the place was practically a monastery. One female employee and she was a secretary... MacTavish wouldn't have lasted very long with those hiring practices at Fermilab, where diversity was official policy, there were dedicated programs for recruiting and training women and minorities, and there had still been complaints about not enough female scientists and staff.

"Edmond?" Matt echoed, a little exasperated. "Did they change the name of this place to Edmondlab while I was gone? Can't you just tell Dr. MacTavish I'm here and let him decide if he'll see me?"

The secretary frowned, weighing the consequences in her mind. "All right," she said after a moment, reluctantly and making it clear this was against her better judgment. "I'll tell him, but this is on your head, remember." She pushed a button on the startlingly antique-looking intercom. "I know you're busy, sir," she said when MacTavish answered and sounded annoyed by the interruption, "but there's somebody here who insists on seeing you. He says his name is Matt Dawson."

"Och, good!" came the scratchy reply. "I've been wanting to see him myself! Send him in!"

The secretary was plainly taken aback. Matt just smiled indulgently at her and went on into the inner office where he had talked to Dr. MacTavish the night before.

The scientist was sitting at his desk and going through a file of what seemed to be damage reports. The ever faithful assistant sat in a chair in front of the desk with a sheaf of papers in his lap, and was not happy.

"Dr. MacTavish!" Edmond exclaimed indignantly. "We have ten more reports to go through!"

"We've been going through them all morning and I'm tired of it!" MacTavish snapped. "I'm a scientist and here I am tied down with all this administrative muck! I haven't seen anything yet this morning that you couldn't have handled on your own." He waved vaguely with his hand, dismissing Edmond. "Take the rest of these papers and go through them yourself. I'll sign whatever needs to be signed later."

Edmond stood up with an almost hurt expression. "Very well, sir. If that's what you want..."

"It is indeed."

Edmond passed Matt on the way out, and shot him a glance that was little short of venomous. The reigning court favorite didn't like being dismissed in favor of the newcomer, Matt guessed. This could get ugly, but what could Edmond possibly do to him that would have any more effect than making faces? Other than insult him, that is.

"You look disgusting," Edmond muttered to Matt. "Why don't you shave?"

Matt rubbed the beard on his chin. "I don't think I can."

"Then at least put on a tie!" Edmond snapped. "This is a scientific institution, not a holiday camp!" He stalked out of the office, closing the door behind him not at all gently.

"Careful," MacTavish said as Matt sat down in the chair in front of the desk. "I don't have very many chairs left. Fine assistant, that Edmond," he added, "but he can be a wee bit tiresome at times. I'll be with you in a moment after I finish up this form here. All this keeps me from my proper work, but it has to be done. I hope master scientists on your world don't have to write up reports and fill out endless forms like this after a raid by an arch-criminal!"

"It usually isn't a problem," Matt said.

"No? If we find a way to send you back to your world, perhaps I should accompany you." MacTavish went back to the form he was filling out, and as Matt waited quietly, he checked off some boxes, scribbled some notes, and finally signed it with a flourish. "There!" he exclaimed.

"Done with that lot, anyway." He shoved the paper aside and looked up at Matt. "So, how are you adjusting to our world?"

"That's what I wanted to talk to you about," Matt replied. "I was trying out my powers this morning, and..." He told MacTavish about his excursion over Chicago and points north, and running into the painful noise and seeing a blue energy dome that seemed to be producing it.

"Well, laddie," MacTavish replied, "just by pure chance, you found Garth Bolton's estate."

"That's what that was? But how could it affect me like that?"

"It's his wee spread up in Kenilworth, though as I recall he bought up some property to the west of the actual town and added it in. That included a golf course, which was about as much vacant land as you might expect to find in the Chicago suburbs, and he built his laboratory and manufacturing complex there. Now, when you're just an ordinary man without any hyper-powers and your worst enemy is a man with hyper-hearing and vision, how do you keep him from spying on you and watching your every move so he can stop you just when you start to do something nefarious? Over the years, Bolton determined from his battles with Astroman what the limits of his powers were, then devised optical shields and sonic interference generators that would keep even someone with hyper-powers from being able to see or listen to what was going on under that energy dome.

"The reflectivity bit was actually a later innovation. When Bolton first put up the dome, it was an opaque milky white with a lot of swirling in it, but people who lived around there complained about it being a terrible eyesore and the seething energy displays gave them headaches every time they looked in that direction. So he changed the dome's configuration to a big hemispherical mirror that wasn't so hard on the eyes, about the only time I've ever heard of him acceding to a request like that instead of just going ahead and doing what he wanted. But even Garth Bolton has to live in this world and get along with the neighbours, I suppose, or else he decided he was too great a man to be wasting his time fighting with the zoning commission. As for the hyper-noise, normal people aren't affected by it because they simply can't hear it, but for someone with Astro-powers, I gather that it must be fairly painful."

"Try excruciating," Matt replied with a grimace from the memory. "I'm surprised my ears aren't bleeding. I'll have to remember to avoid going near the place in the future." Then he mentioned the encounter with a flying dog.

MacTavish nodded. "Aye, that was Astroman's dog. Helio, he calls him."

"But where did this, er, Helio come from?"

"The official version is that he came from Astroman's own world, Helionn, as a puppy—"

"There are dogs in outer space?"

"I suppose if you accept perfectly human-looking people on another planet, dogs aren't that much of a reach."

"And he named his dog after his home planet?"

MacTavish shrugged. "It might have been a coincidence. I once knew a man who called his dog 'Terry,' and I'm sure he didn't name it after *his* home planet. Terra, if you take my meaning. People name their pets all kinds of things. Any road, the story goes that Astroman's father put Helio in the spaceship along with the wee bairn for company. The problem with that is that Helio wasn't known to exist until Astroman was in his teens, so where he was before that is rather mysterious. Not only that, Earth dogs certainly don't live for forty-odd years, but perhaps dogs on Helionn did. Or perhaps people and animals with hyper-powers simply live longer. If that's the case, you may be here long after the rest of us are gone."

He sighed and brought his fist down on the stack of papers. "This red tape be damned! I want to do some science! He stood up and came around the desk. "Let's go over to the infirmary. I'd like to run a few tests on you and your powers."

"Eh?"

"Just out of curiosity," MacTavish said. "It's never been understood *how* Astroman has these powers, some of them defying everything we think we know about proper physics and biology. There's been speculation that Helionn was larger and more massive than Earth and hence had a greater gravitational attraction. So for Astroman to come here was like an Earthman going to Mars and being stronger in the weaker gravity. But that never made sense. If Helionn's gravity was so much greater that coming here would make such a significant difference, the human form would need a radical redesign. That is, legs like thick pillars and so forth, but he looked to be normally built. Even if he could jump further than the average Earthman as a result of a difference in gravity, it certainly didn't explain outright flying. We mostly don't hear that theory anymore, except from people who haven't kept up with the changing fads and fantasies.

"Now the idea is that Astroman's powers are derived from some special radiation from our sun that for whatever reason other stars do not emit. This is pure blather, explaining the inexplicable with impressive-sounding nonsense. You might just as well say his powers are actually psychic in nature and his hyper-strength is due to telekinesis or some such rot. It still doesn't answer the question— how *can* Astroman do what he does? So far as I know, the scientists who examined him never came up with any good answers, but now here you are, right here at hand. I could spend a year just analysing the contents of your wallet with the strange banknotes of the future and the credit card with a magnetic strip, not to mention the car key that emits a signal to unlock the door and the boot, but a living specimen — ah! Pure gold for a scientific mind! If you don't mind, of course…?"

Matt shrugged. "Sure, why not? There's a lot about all this that I'm curious about myself."

As they walked down the hall, MacTavish asked, "How is science conducted on your world, by the bye?"

"Through institutions, mostly," Matt explained. "Universities, industrial R&D labs, some private research centers…"

"What an uninspired way of doing things!" MacTavish exclaimed. "It sounds so… so collectivised! Are there no forward-looking savants such as myself, running ahead of the pack and leading the way?"

"Well, there are authorities in various fields," Matt said, "but not in the way you mean. Science is so specialized that each scientist contributes a little bit here and a little bit there, but nobody is very far out in front of the leading edge. We have quite a few disputes about priority as a result, and if somebody doesn't discover something one week, somebody else will the next. Except for classified military work and industrial trade secrets, all research gets published, and everybody in a given field knows pretty much what's being done."

"Amazing…" MacTavish murmured. "I wouldn't dare publish the results of most of my work! I have too many competitors… and too many enemies! They would take advantage of my blockheaded generosity and use my work to destroy me. Some might use it for criminal pursuits or even to take over the world. Like Garth Bolton for one."

It apparently wasn't enough to just do science on this world. The successful scientist also had to assemble and administer his own organization as well as fight off unscrupulous rivals. Matt had a vision of Tesla hiring guards for his laboratory in case of an attack by Edison's men. When did they have time to do their actual work? And how had things come to this? Matt guessed the answer might be poorly written patent laws here. Without adequate legal protection for their ideas and discoveries, scientists and inventors may have been forced to extreme measures to protect themselves. One more thing to research if he ever found some spare time and a library…

"It sounds an interesting place, this Fermilab of yours," MacTavish added, "but too big, much too big for an independent savant such as myself. Give me a cosy, comfortable, small lab like this, a few willing helpers, and I'll astound the world. As Edison showed, a master and his disciples are the ideal team."

"Maybe so," Matt said, "but I think science just got too big for us to do it that way. One man couldn't come up with billions of dollars for a particle accelerator."

"True enough," MacTavish agreed, "but I do all right by licensing my inventions and using the profits to support further research. I must also admit that the government has also been known to slip me a few quid for specific projects now and then, but that's something we don't talk about."

That sounded interesting, but Matt sensed MacTavish had said all he was going to about it and changed the subject. "Speaking of disciples, how's your assistant doing? The one who was shot last night, I mean?"

"Critical at last report," MacTavish said sadly, "but I'm sure he'll pull through. Poor lad... he fought valiantly against overwhelming odds in our defence. Good thing you showed up just then, else he would have died for certain."

"Just what do you make here that somebody would send a small army to steal it?"

"All in good time, laddie," MacTavish said with a dismissive wave. "All in good time." He stopped in front of a wooden door with faded gold lettering on the frosted glass window reading "Health Department." "Ah, here we are."

Inside was a run-down dispensary suited for little more than emergency first aid in case a clumsy lab assistant spilled acid on himself or didn't ground a live wire properly. What there was, MacTavish proceeded to use on Matt. He weighed him on the scale, took his pulse, and listened to his heart and lungs with a stethoscope. Getting a reading of Matt's blood pressure was out of the question, however, since his arm couldn't be squeezed. MacTavish then collected samples of any fluid or secretion he could get at, such as tears, saliva, and even ear wax.

"Splendid!" he exclaimed when he was working over Matt's ear. "You've got a pimple here!"

"That's good?" Matt asked.

"Of course it's good. Now I can get some pus and blood. I'd like to do a little culturing of your resident microorganisms to see how they fare outside your body and make sure you aren't harbouring some hyperbug that would infect everyone on this Earth with an incurable fatal disease."

"Is that a risk?"

"Some, but we're all still here forty years after Astroman came, so I suspect your germs won't thrive in this environment. Now, would you be so kind as to squeeze that pimple for me?"

When that indignity was finished, MacTavish tried to collect a sample of Matt's hair. Scissors didn't work at all, however. They didn't break, but simply refused to cut. Matt finally had to pull a few strands out with his fingers. An experiment with shaving failed completely, since the sharpest razor had no effect on Matt's darkening cheeks.

"It's like trying to shave a statue," Matt said, urgency slipping into his voice as he realized the implications. "Look, Doc, if I can't get a haircut or a shave, I'm going to look like Bigfoot in a few weeks."

"I'll do the best I can, laddie," MacTavish said, a little too lightly for Matt's peace of mind. Now let's see how good your eyesight is."

What followed was a test of Matt's vision using the eye chart on the wall. That was fun because he was able not only to read the tiniest row of type from across the room but also the minuscule printers' union logo beneath it. Dr. MacTavish took endless notes on a clipboard, saying little beyond an occasional "Hmm!"

Besides the blood pressure problem, the other major hitch of the day was the X-ray machine, as MacTavish was unable to get any results at all. Matt's body proved to be opaque to X-rays, period.

"All in all, you seem quite sound," MacTavish summed up at the end of the examination. "You have a pulse, all your parts are in working order... How do you feel, by the way? In general, I mean."

"To be honest, a little numb," Matt told him. "I can't feel things the way I used to. In some ways I'm more sensitive, but in other ways I feel somehow cut off from the world."

"But well otherwise, I take it," MacTavish said, glancing at his notes on the clipboard, then added a little grimly, "Let's just hope you stay that way."

"Can your world's germs even affect me?" Matt wondered.

MacTavish shook his head. "Not the problem. It may be fine in most respects to be invulnerable to threats from the outside, but your own body might well betray you from the inside. What if you develop appendicitis or a cancerous tumour? If a doctor can't cut you open, you could die of something that would be easily treatable for mere mortals."

Matt gulped. "It sounds like this invulnerability thing has its down side."

"You're young yet and by all indications perfectly sound at present, so you shouldn't have to worry. For a while, at any rate." MacTavish slapped his clipboard. "All right, then, let's try something more spectacular."

They moved to a laboratory that probably first saw service as the former college's gymnasium. Though currently not in use, it was filled with unidentifiable masses of machinery and scattered workbenches under shielded lightbulbs dangling from the high ceiling on long cords.

MacTavish ran Matt through another series of tests. These were crude and improvised with anything handy, less to measure anything with precision and more to simply show that Matt was off the scale. He could lift as many tons of heavy machinery as he could balance. Enormous jolts of electricity didn't faze him.

The one disappointment was hyper-breath. Matt could expel air with enough force to do some damage, but only so much at a time. Since his lung capacity was finite, probably not much more than that of an average man on this world, he couldn't inhale enough air at one time to put out a forest fire with one mighty puff, as Astroman was apparently alleged to do.

If he stared long and hard at an object, on the other hand, he not only saw it in nearly infinite focus, but after a certain point he could see inside and then *through* it. His X-ray vision fell off with increasing density of the material he was trying to look through, however, and seeing through copper was about his limit. He could not see through a sheet of lead, not because there was anything particularly magical about lead as such, but simply because it was too dense. Silver, almost as dense as lead, was as opaque to him as anyone else, as were materials denser than lead, like gold.

If he really stared at an object, it would start to smoke, then burst into flame or melt.

The last left MacTavish dumbfounded. "Eyes receive radiation — they don't emit it!" he exclaimed.

He looked into Matt's eyes with various instruments to see if their structure was somehow different, but as far as he could tell, Matt's eyeballs were just eyeballs.

"I wonder if it has something to do with focus," MacTavish muttered half to himself, "like using a magnifying glass to concentrate a ray of sunlight, but it still doesn't explain how the light beam would be projected *from* your eyes..." He finally shrugged. "I knew Astroman was supposed to have this power but I just never really believed it. I can't explain it."

Matt couldn't, either. He had read somewhere that the ancient Greeks had a theory of how eyesight worked that was oddly like modern radar. That is, the eyes saw by sending out rays of some kind that returned with information on what they had encountered. It was an ingenious concept but devised before the nature of light and the structure of the eye were understood, and it didn't seem to apply here. Matt just made a mental note to be careful how he looked at things until he had his various "visions" under better control.

Finally, Dr. MacTavish gave up on the tests, unable to think of anything more for Matt to do. They sat down on a workbench and the scientist announced his results. "What can I say, lad? You're not infinitely powerful and there are some limitations, as you learnt to your cost when you encountered Garth Bolton's defences, but for all practical purposes... you're *hyper*."

"I already knew that much," Matt said in some exasperation, since two hours of tedious and tiresome examination still hadn't produced any explanations worth taking seriously. "But *why* am I hyper?"

MacTavish shrugged. "I don't really know the answer to that. I suspect it has to do with that fact that you're from another universe. You're in this universe but not *of* it, so your relationship to your surroundings has changed. There's more to it than that, but I'll have to study you further. You're quite a prize, you should know. After all these years of Astroman seemingly violating all the known laws of physics, we can finally put him and his powers on a sound scientific basis. I mean, it was hard enough to believe when it was just him, but then came his dog and now his cousin, and with each new addition to the family, the whole thing became that much more unbelievable—"

"Wait a minute," Matt said in astonishment. "Did you say his *cousin*? There's a whole family of Astropeople?"

"Just the cousin. That's Astrogirl, and she's a bonnie lass of about twenty. He's been missing for two weeks or so, but she's been seen recently."

"A cousin, too..." Matt mumbled. It almost seemed too much along with everything else he had heard.

"I can see the questions you're about to ask, lad," MacTavish said, "and I have to admit that I'm no specialist on Astroman. Let's go to the library."

That's right, Matt thought. *This is 1967 — too soon for the Internet and Google*. If you wanted to find out about something, you had to do it the old-fashioned way. No Wikipedia here.

The library was in another building on the campus, its dark rooms filled with shelves of dusty books. Most had been inherited from the defunct college and left where they were because no one had ever had time to go through them to see what was worth keeping. Matt made a mental note to give the history section a look when he had a moment to see if he could determine where this world had diverged from his own. Only the room with physics books looked as though it had seen any use in recent years, and it suffered badly from the lack of full-time staff.

Stacks of new magazines and uncatalogued books covered the checkout desk, and people who returned borrowed books evidently weren't any too fastidious about reshelving them where they belonged.

"I really should hire a proper librarian just to put this place in order," MacTavish said in partial apology, "but with one thing or another..."

"Sounds like a good job for Edmond," Matt suggested.

Dr. MacTavish chuckled. "Nae, too valuable where he is. Can't spare him. But if you ever have a free afternoon, laddie..."

More like a free week, Matt thought, looking at the heaps of books and magazines.

Dr. MacTavish riffled through several drawers in the ancient-looking free-standing wooden card catalog, then checked the shelves in the appropriate section — they did have the Dewey Decimal System here — but came up empty.

"Hmm, it seems we don't have any books on Astroman specifically. Of course, a great deal has been written about him over the last twenty-five years, but we're missing the popular-level surveys of his life and career that the catalog insists we have. I'm not surprised since quite a few books walked out with the last of the staff and students before I bought the place. Nonetheless, there ought to be something in the serials."

That meant the magazines, though Matt had a brief flash of some actor playing Astroman in a fifteen-chapter black-and-white movie shown in weekly installments at the local Bijou. For all he knew, something like that might have even existed here.

"We do still have all manner of abstruse papers in the physics journals desperately trying to make sense of Astroman's powers," MacTavish reported after a quick scan of the listings, "but they wouldn't be what you want. We now know they're all wildly off the mark anyway. This might be your best bet, actually..."

It was the current issue of *Newsweek*, lying on top of the clutter on the front desk where it had been casually tossed after the mailman had delivered it a couple of days before. The cover was stark and simple, showing a giant question mark superimposed on a stylized winged "A" emblem and the headline, **WHERE IS HE?**

"I'm afraid that's all we have," MacTavish said. "It'll give you the background, anyway. I'm sure you'll have more questions, but for those answers, you'll want to enquire at the Astroman museum in the city."

"He has his own museum?"

"Certainly. He's been quite the public figure for a quarter-century and people are naturally curious. Whether the museum is accurate or if it's really a way for him to tell his story the way he wants it told, I can't say. Any road, it might give you a few hints."

MacTavish went back to his laboratory, saying he had an idea or two about Matt's condition that could be worth trying out, but not sounding any too hopeful. With a sigh of resignation and a reflective rub of his beard, Matt went to the dining hall, found a bottle of Coke in the refrigerator, and retired to his dorm room to read the *Newsweek*.

Old habits died hard. He could have just as comfortably read the magazine suspended in mid-air a mile high as stretched out on a bed, except that a mile high there wouldn't have been any place to put the Coke bottle between sips. Speaking of which... it was nice that they had something as familiar as Coca-Cola here, but that was understandable since it dated back into the 19th Century, probably well before the respective histories of the two Earths began to seriously diverge. It seemed to taste the same, too, though with his extended perception, Matt's sense of taste was now more like a chemical analysis of the various ingredients and he had trouble combining them into the overall flavor. He was hearing the individual instruments instead of the symphony. *Maybe Pepsi could hire me to crack Coke's secret formula...* he thought idly as he read through the *Newsweek*.

Skimming the news and feature articles, Matt began to sense something of this world's prior history. Perhaps his world and this one were somehow linked, accounting for why they were so similar, though there was obviously some room for variance. The two histories had roughly mirrored each other through World War II, allowing for some minor differences in people and events, but after that there seemed to be an increasing divergence, culminating in the 1967 Matt saw around him. Although 1967 had been nearly thirty years before Matt was born, he had some idea of what the '60s looked like from books, documentaries, and old movies and TV shows, and this world wasn't quite it. Wasn't 1967 the year of "the Summer of Love," with hippies and protest marches and the war in Vietnam? None of that seemed to be going on here, and American society was either at peace or just very quiet. The mass media was even still making fun of beatniks as a comical fringe element. It also looked as though the current generic-looking young President had never been assassinated and was into his second term.

Then Matt thought he had it. This world was 1967 as somebody in 1963 or so might have imagined it would be, a continuation of what was going on just then without the unpredictable upheavals that actually resulted in the years that followed in Matt's history. The baseline was also a noticeably backward 1963, perhaps 1963 as perceived by someone who had come of age in the '40s or before and had never adjusted to the

'60s or even kept up very well. It was as though the Great Society hadn't happened but the New Frontier had gone into extra innings, with some of the New Deal still lingering in the background.

At least that was Matt's initial impression, though he'd probably be weeks or months working out all the details as to why this world was the way it was. He could only hope that he wouldn't be there that long. Now the more immediate question was who this Astroman was.

He soon had something like an outline. Besides the articles, which presupposed considerable familiarity with Astroman on the reader's part but nonetheless imparted much of the background in passing, the magazine even had pictures of him.

The obvious feature was Astroman's uniform. As Matt remembered the comic books of his childhood and their later live-action movie adaptations, free-lance adventurers and crimefighters were depicted wearing garishly colored skin-tight costumes much like those of circus acrobats. He had once been startled to come across a full-color reproduction of an 1890s circus poster in a book somewhere and see a troupe of acrobats wearing costumes almost identical to those worn by that sort of comic-book character. The only differences were the acrobats' handlebar mustaches and the lack of any distinctive insignias on their chests.

Unlike comic-book characters or acrobats, however, Astroman's taste in costumery was more subdued. His uniform was a rather sober dark green with white trim. Instead of being tight-fitting to the point of an extra layer of skin, it was more of a green tunic over green slacks, perhaps based on a military uniform in use wherever he came from. Its more theatrical elements were the elbow-length white gauntlets flared at the ends, a long green cape, and the knee-high white boots. At his waist was a white belt, while a white winged "A" emblem on his chest contrasted vividly against the green background. He also had a mask, a dark-green half-hood that covered most of his face except for his mouth and chin. The mask stopped just above his eyebrows, leaving his upper forehead and tousled brown hair free, but each ear was covered by a hard white disc. While the purpose of the ear-coverings was unknown, they were thought to be radio receivers. Or perhaps they had no purpose at all other than to make the mask look cool.

While the mask left little of his face exposed, he did seem to be a good-looking specimen of perfectly human manhood. He was also solidly built with a massive, muscular body. Having put in his share of gym time, Matt had to wonder how Astroman kept in shape in a world where lifting a car over his head and then throwing it was no more effort than tossing a water balloon.

The gloves certainly made sense if Astroman had a secret life as a private citizen. Without them, he would have been leaving fingerprints everywhere. The mask made even more sense, since celebrities are recognized on the street all the time even in casual clothes and without their usual stage make-up. There was no way he could have convinced people, especially people who knew him in both roles, that he was really two different and unrelated individuals if he did nothing more than, say, wear glasses in his civilian guise and comb his hair differently. On Matt's world, of course, with half a century's worth of technical advances since 1967, facial recognition technology would have identified him immediately.

The idea of putting on a costume to fight crime hadn't come out of nowhere, as this world had a tradition of independent masked detectives grudgingly tolerated by duly constituted law enforcement agencies that couldn't otherwise cope with some of the really bizarre criminals. Most of the free-lancers seemed to rely on gimmicks, but some may have actually had extraordinary powers thanks to the wacky physics here, if not to Astroman's extent. Matt's impression was that Astroman was considered the first and foremost in his field while the others were just pale imitations and also-rans.

Boiling down the articles and accompanying sidebars, Matt gathered that Astroman was around forty years old and his public career dated back about twenty-five years. He was first heard of as the teenage Astrolad in the small town of Centerburg, Ohio. (Astrolad? Why not Astroboy? Or was that name already in use somewhere?) He then spent four years in Columbus, the state capital, presumably when he was in college. After transitioning to Astroman, he had worked out of Chicago as a freelance first-responder ever since. If he had an unknown alias, no one had ever been able to find it out. It seemed to Matt that any halfway competent private detective with an afternoon to kill could have uncovered Astroman's secret civilian identity in short order by going through the Centerburg High School yearbook of the appropriate year and looking for likely males who had gone on to Ohio State and were now known to be living in Chicago — how many could there be? — but maybe Astroman had done something to cover his obvious tracks.

Astrogirl figured in one of the pictures. It wasn't a close-up, unfortunately, but Matt saw that she had shoulder-length blonde hair styled in a '60s flip and wore a costume that was a girl's version of Astroman's. The main difference was that instead of a half-hood over her head like Astroman, she wore a more traditional green domino mask that mainly covered the area around her eyes. Matt couldn't see that it hid very much of her face. Also, the tunic was extended to mid-thigh or so as a skirt, and instead of wearing slacks her legs were bare above her knee-high white boots. She looked like a figure skater or a cheerleader for a high school with a name that started with "A."

Astrogirl was about twenty but had been active only for the last three or so years. Though she apparently had the same powers her cousin did, she was not seen in public as often, and little was known about her. A compilation of sightings had led to the suspicion that she lived some-where in downstate Illinois and not with Astroman, who was believed to live in Chicago itself, and she presumably had a private life of her own.

Where the Astros had actually come from seemed to be a matter of dispute. The official version was that they had been sent to Earth from a now-destroyed planet called Helionn, which had had an advanced civili-zation inhabited by human beings more or less identical to Earth people. Artists' conceptions of life on Helionn tended to 1930s pulp-magazine cover super-cities — nothing said "city of the future" like elevated high-ways between skyscrapers, never mind how practical they were — but there were alternate versions with more alien concepts like cities that resembled ice sculptures. Looked rather chilly, Matt thought. Other speculations ran to the Astros being weird genetic experiments grown right here on Earth like clones in tanks filled with nutrients, never mind the claimed extraplanetary origin story. No one seemed to know for cer-tain, but whatever the real story was, Astroman and Astrogirl had immense powers that were genuine but couldn't be scientifically explained.

The point of the lead *Newsweek* article was that Astroman was miss-ing. He had not been seen for two weeks, even failing to show up for several scheduled public appearances to promote various good causes without calling to cancel. The Astroman Foundation, a corporate entity that existed to perform the necessary legal functions for a man who had no legal existence, was refusing to comment and bravely insisting that everything was just fine. Unnamed sources indicated, however, that behind the Foundation's closed doors the officers were in a state of near-panic after two weeks of not hearing anything from the big guy. Unfin-ished business that couldn't be taken care of without personal instruc-tions from Astroman himself was piling up alarmingly. For her part, Astrogirl hadn't gone missing, but all she told reporters who tried to cor-ner her for a comment was, "Don't worry, he's just on a secret mission," and then she flew away.

One reporter with more nerve than sense disguised himself as tem-porary kitchen help and managed to bluff his way into Garth Bolton's heavily guarded lakefront estate in Kenilworth. The reporter confronted the renegade scientist at poolside, where Bolton sat in a deck chair under an umbrella while a bikini-clad former model manicured his fingernails. Since the reporter was Johnny Larsen, one of Astroman's few personal friends, the resulting interview was perhaps somewhat less than objective, with Larsen accusing Bolton outright of killing Astroman somehow. Bolton replied that if he had, he wouldn't feel any qualms about killing Astroman's friends since he wouldn't have to worry about retribution, but he honestly didn't know any more about it than anybody else. Bolton's hired thugs then frog-marched Larsen off the premises, told him not to try that again if he knew what was good for him, and gave him a boot in the posterior to assist in his departure.

Just when Matt was finishing the magazine, someone knocked at the door.

"Come in," he said, assuming it was Dr. MacTavish. He wanted to talk to him anyway, and ask some questions to fill in the holes left by the magazine's account of things

Instead, however, and Matt's spirits sagged a little, it was Edmond, carrying a small box.

"I have a present for you from Dr. MacTavish," the officious assistant said coldly. "Since we are not running a coffee shop where beatniks play bongo drums, we prefer for our personnel to present a clean-cut image at this facility."

For his part, Matt preferred to sport a little facial hair, but Edmond's emphasis was on petty little rules to be followed. It was a game of Simon Says, with what Simon actually said unimportant. What mattered was who got to be Simon. Besides, on Matt's world, insisting on shaved faces at a scientific research facility would have resulted in the most irreplaceable personnel walking out.

"What do you want me to do?" Matt demanded. "Pull my beard out one hair at a time?"

"That won't be necessary," Edmond replied. "Try this."

He set the box on the room's small table and opened it. Inside were a razor, some two-edged razor blades of a type just about extinct on Matt's world, a bottle of water, and a small plastic container filled with what appeared to be shaving cream.

"We tried some experiments in increasing energy levels this afternoon," Edmond went on. "The process seemed to work to some extent on inanimate objects. As for living things, we succeeded mainly in frying a few mice. At least now you should be able to shave."

Energy levels? While Matt tried to puzzle that out, Edmond left, his duty done.

Matt took the improvised shaving kit down the hall to the shower room to try it out. It wasn't the smoothest shave he'd ever had. On his own world, he would have thrown out a blade that felt this dull. Its energy level, whatever that was, was still apparently rather less than his own. Nonetheless, the shaving cream and water did have some effect in softening his beard and he was able to make a little headway against the hair on his face. He was sorry to see the beard and mustache go, but it was a sacrifice he'd have to make to live on this world.

At any rate, it was a shave, even if he would probably have to put up with a certain irreducible degree of five o'clock shadow. Feeling somewhat refreshed and a little cleaner, Matt went to the dining hall for dinner.

Again the food didn't sit very well, and he had to hope that he could adapt over time to eating on this world. Perhaps the real wonder was that he was able to get any nourishment out of it at all. He felt a little better after a walk around the grounds, then decided to take a flight after dark to see how night-flying went. Not wanting to risk getting lost in the darkness above the confusing welter of lights of semi-rural Illinois, and still not feeling entirely up to spec, he cut it short and went to bed early.

As he lay in bed listening to his stomach gurgle, he wondered how Dr. MacTavish was able to make objects at least semi-hyper. If the process worked on his own world... He fell asleep thinking of commercial applications like indestructible drill bits and grinding wheels.

Chapter Four: **Battle with Berserko**

The next day dawned bright and clear.

After getting up, Matt made another attempt at shaving. Even though the results weren't as smooth as he'd like, he was just glad that he could look reasonably presentable in public thanks to the higher-energy razor blade, shaving cream, and water. It was too bad this world's 1967 still preferred the clean-shaven look for men. If he'd arrived in the '70s, he might have been able to get by with a beard and mustache. He'd still have to figure out how to trim them, but at least shaving wouldn't be a daily obligation.

He still had no idea what was meant by "energy levels," which sounded for all the world like the "vibrations" so beloved of psychic mediums and the various pseudo-scientific frauds and cultists of his own world, a portentous term that sounded fraught with meaning but actually explained nothing. But Dr. MacTavish was a working scientist who actually got results even if he sometimes didn't use the same words Matt did, so surely he knew what he was doing and had an explanation behind all this.

In addition to a high-energy shaving kit, Matt now had clean clothes. Edmond had sent out for several new changes of clothing for him, doubtless less out of consideration for his well-being than a realization that the clothes that had come with Matt were products of the other dimension and should be analyzed and tested as well. Edmond's insistence that the staff should observe the dress code also showed in the inclusion of a suit coat, a couple of neckties, and even a fedora. Did men still wear hats on the street here? By this time, it wouldn't have surprised Matt in the least.

Nothing that directly concerned him seemed to be going on that morning. Edmond had refused to answer his questions when he dropped off the clothes, tersely saying that experiments were continuing and all would be made clear in due course once certain hypotheses had been tested. As for Dr. MacTavish, he was in some undisclosed location and not to be disturbed, presumably tending to said experiments. Shut up and don't bother us, in other words. That left Matt on his own.

With nothing else to do that morning, he decided to follow up on Dr. MacTavish's suggestion and fly into Chicago to see if the Astroman Museum might answer some of his questions. He wore the suit coat and a tie, but the hat would have been impractical for flying. Since he would have to take it off inside the building and either check it in somewhere or carry it, he left it behind no matter what the quaint native custom was.

The Astroman Museum turned out to be an adjunct to the Museum of Science and Industry well to the south of the tall buildings of downtown Chicago (the "Loop," as natives of both worlds called it) on Lake Shore Drive. Just to the east was Lake Michigan, vast and sparkling blue in the sunlight, while the University of Chicago campus lay to the west. From the air on that warm and cloudless July day, the main building of the museum looked about the same as it did on Matt's world, a massive domed pseudo-Greek temple left over from the 1893 World's Fair.

The Astroman annex was at the rear, where the Henry Crown Space Center should have been. It was a round, pillared building that reminded Matt of seeing the Jefferson Memorial on a long-ago school trip to Washington DC. Only this building had a heroic-sized statue of Astroman standing arms akimbo on top of the dome, marble cape forever billowing.

Matt landed in the back, near a loading dock, hoping no one had seen him. Actually, if anyone had, the sight of flying people in the sky was probably so common in this world that no one would think it was unusual. Especially not in the vicinity of this particular museum. Even if Astroman was missing, Astrogirl must have dropped by now and then.

He walked around the building to the front, and on the way noticed the cars in the parking lot. Most were Fords, Chevys, and Dodges, to judge by their chrome lettering. The body styles were oddly old-fashioned, as though the designers had decided 1963 was such a good year that they would rerun it with just a few changes from then on. No Japanese cars were in sight and the only obvious import was an old-style Volkswagen Bug. Matt wondered if America's balance of trade was considerably better on this world. A yellow school bus was also parked in the lot, suggesting that Astroman was considered important enough in this world that teachers thought his museum rated a field trip. It was July but evidently some sort of summer school class was involved, since there was a sign on the side of the bus referring to a "Summer Enrichment Program."

Near the front of the building, an elderly man in a worn and rather shabby suit stood on the sidewalk probably some legally specified distance away from the steps leading up to the entrance. He carried a hand-lettered sign reading **THERE IS ONLY ONE TRUE "STAR-MAN"** in one hand and in the other was a fistful of dreary-looking religious tracts. With his extended perception, Matt could see from their covers that they were in crudely drawn comic-strip format and warned against placing trust in "false prophets" like certain individuals claiming to be from other planets. Apparently Astroman wasn't *quite* universally beloved. Although the proselytizer smiled at him from where he stood a hundred feet away and called something about "free literature," Matt pretended he couldn't hear him even though he could have easily tuned in on the man's heartbeat if he listened hard enough, and went up the steps.

He paid a modest admission fee at the door, using money that Edmond had grudgingly doled out to him before he left the laboratory, and went on inside.

In the entrance hall was a bulletin board labeled **ASTROMAN'S LATEST EXPLOITS**. On the board itself were pinned a few newspaper clippings several weeks old and a hand-lettered sign reading:

AWAY ON A MISSION.
WILL RETURN SOON.

Even if Astroman was a man who had everything, the museum had to support itself and could probably be forgiven a little shameless huckstering. Next came the inevitable gift shop selling various souvenirs like pens, pencils, rulers, and metal pin-on buttons emblazoned with the stylized winged "A" symbol, all duly marked with the tiny but almost as important "R" in a circle. (Hadn't refrigerator magnets been invented here yet?) Numerous books were on display, ranging from some meant for children (*Astrolad Saves a Puppy* and *The Mightiest Boy in Centerburg*) to thick tomes for adult readers with titles like *The Astroman Story* and *Helionn: The Doomed Utopia*. Nearby was a revolving spinner rack with a sign aimed at attracting the small fry: **HEY, KIDS! COMICS!** It was filled with authorized *Astroman* comic books featuring the main man, but whether they were his actual adventures or just imaginary stories, Matt couldn't tell. Another rack offered postcards. If Matt had wanted one reproducing a painting of Astroman looking proud and majestic with his cape waving in the wind as he stood on a mountaintop, he could have bought it here, except who was there to send it to?

Helio the Astrodog also came in for his share of licensed merchandise, including any number of different stuffed plush dolls all complete with capes. There were also plush dolls of other animals with capes, like cats, horses, monkeys, and even turtles, but they were presumably fictional, maybe characters from the comic books.

Astrogirl wasn't nearly so well represented. Other than for a few moppet-sized Astrogirl costumes hanging from a rack in the back (next to a sign warning the purchaser that the costumes did not give the wearer the power to fly so don't let your kid do anything stupid) and what seemed to be a repurposed Barbie doll, there was fairly little merchandising capitalizing on the latest addition to the family. Perhaps she was still too new.

Not finding anything in the gift shop he wanted to buy — well, one of the books might have been helpful for background information but Edmond hadn't given him enough money — Matt continued into the main exhibit hall. Since it was a weekday morning, the museum was nearly empty. The only visitors were a few stray tourists from out of town and a noisy class of fifth grade or so children on a field trip, probably the kids from the bus outside whose summer was being enriched by being stuck in school.

The rotunda under the dome was dominated by a huge three-dimensional display perhaps thirty feet in diameter depicting an exploding planet, the stays and struts supporting the individual chunks artfully disguised as simulated gouts of flame from the brightly lit central orange and red plastic fireball. In front, a little rocket ship was caught in the act of speeding away, held up by a curving rod made to look like its exhaust.

Thinking he might as well start at the beginning, Matt took a seat in a small auditorium off the main hall and sat through an introductory film and recorded lecture called *The Legend of Astroman*. Unfortunately, he had to share the auditorium with the fifth graders, who didn't exactly sit quietly and watch the show with rapt attention. Maybe they had heard it all before, but they were restless and seemed bored.

The presentation was a multi-media combination of drawings, limited animation, and live-action footage, reminding Matt of a planetarium show that used every flashy trick known to get around the fact that the budget hadn't been large enough for real animation. Somehow managing to tune out the babble of the kid next to him despite having a sense of hearing capable of perceiving the sound of paint drying (a faint crackling and rustling), Matt listened to the film's slickly professional narrator (him they could afford) recount the basics of the Astroman story. Some of it he already knew from what he had read and been told the day before, but the film fleshed out the details.

An arrow pointed to a bright star in an observatory photograph of the night sky.

"Astronomers call this star Delta Pavonis. Some twenty light-years from Earth, this was the sun that warmed the planet Helionn — the home of Astroman!"

With that, the picture changed to a cloud-streaked planet that looked much like a photograph of Earth from space artificially tinted green.

"Helionn! The home of an advanced culture of human beings like ourselves, but doomed to destruction!" A series of slow pans across still pictures showed artists' conceptions of impossibly noble people in vaguely Grecian costume strolling through futuristic if architecturally improbable cities. Astroman himself may have been indistinguishable from a man of northern European descent, but according to the pictures, all of Earth's races had analogues on Helionn as well.

A drawing of a noble Helionnite facing a council of elders introduced Jarn Thelnarr, a leading scientist who had discovered that Helionn had a geologically unstable core and was about to explode. Failing to convince the council to evacuate the planet, he worked on his own to at least send his wife, Rhisha, and his infant son, Karsten, to safety on distant Earth. In the end, Rhisha chose to stay with her husband, leading to the beautifully painted scene of a miniature rocket speeding away just ahead of the hurtling debris of the exploding planet.

"Little Karsten soon reached Earth," the narrator went on. "His spaceship landed in Ohio, where he was found by a kindly family who adopted him and raised him as their own son. For security reasons, their identity remains a secret to this day, but despite their anonymity we can salute them, for with their love and care they nurtured the baby from space into the hyper-powered crusader for law and justice we now know as Astroman! He made his first public appearance as the teenage Astrolad in Centerburg, Ohio, and any criminals so foolhardy as to try to rob the bank or the hardware store in that town soon learned to regret their folly! The boy could fly, lift great weights, and see through walls! There may not have been much crime to battle in a small town like Centerburg, but certainly having Astrolad around didn't hurt!"

(Film clip of adult Astroman returning to Centerburg as a guest at some local celebration. Kid of about nine or ten looks up at him in awe and burbles, "You're not just some actor in a costume! You're *really* super-duper!" *Well, wasn't that priceless.* Matt was mainly surprised that the expression "super-duper" existed here, rather than something like "hyper-dyper." Sounded too much like "diaper," maybe.)

"As Astrolad grew older, he turned his attention to larger cities. He spent four years as a young man in Columbus, Ohio, and long-time residents of the Ohio State University area say the campus was never safer before or since! Then Astroman appeared in Chicago, where he has been to this day, though of course he will fly to the scene of trouble any-where around the world! Because he has such great power, he has sworn to use it for good, and has dedicated his life to the service of humanity!"

The presentation concluded with stirring march music over a montage of newspaper front pages that summed up Astroman's career to date. Foiling bank robberies, apprehending master criminals, saving sinking ships, putting out forest fires, bringing supplies to disaster victims... quite a busy fellow, that Astroman. It was to the point that Matt had to wonder if he had any time for himself.

The film ended with a list of credits and a blurb to the effect that it had been produced by Seale & Shuhmacher Studios in Cleveland, O. *At least it wasn't boring*, Matt thought, and started to get up.

But wait — there was more! *The Legend of Astroman* had been made before Astrogirl was introduced to the world about three years before. Instead of reediting that film to include her, the Museum had tacked on a short, second film called *The Legend of Astrogirl*, obviously made by other hands with an even lower budget.

Matt hadn't been able to understand how Astrogirl could be twenty years younger than Astroman if Helionn had exploded when he was a baby, but this film explained it with a series of colored line drawings. A small colony on one of Helionn's moons had survived the disaster, and Astrogirl was born sometime later. To Astroman's uncle and aunt, coincidentally enough, accounting for the cousin connection. Despite a valiant effort to make the colony self-sustaining, the lack of fresh supplies from the mother world sealed its fate in the long run. As the last colonists died, Astrogirl was sent to Earth just as her cousin had been, only she was fifteen by that time and not a baby.

When she arrived on Earth, she found Astroman at once, but her existence was not immediately announced. Instead, Astroman trained her in secret for about two years before she made her public debut. At that point in the narrative, the illustrations changed from artists' conceptions to actual photographs, and the film then traced her career to date. The succession of newspaper headlines and TV news footage suggested that she had put her share of master criminals behind bars, but preferred to help out in natural disasters, illustrated by shots of her rescuing children stranded on the roof of a house all but submerged by swirling flood-waters, putting out a forest fire in Yellowstone National Park, and ferrying frightened woodland creatures to safety ahead of a volcanic eruption.

In her photographs, Astrogirl appeared as an athletic blonde of medium height. Her costume was the same skater/cheerleader number Matt had seen in the *Newsweek* picture, though it had gone through some minor modifications over time. The headband was not a particularly good look, Matt thought, and fortunately she didn't wear it for long. From her close-ups, Matt saw that under the mask she had a pretty face with blue eyes, an upturned nose, and a faint dusting of freckles. There had to be more to the story than parallel evolution to explain how anyone who looked like that could be a native of another planet.

Matt also reflected that if Astrogirl had turned up on his world, she probably would have started calling herself the more politically correct Astrowoman the minute she turned eighteen, but maybe trademark and merchandising considerations, not to mention TV deals, would keep her as Astrogirl well into her twenties.

Since there was relatively little material to work with, the film was soon over. On the way out of the auditorium, a little girl walking next to Matt suddenly exclaimed, "Hmph! What a bunch of lies!"

Startled, Matt looked down at her. She was tall for her age and thin, and wore glasses.

"Lies?" he asked, wondering if someone really did know more about all this than the official story let on. "What do you mean?"

The girl seemed happy to set the grown-up straight. "My mother says Astroman isn't from space at all. He's from right here on Earth!"

That sounded reasonable, but... "Then how did he get to be hyper?"

"Mom thinks he's some kind of Nazi experiment. You know, breeding a superior race and stuff."

It took Matt a moment to recover from hearing a little girl say something so stunningly wacko with a straight face. "Isn't he a little old to have been a Nazi baby?" he had to ask. "He would have been born way before the war." Around 1927 if he had it figured right, and the Nazis didn't take power in Germany until 1933.

Almost gleeful with the chance to display her secret knowledge of things *they* don't want you to know, the girl went on to elaborate. "Mom says the Nazis probably kidnapped him as a little boy and did weird things to him, then planted him in America because Astrolad appeared around the time the war started, and then maybe the CIA took him over after the war. They wanted a hyper-hero who would do what big business told him to do and beat up people who didn't go along. Mom says he's just a hyper-reactionary and not progressive at all."

Rather advanced for a fifth-grader, Matt thought, but then she was just repeating some conspiracy theory she had heard at home from her parents. Even at that, it sounded highly unlikely. After all, he had the same powers Astroman did and as far as he knew he wasn't a Nazi-CIA plot. Where Astrogirl fit into the theory, who knew.

"Hmm. I don't think your mother quite has the right idea—"

"My mother wouldn't lie to me! You called my mother a liar! I'm gonna tell! Miss Stapleton!"

The girl's yelling brought her teacher over and Matt found himself embarrassed and hard-pressed to explain.

Miss Stapleton just shook her head tiredly. "Don't worry about it. Carla's mother is a political science professor at one of the local colleges, so you can imagine that she brings all kinds of ideas to school."

"I see..." Matt muttered. It was probably only to be expected. With the only available explanation for Astroman's origin and powers so fantastic, some people would try to come up with alternate theories that, at least to them, were a little more believable. Without any facts to back up the speculation, however, their theories were just projections of their own pet beliefs. A left-wing college professor saw Astroman as a Nazi plot, but a real Nazi would probably denounce him as some kind of Jewish creation.

The teacher assembled her flock and led the kids to go look at something else, and Matt was relieved to see the last of them. Since it was nearly noon by this time, he stopped in the museum snack bar for an Astroburger and a Karsten Kola. By now he was getting on better with the local food, but he had a suspicion that this was one instance where he could be glad he had what amounted to a cast-iron stomach. After lunch, he wandered through the museum and took in the exhibits.

One particularly striking display was billed "Astroman Brings Peace to the Middle East." Most exhibits were loudly triumphant, but this one was conspicuous by being almost apologetic. The explanations accompanying the newspaper headlines and desert dioramas emphasized Astroman's youthful idealism and how he had not yet learned the restraint that comes with maturity.

When an Arab-Israeli war broke out, a then still young Astroman flew to the Middle East and stopped it by a simple but drastic measure. He kidnapped the Egyptian and Israeli leaders and tried to make them settle their differences one on one in front of their respective armies. If the conflict had been this world's premature counterpart of the Six-Day War, it ended five days early, as the leaders of neither side were eager to fight personal duels.

Instead of praise and the Nobel Peace Prize, however, Astroman got only a firestorm of criticism from all quarters. The Arabs were convinced that their tanks would have rolled into Tel Aviv if he hadn't interfered, but most critics were certain that he had actually saved the Egyptians from a military disaster. Besides, the Israelis didn't start the war. They were attacked in cold blood, so why subject their leaders to the same humiliation as the truly guilty parties? The President of the United States called Astroman to the White House for a private conference that was later described by insiders as a trip to the woodshed, and he gave up overt meddling in foreign policy after that.

The only thing was, Matt realized, without the controlled experiment of a duplicate Earth where Astroman didn't take a hand, no one appreciated what he had accomplished. Shaken by the experience of staring at each other in a makeshift arena with a hyper-powered American urging them to settle their dispute themselves instead of making thousands of young soldiers die in their place, the Israeli and Egyptian leaders established a commission to resolve their differences short of war, and that led to the creation of a joint administration over the Sinai Peninsula and the Gaza Strip as a semi-autonomous Palestinian homeland. The Egyptian President would have agreed to almost anything rather than face that mean-looking Israeli general with the eyepatch again, and that part of the Middle East had been quiet ever since. No more Arab-Israeli wars, no more Palestinian terrorism or uprisings...

If the museum staff only knew, Matt thought as he came away from the exhibit, they wouldn't have been so apologetic. That stunt might have actually been Astroman's greatest achievement.

He must have looked lonely or else she didn't have much to do in the nearly deserted museum and was bored. He was approached by a pretty red-haired girl in a green and white museum guide's uniform of knee-length skirt, jacket, and boots somewhat resembling Astrogirl's costume though with a green garrison cap that looked like a flight attendant's hat and a modest white winged "A" emblem on the jacket pocket.

"Hi, I'm Laurie," she said with a dazzling smile. "Can I show you around?"

Matt had no objection to pretty young girls paying attention to him. "Sure. Where do we start?"

"Well, there's a copy of the manuscript that Jarn Thelnarr put in the rocket with baby Karsten..."

A few photostats of hand-printed sheets lay in a place of honor in a glass case, surrounded by a diorama of Jarn Thelnarr in Grecian tunic applying pen to paper. Matt glanced at the pages through the glass, expecting to see an example of Helionnian script. While the language may not have been English, to his surprise the letters were Latin, though more angular. For that matter, the language seemed somehow familiar. It reminded Matt a little of German, but it wasn't that.

"Is that an Earth language?" he asked.

Laurie nodded with a smile. "I see you're not up on the Astroman Legend! Believe it or not, Jarn Thelnarr wrote that letter to his son in *Swedish!*"

Laurie had expected that little tidbit of information would startle Matt, and it was so out of left field that it had the anticipated effect. This world was just full of surprises...

"No one knows why, either," she went on. "Maybe he had the mistaken idea that Swedish was the dominant language on Earth, or perhaps he expected the rocket to land in Sweden and it went off course for some reason and came down in Ohio instead. That's not all of the letter since Astroman released only a few pages, but what we have has been translated and it's basically Jarn telling his son where he came from and why he was sent to Earth. For years, that letter was all we knew of what life was like on Helionn. Then Astrogirl came and of course she could tell us more because she grew up in a Helionnian colony."

"I wonder what could have been in the rest of the letter?" Matt said, thinking it might have answered some of his questions about the hows and whys of being hyper.

Laurie shrugged. "So does everyone else. Maybe it's just too personal. Anyway, he must have some good reason for holding it back."

The next exhibit was visitor-participation. "Match Your Strength With Astroman's!" read the sign. A section of railroad rail cut to about ten feet long and bent into a U-shape rested on a concrete pedestal and visitors were invited to try straightening it. Mounted on the wall in back of the exhibit was a series of enlarged photographs showing Astroman bending the rail at the museum's opening-day ceremony.

"Why don't you try it?" Laurie suggested.

Matt forced a smile. "I'd better not. Your boss might get mad if I ruined the exhibit by unbending it."

"I don't think that's much of a risk," Laurie said dryly. "Go on, try it!"

"Oh, all right," Matt said reluctantly.

He stepped up to the pedestal and placed his hands on the ends of the rail. As he gripped the steel, he had the sense that he *could* bend it if he chose to. Instead, he let his hands rest lightly on it and faked a little grunting and straining.

Then he turned to Laurie with a sheepish grin. "Nope, can't do it."

"I don't think you tried very hard," Laurie said with mock disapproval.

Just be glad I didn't...

Next was the "Astroman's Greatest Foes!" exhibit, illustrated with huge blow-ups of newspaper headlines and photographs as well as a row of wax dummies representing said Foes, some in outlandish costumes. A few were ordinary criminals ranging from bank-robbers to organized gang-leaders on the Al Capone level, but others had adopted colorful personas and specialized gimmicks, as though criminal psychology on this world carried with it a penchant for publicity and notoriety that seemed better suited for professional wrestlers. A few foes were downright bizarre. One looked like an elf who wore a funny cap something like an undersized top hat. For lack of a better name, the newspapers called him Mr. Qwertyuiop, and over several years he had appeared every few months to play tricks on Astroman and the citizens of Chicago.

"He hasn't been seen in a while," Laurie added. "We don't know where he came from but we hope he'll stay there from now on. Even if he wasn't really malicious, his pranks were annoying."

There was also a creature called "Berserko," depicted in a series of models and line drawings as something like a cartoonishly caricatured version of Astroman.

Laurie passed over the display quickly, promising, "You'll see more of him later, at the end of the tour."

Finally, they came to Garth Bolton, a coldly arrogant-looking man with thinning hair in a business suit, who appeared to be in his well-preserved sixties. *So that's what he looks like*, Matt thought. Since he had heard almost as much about Bolton as about Astroman since coming to this world, Matt read the accompanying description curiously.

The museum's account of Bolton was oddly vague, sticking rigidly to the published record of newspaper articles and court proceedings. Besides being a renegade scientist (a concept Matt found difficult to wrap his brain around), Bolton was also a local Mr. Big with enough money and behind-the-scenes power and influence to corrupt any number of politicians and judges. The record spoke of iron-clad court cases against Bolton that were mysteriously dismissed out of hand and convictions for crimes most foul that were inexplicably overturned on appeal on the slimmest of technicalities. Bolton had been in prison several times but never for very long. Even master criminals had feelings — or lawyers — and the museum directors apparently felt discretion was better than explicitly stating what everyone felt about Bolton. He was too notorious to ignore, too powerful to offend.

Looking at the exhibit, Matt actually felt a twinge of reluctant respect for Bolton. Powerful as the renegade scientist was, he was still a mere mortal and Astroman could squash him like a bug if it came to that. Being able to match a hyper-powered enemy for years on end with just his wits took some kind of genius, though it certainly helped that Astroman evidently had a strict ethical code that didn't allow him to kill anyone. Matt remembered the badly wounded lab assistant lying on the floor in a pool of his own blood and wondered if perhaps Astroman should have just grabbed Bolton some dark night, flown him out over Lake

Michigan, and dropped him from a mile up. Bolton disappears, nobody's the wiser, end of problem. But Astroman didn't work that way, and Matt had to admit that he probably couldn't bring himself to do it, either. Killing someone, even someone who arguably deserved it, was just a bridge too far.

Besides Foes, Astroman also had Friends. An accompanying exhibit showed how for jobs that required extra hands he had occasionally teamed up with some of this world's other colorfully costumed and sometimes even downright weird hyper-heroes, with names like the Streak, the Sea King, and Gladiatrix. He and a hero based out of New York City called Knightfox had worked together the most as what was dubbed the Earth's Greatest Team, even though it seemed at first glance like a mismatch since Astroman had enormous powers and Knightfox didn't. To go by the explanatory texts and photo captions, the partnership had worked for solving subtler crimes because Knightfox had a detective's expertise in following clues and making deductions while Astroman was more straight-ahead muscle without ever having had a need to develop much finesse. Knightfox had since retired, however, and Astroman had gone back to working alone.

Just before the end of the tour, Matt and Laurie stopped in front of an exhibit showing the Astro-Family. Lifelike, life-sized wax dummies of Astroman, Astrogirl, and Helio stood tall and proud in front of a green, blue, and white half-globe of Helionn ten feet in diameter. Since no actual maps of Helionn were available, the oceans and continents were probably imaginary. Matt's attention zeroed in on Astrogirl. With her dazzling smile, she struck him as more than a little fetching.

"Is she really that pretty?" he asked.

"Oh, prettier," Laurie said. "The figure doesn't do her justice. They were so advanced on Helionn that I'm sure they could modify their genes, so all the men were probably handsome and all the women must have been very beautiful."

There were about three maybes in that sentence, suggesting that very little was known with any certainty about Helionn. In any event, even if all the women on Helionn had been beautiful, only one was left now, but she definitely made the claim plausible.

The last exhibit before the exit was a life-sized statue of the aforementioned Berserko, caught in a pose of stepping forward with an outstretched hand, as though about to shake hands with someone. The statue was on the floor rather than on a pedestal, and not blocked from public access by any barriers. A sign offered patrons the opportunity to **SHAKE HANDS WITH BERSERKO!** Matt wasn't sure why anyone would want to. Berserko was just a sad parody of Astroman. He — or it —

wore a patched, dirty, baggy, and badly faded Astroman costume that seemed to be a part of him the same way a toga was part of a statue of Julius Caesar, and his face and hands were craggy planes and angles, as though roughly carved out of rock, with overly bright and smeared colors. He looked like a sad clown version of Astroman.

"And here is the highlight of our museum's collection," Laurie said proudly. "This is Berserko. No, it's not a dummy, not a statue, not a replica. It's really *him!*"

She launched into the long and pathetic story of how Berserko came to be. A scientist-savant had a scheme of creating artificial life by using a human being as a pattern, but replacing carbon atoms with silicon. It didn't work with regular people as models for some reason, but using Astroman had resulted in a creature dubbed "Berserko," a crude parody of Astroman with rock-like features. Unfortunately, trying to duplicate Astroman overloaded the equipment, and in the inevitable explosion the machinery was wrecked, the scientist was killed, and his notes and plans were destroyed. It was as though some larger destiny was making sure Berserko would forever be the only one of his kind and there could be no others. Just one dull-witted hyper-being as strong as Astroman himself was probably enough, however.

Being childlike as well as powerful, Berserko caused enormous problems until Astroman managed to shut him down. Astroman insisted in response to later criticism that Berserko wasn't alive in some technical sense, being made of "non-living" silicon, and was only a highly complex machine, which meant turning him off wasn't really killing him. Even so, Berserko seemed to be conscious and aware, he could talk to a limited extent, and he acted independently if not wisely, so the assertion that he was only a robotic simulation of life sounded weak and may have been something Astroman had to talk himself into believing.

An exhibit off to one side depicted the "Deactivator" Astroman had used. The business end was a gleaming metal rod or wand about a foot long that projected some kind of ray, connected by a thick cable to a box worn as a backpack and somewhat resembling a high-tech portable leaf blower. Berserko would have had to be impossibly naïve to approach with a smile and an outstretched hand someone wearing that rather menacing-looking thing, but a diagram showed how the wand was hidden inside Astroman's sleeve with the backpack unit covered by his cape.

"It was very sad," Laurie finished. "Astroman had to trick Berserko within range of the Deactivator, and he did it by pretending to make friends with him. Berserko came forward to shake hands with his new friend, only to be 'turned off.' But it was best this way. Berserko was too powerful and too irresponsible to be allowed to roam free. Astroman had

Dwight R. Decker

to put him out of action. Now Berserko himself stands here, greeting the guests of the Astroman Museum as an actual memento of one of Astroman's strangest and most touching adventures!" She smiled a little sheepishly as she realized how theatrical she must have sounded. "Er... sorry! I kind of turned on my canned lecture there. I give that speech a couple of dozen times a day, you know."

Her voice turning lower and more confidential, she added, "The really sad part is how people make fun of Berserko just because he was stupid and talked funny. The *Astroman* comic books have a regular series about him and his imaginary relatives on a whole planet of Berserkos and how dumb they are. It's supposed to be hilarious comedy, but it's pretty heavy-handed and just laughing at somebody because he isn't very smart. I think it's a little cruel myself, but maybe it's a way for people to reassure themselves that someone who really can be a dangerous menace is actually harmless."

While Berserko was another audience-participation exhibit and patrons were invited to shake hands with him, "shake" was hardly the right word. Being made out of solid silicon, he was literally petrified and as immobile as Gibraltar, and probably at least as resistant to damage as the bent rail. The museum didn't have to worry about vandals or souvenir hunters breaking off fingers. At the end of the day, it was probably enough for the cleaning lady just to wipe the grease off his hand.

Still, Matt thought as he watched some giggling tourists take each other's picture while shaking hands with the frozen clown, what a way for even a mentally deficient parody to end up.

Then he remembered something Laurie had said. "What was that 'Deactivator' you mentioned?" he asked. "How could it turn Berserko off?"

"I'm not sure," Laurie admitted. "I think one of the books about Astroman talks about it a little, but not much is really known. Apparently Astroman knew enough of the theory behind the original duplicating machine that created Berserko that he could have some other scientist-savant make something for him that would affect Berserko somehow. Just how it worked is a mystery."

"He could turn Berserko off because he was a menace but he lets Garth Bolton go free?"

"Berserko didn't have Constitutional rights," Laurie pointed out, then murmured, "or every judge and prosecutor in the state in his pocket."

Meanwhile, the tourists had finished and were headed towards the exit, leaving Berserko available.

"Want to try it?" Laurie asked.

"I'm not sure if I should," Matt said uncomfortably.

Laurie laughed. "Don't worry he won't break!"

"It isn't that..." Matt started to say, but trailed off. It seemed silly to admit that he simply felt sorry for the poor goof. But if Berserko was turned off, inert, no more than a lump of rock, what would be the harm?

Meanwhile, the fifth grade class was moving in behind them, forming into a line. Besides their teacher, they were led by their own guide, another young woman in a uniform identical to Laurie's, and seemed to be winding up the tour. Matt got the impression that he was holding things up and they were politely waiting for him to do the handshaking bit so they could run the kids past Berserko and get them back on the bus by a certain time. With twenty-odd kids, it would take them a while to go through the whole class, so the teacher and the guide were probably impatient to get started.

"Oh, why not..." Matt stepped up and put his hand in Berserko's.

Big deal, he thought. It really was like shaking hands with a statue. The hand felt like so much carved stone.

Then he felt a slight tingle, like a spark passing from his hand to Berserko's at the point of contact.

Berserko's hand suddenly turned supple. The fingers tightened around Matt's hand.

And Berserko blinked.

Matt yanked his hand away. "Oh Christ!" he exclaimed in horror. "I think I jump-started him!"

"You did *what?*" Laurie demanded. Then she saw Berserko move his arms, and she screamed.

The fifth graders behind them stirred uneasily. Laurie clamped her hand over her mouth to stifle the scream, and glanced dumbfoundedly at Matt, her eyes wide, obviously wondering how he could have turned the monster on.

Matt took a step backwards as Berserko rolled his head around his shoulders. He could hear creaking and snapping as Berserko moved, as though breaking rocky concretions that had grown over his joints during his long dormant period. Matt had a bad feeling that he had also been recharging somehow during that time, and a hyper-powered menace even Astroman could barely handle was about to revive at full strength.

Berserko opened his mouth with a cracking sound and moved his lips, and a low rumble issued that sounded like gravel grinding together. To Matt's surprise, he understood what the thing was trying to say.

"Where am Astroman? Astroman trick me! Me fix him!"

"Uh, Astroman's not here right now," Laurie said quickly and desperately.

Berserko glared at her. "That not true — Astroman am here!" He suddenly lashed out, thrusting his open hand towards Laurie to push her out of his way.

If Berserko's hand connected, Laurie would be slammed all the way across the exhibition hall and probably badly hurt if not killed outright. Matt saw the movement and jumped in front of her to block the blow. Whatever else Berserko was, he was hyper-powered. Matt felt the impact and staggered back. He brushed against Laurie and that was enough to knock her to the floor.

Matt looked back and down at her. "Are you all right?" he asked worriedly.

She rubbed her head a little dazedly. "Yes, but..." She looked up at him in bafflement. "How did you...? You can't be Astroman, can y— watch out!"

No, he couldn't be Astroman because Astroman would have known better than to look away from Berserko. The punch caught Matt full in the stomach and doubled him up. Matt staggered backwards. Invulnerability trumped hyper-strength, however. Matt didn't feel any pain, and his breath wasn't knocked out. A fight between two hyper-powered people still wasn't the same as a fight between two normal people. If Berserko hit him with the power of an oncoming freight train, there was nothing magical about hyper-powers that made their force any different from that of the freight train.

It dawned on Matt that Berserko couldn't hurt him, but that wasn't the problem. How could *he* fight someone who couldn't be hurt, either? This wasn't the old physics chestnut about what would happen if an irresistible force met an immovable object — this was two irresistible forces colliding head-on.

"You not Astroman!" Berserko exclaimed disgustedly and turned away. He seemed uncertain about his next move, then Matt saw him notice the Astro-Family exhibit down the way and his rocky face took on an expression of sheer hatred. A sudden tensing of his body as he was about to make a move, and Matt could see where he was heading.

Meanwhile, the teacher and guide had seen trouble brewing and were herding the stunned-looking kids away, right into the path Berserko was about to take.

"Get those kids out of here!" Matt yelled.

The kids didn't wait for their teacher or the guide to tell them what to do, and scattered on their own like frightened rabbits.

Except for one little girl, who was more like the classic deer in the headlights and just stood there as though paralyzed by fright, directly in

Berserko's way as he leaped. Carla, wouldn't you know it, the girl who thought Astroman was a Nazi plot. Fate could be capricious that way.

Matt had to be a tenth of a second faster than Berserko. He threw himself forward, managed to grab Carla by the waist, and hit the floor with her as Berserko shot barely inches right over them. Matt even felt the wind on his cheek.

"You knocked me down!" Carla shrieked at Matt. "I'm gonna tell!"

And he had saved her life, not that he was going to get any thanks for it. But there was no time to argue about it with a hyper-menace on the loose, and he sprang to his feet.

Berserko flew down the hall like a rocky torpedo towards the Astro-Family exhibit and tore headlong into the life-sized wax dummy of Astroman in maniacal fury. Chunks of wax body parts and scraps of cloth from the costume whirled in all directions.

Matt watched, appalled. The disturbing part was that Berserko seemed to think it really was Astroman he was ripping apart in his rage.

No wonder he's called Berserko!

The few remaining tourists in the area had realized that something bad was happening and were running for cover yelling and screaming. Among them, Matt had a brief glimpse of Miss Stapleton urging Carla and the rest of her shrieking fifth graders towards the exit.

A museum security guard ran up with his pistol drawn, shouting for Berserko to cease and desist. The threat was pathetically inadequate, as anyone who worked in this place and saw the Berserko exhibit every day should have known, and Berserko ignored him. The guard fired several shots point blank at the monster, but Berserko didn't even feel them. The bullets flattened into lead splotches as they struck but had no other effect. Since his costume was an integral part of him, the bullets didn't even rip or tear it. The guard then retreated from the scene, realizing he didn't have a prayer of stopping Berserko, and went to help a couple of tourists out the door.

Matt had absorbed enough from Laurie's lecture to know that Berserko had never been a pushover even for Astroman, who had defeated him in the past only by ingenious stratagems rather than by force. With that hyper-powered, rock-like body, Berserko might have even been relatively much stronger than Astroman or at least not slowed down by pain or injury.

Matt felt responsible for turning Berserko back on even if it had been unintentional. The problem now was stopping him before he hurt or killed someone. Turning him off again probably wasn't as simple as finding a button on the back of his neck and pushing it. Then he remembered something else from Laurie's lecture.

She had just gotten to her feet again when he turned towards her.

"That 'Deactivator' Astroman used to shut him down!" he exclaimed. "Please tell me that's the real thing the museum has on display!"

"Er... I think Astroman kept it," she replied. "All we have is just a replica!"

Oh, great... They had the real Berserko here but the thing that turned him off was just a model. Not exactly good planning. And Matt's brain was a little short on ingenious stratagems at the moment. Given a day or two to think about it and look up old newspapers to see how Astroman had managed to trick Berserko before, Matt might have come up with something, but he needed an idea *now*. To complicate things, Berserko may not have been a genius but having been tricked before, he would probably be wary of anyone trying to pull an ingenious stratagem on him.

The only thing Matt could think of was to lure Berserko away from the museum. What he would do with him then was another problem entirely, but at the moment he had to make sure the monster couldn't hurt anybody. He raced down the hall to the Astro-Family exhibit — or what was left of it.

"Berserko!" he yelled as he approached.

The dim-witted parody abruptly stopped tearing the Astrogirl and Helio dummies apart and looked up suspiciously. "What you want?"

"It's me — Astroman!" Matt shouted. "How do you like my secret identity? I'm here to turn you off again!"

How much of the threat Berserko really understood wasn't clear, but he did recognize a threat plain and simple. His reply was a muffled "Rarrgh!" and he suddenly launched himself at Matt.

Matt's first thought was to turn and fly out the nearest window if he could find one, hopefully leading Berserko out of the museum, but in that second he had something like an idea.

His ex-girlfriend had once developed a sudden enthusiasm for karate and nagged him into joining her class. In the few weeks her interest lasted before she went on to something else, he had learned a few basic moves.

Meanwhile, Astroman had spent his whole life infinitely stronger than everyone else on Earth, and Berserko would have been the only opponent he had ever faced on anything like equal terms. No wonder Astroman had been at a loss dealing with Berserko, no wonder he had to rely on ingenious stratagems to dupe him. He had never learned how to fight.

Berserko was stronger, but Matt could use his strength against him. Berserko leaped at Matt, and Matt grabbed his arm, slid under him, and tossed him over his shoulder. Berserko flew into a display case containing replicas of medals Astroman had been awarded from various grateful governments for services rendered. The case collapsed in a spray of glass shards and beribboned decorations.

Berserko came up with a roar of primeval rage that rattled even hyper-eardrums and threw himself at Matt again. Like Astroman, Berserko had never learned how to fight, either, but made up for it with blind fury. When he threw a punch that would have smashed in the front of a speeding locomotive, Matt could easily see it coming. He deftly dodged and the rocky fist shot past his cheek.

With the monster off balance from the missed blow, Matt slammed his own fist into Berserko's jaw. The monster's head jerked back from the impact, but it looked as though Berserko hadn't even felt it. It really was like slugging a statue. About then Matt realized that maybe standing toe-to-toe with Berserko wasn't such a good idea after all.

Berserko fired another punch at Matt that would have knocked an elephant end over end backwards. Matt parried it and the bizarre battle was on. They fought up and down the hall, Berserko roaring in rage and flailing away, unable to connect as Matt weaved and dodged, and Matt responding with blows that connected but accomplished absolutely nothing. Berserko could rush Matt, and Matt could flip him into the wall, but Berserko would just crash through and come up again without being slowed down in the least.

Matt caught a brief glimpse of Laurie looking on with wide eyes and open mouth as it dawned on her that the young man she had given a guided tour of the Astroman Museum had turned out to be hyper himself, then she whirled and ran for the exit.

The property damage was immense and mounting. Berserko didn't care what he destroyed, and at times even seemed to be smashing more than he had to, exhibit after exhibit, display case after display case, as he stormed through the museum after Matt. The last of the tourists had already cleared out by the time Berserko shot through the huge display in the main hall of Helionn in mid-explosion, smashing into the simulated fireball in the center in a burst of shattered red and orange plastic. The delicately balanced assemblage of supposedly flying chunks of Helionn's crust promptly collapsed in a deafening roar. The display had shown Helionn halfway to destruction, and Berserko had finished the job.

At that point, Matt realized he was standing by the exhibit with the bent steel rail. Maybe that would get results. He tore the rail out of the pedestal in a spray of concrete fragments, grabbed each end, straightened it, and as Berserko charged in a new attack, slammed it full force against the side of the monster's head.

The impact bent the rail but barely knocked Berserko back a little. Matt had succeeded only in deflecting Berserko's attack by distracting him for a moment. As for physical damage, not even a scratch. The fight was turning into a stand-off.

It must have penetrated even Berserko's diminutive reasoning faculty that continuing the fight would be pointless. He couldn't get his fists past Matt's defense and Matt couldn't hurt him. Or maybe he just got bored. He abruptly broke off, turned, and leaped straight up, drilling into the ceiling in a shower of plaster and wood debris. A smashing noise from overhead as Berserko burst through the roof was followed a moment later by a loud crash outside the building, as though something large and heavy had hit the ground and shattered.

Matt paused to take a deep breath. He had been lucky. If Berserko had been intelligent or at least knowledgeable about human physiology, he would have seen that Matt was tiring. Berserko might not have been able to beat Matt outright, but he could have worn him down by stretching out the fight a little longer. Matt couldn't even guess what kept Berserko going so relentlessly.

He leaped up through the hole in the ceiling, following Berserko's trail through the roof and out into the open air. What he would do, or even could do, if he caught up with him was a problem he would deal with when he came to it.

Climbing into the sky above the museum, Matt saw that a crowd had gathered outside, mostly the visitors and staff, and heard a collective murmur and gasp as the spectators caught sight of him.

A cloud of dust was rising from the side lawn. In smashing his way through the roof, Berserko had knocked over the statue of Astroman standing on top, and it lay in pieces on the grass below. Matt hoped nobody had been standing under it when it fell, and was relieved to see that the crowd was mostly around front and there was no rush to the rubble to pull bodies out.

Above him, Berserko was a tiny green and white figure climbing fast into the cloudless blue sky. Matt threw every last ounce of his strength into catching up, although still not quite sure what he could do if he did.

Berserko soared higher and higher, and Matt doggedly followed. The city and the lake shrank beneath him into an abstract, colored map, and still Berserko rose. First one mile, then two.

At three miles and climbing, Matt gasped. He was gulping for air that his lungs were still not used to processing completely, and there just wasn't enough no matter how much he took in. Berserko kept rising above him, seemingly unaffected.

Finally, when Matt's vision started to blur and was filled with dancing black spots, and his head was spinning and his lungs were burning, he gave up the chase. Berserko may not have needed to breathe, but he did. If Berserko was headed for some favorite hiding place on the Moon, say, Matt could only let him go. At least there he wouldn't cause any trouble.

As Matt turned to go back down, he saw the shrinking green and white dot of Berserko's costume high above him, disappearing into the infinite blue expanse of the sky.

Chapter Five: **The Power of Love**

Matt's better judgment told him he should fly straight back to Mac-Tavish Laboratories. Returning to the museum would just mean he would be in for a lot of questions he didn't want to answer.

But Laurie had been cute and friendly, and he wanted make sure she hadn't been hurt in the battle.

Of course, he *knew* she hadn't been hurt, unless some flying debris had hit her when he wasn't looking. No, this was another need making itself felt. If Matt was going to be on this world for some indefinite length of time, he ought to make some friends. Especially of his own age, and better yet, female. Dr. MacTavish was all right, but the old savant had his limits. Matt was thinking more of long evenings of cuddling on the couch, and Laurie *had* been cute and friendly.

What if she already had a boyfriend? The rule on Matt's world — "The good ones are already taken" — probably applied here, too. But even as "just a friend," Matt decided, it would be worth improving the acquaintance. Since she worked for the Astroman Museum and knew the subject, she might be able to answer more questions as he thought of them. More immediately, he should probably tell someone that Berserko had gotten away and Laurie would know the toll-free number to call, or whatever the procedure was on this world for reporting a hyper-powered menace on the loose.

With his hypervision, Matt could see the crowd was still milling in front of the museum, if anything larger than before, and that police cars and fire engines had arrived. If he landed in the middle of all that, he would be in for endless complications.

Landing discreetly wouldn't be simple, either. As a speck in an otherwise empty sky, a flying man would be visible for miles around. It would be hard to land within walking distance of the museum without being spotted.

The answer seemed to be coming in low. Matt flew several miles south, then east out over the lake. He went down to a few feet above the water and turned back north.

He came ashore on a deserted beach just south of the museum and walked the rest of the way. No one paid any attention to him as he joined the crowd, held back by a police barricade set up in front of the museum steps. His clothes were a little rumpled but had somehow come through the fight intact, and once he had brushed the plaster dust off, he looked like any other civilian. The one glaring omission was his lack of a hat since most of the men in the crowd wore them, but it was an emergency situation in which decorum was at best secondary and it might not attract too much notice.

Even seen from the ground, the domed roof of the museum was obviously damaged, with a gaping hole in it and the fallen Astroman statue lying in pieces below. Judging from what Matt heard being said around him, most people were convinced that Berserko had fought with Astroman himself.

"In a way, it's a relief," one woman was saying. "It shows Astroman's still around. I'm afraid to think of what might happen if he were gone and there wasn't anybody to stop Garth Bolton and all the other master criminals."

"But why wasn't Astroman wearing his costume?" a man nearby demanded. "Why doesn't Astroman go on the news and tell us where he's been and what's going on? I think somebody's covering something up."

Looking around the crowd, Matt soon found Laurie. She was standing with a short, dumpy, and very agitated middle-aged man in a dark suit speckled with plaster dust — probably her boss, the museum director — as he was being interviewed by a TV news reporter. The reporter's microphone was the size of a policeman's nightstick and the camera was on the scale of an orange crate mounted on a tripod almost as tall as the man operating it. Thick cables connected the camera to a nearby panel truck with the letters "WGN-TV" on the sides. Words like "miniaturization" and "camcorder" didn't mean much on this world.

"No, I *don't* know how Berserko got turned on!" the museum director was exclaiming. "Astroman assured us Berserko was perfectly safe and so much rock when he gave him to the museum. And no, of course not! We wouldn't have exposed the public to Berserko if we had known there was any danger!"

The reporter mumbled a question.

"No, I don't even know who he was fighting with!" the director snapped. He turned to Laurie. "You saw the fight. Was the other guy

Astroman in disguise? One of the guests said they heard him tell Berserko something like that."

"I don't think so," Laurie said as the reporter shifted the microphone to her. "He was too young to be Astroman. That may have just been something he said to get Berserko's attention."

"Well," her boss added, "that means there's two of them now. I don't know who else could trade punches with Berserko and still be alive."

The reporter took the microphone back and faced the camera. "There you have it. First confirmation of the rumor that Berserko's mystery opponent was not Astroman but a second and younger hyper-powered man! Now all the world waits breathlessly for the answer to the fateful question, 'Is he friend... or is he foe?'"

They do get dramatic on this world, Matt thought.

Laurie gestured to the reporter for the microphone again. "I think I can answer that. I gave him a tour of the museum before I knew he was hyper. He seemed intelligent and curious, but there were a lot of things he didn't know about Astroman that anyone who's been living on Earth for a while should have known. I think he just got here from somewhere else. Maybe he's the last survivor of that colony Astrogirl came from. He seemed nice when I talked to him, and he tried to protect people during the fight. I think he's a friend, not a foe."

Hearing her say that gave Matt a warm feeling. Some kind of personal bond really had been formed during the tour, and perhaps it could be the basis of a friendship.

After the interview was over, the TV reporter collared somebody else to stand in front of the camera. The old man with the sign and religious tracts actually did have something interesting to say about seeing screaming tourists running out of the doors and then Berserko blasting his way through the roof and the statue toppling. At least until he started rambling about how the fall of Astroman's statue was symbolic of the futility of putting one's faith in mortal heroes, and then the reporter started looking around desperately for some other eyewitness to talk to.

Meanwhile, Matt caught up with Laurie, who was now standing somewhat apart from the crowd.

"Hi," he said. "I hope you're okay—"

She recognized him with a start. "You!" she blurted and started to turn and call to her boss. By this time, the director was some distance away and in the middle of giving a statement to a couple of police officers.

"Please — no!" Matt muttered urgently. "Can I talk to you? In private, I mean."

Laurie hesitated. "I'm not sure... just who are you?"

"I'm not a 'foe,' if that's what you're getting at. Besides, I—"

"What about Berserko?" Laurie suddenly demanded. "How could you just turn him on like that?"

"I didn't do it on purpose," Matt protested, looking worriedly around to see if anyone was listening. Laurie's voice was growing a little loud. Fortunately, they were standing away from the nearest bystanders and no one seemed to have heard. "You were the one who insisted I shake hands with Berserko, remember? How was I to know I'd start him up by just touching him?"

Perhaps realizing she was not entirely without some responsibility in what had just happened, Laurie changed the subject. "What happened after you two flew off? Did Berserko get away?"

"I'm afraid so. I have to breathe but I don't think he does, and he flew higher than I could. You should probably let someone know he's out there somewhere. Can we go somewhere a little more private? I need to talk to someone."

Laurie softened. "Well... all right." She thought for a moment. "I've already given a statement to the police and they know how to reach me if they think of more questions, which they probably will. I'll tell them that Berserko's still on the loose, but they probably have that figured out already. If I tell someone now, they'll wonder how I suddenly know that when I didn't mention it before, then they'll notice you standing here and I take it you want to stay out of sight for the moment. Anyway, thanks to you and Berserko, I have the afternoon free — and probably the next month at least — and I was about to head for home. My car's in the lot, so maybe we could talk over dinner? Or do you hyper-people live off sunlight?"

People really think that? "If we do, my stomach hasn't found out about it yet."

Laurie's car was the battered Volkswagen Beetle Matt had seen earlier. "It's not much," she admitted, unlocking the passenger-side door for Matt, "but I'm just a student working a part-time job and it gets me around. I can't fly... like *some* people I know."

"Hey, I'm not complaining," Matt said as he opened the passenger door and clambered inside. He leaned over and unlocked the driver's door as Laurie walked around the car. She opened the door and climbed in. "Old-style VW bugs like this are pretty much extinct on my world now, so it's pretty cool to actually ride in one."

Laurie stared at him as she settled in her seat behind the wheel. "Wait a minute. You're not telling me they had Volkswagens on Helionn, are you?"

"I never said I was from Helionn. That may be Astroman's story, but it's not mine. Say, I worked up an appetite beating on Berserko. Do they have Chicago-style pizza here?"

"This is Chicago," Laurie said a little blankly, "but I'm not sure what you mean. Pizza's pizza, isn't it?"

"I was thinking a nice deep-dish pizza an inch and a half thick would hit the spot right about now, with something to wash it down."

Laurie turned the key and started the car. "I think I gained two pounds just hearing you describe it, but I've never heard of pizza like that. If that's Chicago-style, it must be some other Chicago."

"You're right about that," Matt said. "But what about Berghoff's? Do you have Berghoff's?"

"If you mean that German restaurant in the Loop, ja, dot ve do haff. Now, how about some explanations?"

As Laurie drove north on Lake Shore Drive towards downtown Chicago, Matt told her his story to date. Though he still wanted to avoid major publicity until he knew his way around this world a little better, he didn't see any particular reason to keep his origin a secret from Laurie.

She was shocked. "But if you're from a parallel Earth, where did Astroman come from? I mean, all that stuff about Helionn can't be a complete lie, can it?"

"I don't know," Matt admitted. "Dr. MacTavish told me he'd always had a problem with the idea that a billion years of independent evolution on another planet would produce a creature identical to a human being, and frankly so do I. I'll ask Astroman if I ever see him, but I'll bet that if he did come from a planet called Helionn, his ancestors didn't evolve there."

"Maybe Helionn was a lost colony of Atlantis?" Laurie suggested.

Matt was about to dismiss the idea as hardly worth considering, but bit his tongue. Laurie sounded just serious enough that there might have really been an Atlantis on this world. For that matter, the idea that Helionn was the lost colony of some ancient civilization, whether it was called Atlantis or something else, was more plausible than parallel evolution that exact. How there were two whole Earths and their accompanying universes that were so similar was a different order of problem.

There was a pause in the conversation, then Laurie said, "It's too bad Berserko got away, but without the Deactivator there's no way to hold him. I just hope he stays away for a while. He's caused a lot of trouble in the past, and the only good thing about it is that he isn't malicious. He may be irresponsible and stupid, but he isn't really out to hurt anybody or steal anything. He doesn't eat, he doesn't have a life, so what could he possibly want? He disappears for months at a time and some scientists think he needs to recharge somehow. When he does come out, I think it's mainly because he's lonely. There's a gruesome story about what happened when he tried to pet a kitten he came across — we left it out of the museum display since we have so many children passing through — but I think it shows he does have feelings of some kind and was just trying to reach out. It's sad. He's dangerous, but it's sad."

After leaving the car in a parking garage, they went on to the restaurant. Berghoff's was a Chicago tradition that Matt was glad to see had a counterpart on this world. It was even a little better here since the food was served by pretty girls in traditional Bavarian costumes instead by young men in black dinner jackets and aprons.

They compared notes over dinner about the histories of their respective worlds. From Laurie's account of things, events had proceeded about the same on both worlds, with some minor variations, until sometime after World War II. The '50s just seemed like a lot of confused events that Matt couldn't really follow and would have to do a lot of reading to sort out. Perhaps the presence of a hyper-powered crusader named Astroman accounted for much of the difference. Strangely, no matter how much things deviated from the main line of history, they always ended up more or less tracking the course of events on Matt's world so the two Earths were still roughly similar. If history here had been a TV series, the status quo would be restored at the end of every episode.

After that, it sounded as though history had stalled sometime in the early '60s and several years had passed without much change. On Matt's Earth, the Soviet Union had joined the Austro-Hungarian Empire in the history books. Here, the Soviets still held Eastern Europe, and their leader, a short, fat, bald man who sounded a lot like Khrushchev, blustered about the superiority of their system but always seemed ready for a summit conference. While an eventual nuclear war between the United States and the Soviet Union was still a potential threat, Laurie's sense of things was that the international state of affairs had settled into a weary equilibrium that no one was likely to disturb.

Closer to home, color television was still an expensive novelty considered a luxury item mainly for the well-off, if not an outright sinful extravagance. Video tape was just now coming to the public's attention, but it was used mainly for professional broadcast and commercial purposes with expensive equipment — the Astroman Museum was experimenting with it for displays — while the idea of home units recording programs off the TV at home for later playback was close to unimaginable and even sounded faintly illegal. Computers existed, but something with the power of Matt's laptop back home would take up an entire room full of cabinets with flashing lights and spinning reels of tape.

The official NASA space program seemed at about the same point, with sending astronauts into orbit relatively commonplace until early that year when a bad accident had temporarily suspended all further launches. Roughly the same thing had happened at the same time on Matt's world, which meant events were tracking to at least some extent. A Moon landing was still being projected in the next couple of years when things got going again, so this world might match Neil Armstrong even yet. Where things were different, however, was that some of the better funded master scientists had private space operations of their own, somehow able to get much the same results with far less money than the taxpayers were spending, and there were rumors that there had already been unofficial landings on the Moon or maybe even Mars, which in this universe was thought to harbor some sort of life.

If I have to stay here... I wonder if those guys are hiring?

The state of the world seemed perfectly normal to Laurie since she had grown up here, and he had to admit that her world had its advantages. If drugs were a problem at all, they were still confined to the outer fringes of society and had not broken out into the nation at large. While crime seemed to be more spectacular and more organized, it probably threatened the average citizen less directly.

The wonders of Matt's universe, meanwhile, fascinated Laurie, and she wanted to hear more. After dessert, she shyly suggested that they go back to her place to continue the conversation. Matt was in favor of the idea. The ice in his heart left by the abrupt and rather acrimonious departure of his last girlfriend was melting fast. Also, something she'd said during dinner hinted very strongly that she was unattached at present, which was certainly heartening.

To his embarrassment, Laurie had to pay for the meal. Edmond had provided him with enough money to get into the museum and buy lunch, but certainly no one could have foreseen that Matt would have a date by evening.

"I'll pay you back when I can," Matt promised, even though he was by no means clear when that would be.

"Don't worry about it," Laurie said. "If I ever get hard up, I'll bring you some coal to squeeze."

"Er... huh?"

As they approached the car in the parking garage, Laurie explained that Astroman was supposedly able to squeeze a lump of coal in his bare fist so hard that it turned into a diamond.

"I'll have to try that the first chance I get," Matt said, still a little dubious even though it sort of made sense since coal and diamond were both forms of carbon. As Laurie unlocked the car door for him, he added, "But I think I'll just end up with a handful of coal dust."

"Why would Astroman lie about it?" Laurie asked, walking around the car. "There's a display case in the museum with some diamonds he made that way. If you and Berserko didn't smash it, I mean."

Matt started to open the car door — and felt something jab his back.

"Okay, buddy," snarled a voice behind him. "Put your hands up and turn around real slow."

What a difference hyper-powers made. Matt was mainly annoyed by the interruption. On the other side of the car, Laurie had been unlocking the door, and she looked up in puzzlement.

Sighing impatiently, Matt raised his hands as ordered and turned around. Standing there was a thug with a gun. The man was about thirty, not very clean, unshaven, and sloppily dressed with a soft billed cap, almost a cartoon caricature of a mugger needing only a little black mask to fully look the part. He had apparently been hiding in the shadows or behind a pillar in the parking garage, waiting for likely victims to come along. With his hyper-senses, Matt should have been aware that someone was nearby, but he had been concentrating on Laurie and not paying attention to anything around him. What had he been thinking earlier about crime not threatening people as directly on this world? Just his luck to run into the exceptional case...

"Good," said the mugger. "Real good. Now give me your wallet and nobody gets hurt."

"This is just not your day," Matt replied. "I don't have any money you could spend, but I do have hyper-powers and I'm getting mad."

"Sure, and I'm Garth Bolton!" the mugger snapped. "Cut the funny business and hand over your wallet, or you're dead."

One of the museum exhibits had described a trick Astroman used to disarm opponents: focusing his heat vision on their guns until the metal was too hot for them to hold. Laurie seemed to be in no immediate danger with a Volkswagen between her and the mugger, and Matt decided to try the stunt himself. He stared fixedly at the gun. For a moment or two, nothing happened.

"C'mon, c'mon!" the mugger urged. "Fork over the dough before I use this thing!"

He waved the gun for emphasis — just as Matt's heat vision finally kicked in.

The gun had moved out of Matt's line of sight and the focused heat beam from his eyes drilled into the mugger's shirt sleeve and arm.

The mugger screamed and dropped the gun. His sleeve was on fire and there was an odor of cooking meat. He went on screaming and tried to put out the fire on his sleeve by slapping it with his other hand.

Matt spun on his heel to face Laurie, still standing on the other side of the car and looking on in amazement. "We'd better get out of here!" he exclaimed. "The police would just ask questions I can't answer very well."

Laurie didn't need to be told a second time. She jumped into the car ahead of Matt and was already backing out of the parking space as he was closing his door. They left the screaming mugger to his agony behind them and raced for the exit to the street.

"I didn't want to hurt him!" Matt insisted. "I just wanted to disarm him."

"Which you just about *did*, literally," Laurie said. "But cheer up. You didn't kill him, after all."

Maybe so, Matt thought as Laurie drove through the Chicago streets towards Lake Shore Drive, but the real problem was his lack of control over his powers. He needed more practice, particularly for the more arcane ones like heat vision, before he could safely use them in emergencies.

Laurie lived in a little apartment in Evanston, not far from the Northwestern University campus where she attended classes part-time. The living room was a little better furnished than the set of *The Honeymooners*, but not by much, and of course her TV was a small black and white model. She turned it on for Matt to watch for a minute or two while she went into the kitchen to get something for them to drink. He took off his suit coat and loosened his tie, then sat down on the couch.

The TV picture was a little hard to watch because he kept seeing the scan lines and focusing on the individual pixels instead of the image as a whole. Looking somewhat away from the picture and following it with peripheral vision helped keep his perception of the image coherent.

A news program was just winding up a report on the fight at the Museum, which didn't tell him anything new since he had been there, though it was a little odd to see a blurry black and white image of Laurie being interviewed for a sound bite when the real thing was just in the next room. Then the program went to coverage of the President's speech earlier that day. The politics were lost on Matt since some deadly dull issue involving tariffs that had no exact equivalent on his own world was involved. What struck Matt more was the fact that this President wasn't any public figure he had ever heard of. Instead, he was just a relatively young politician who might have been played in a movie by some bland fortyish actor, whose part was simply billed as "The President."

Laurie came in with a tray and glasses of something bubbly and joined him on the couch. They started talking and never paid any more attention to the President or the TV. The relationship started to warm up about the time Matt was telling her about his personal, portable, pocket telephone, which had gone missing in the transition between universes.

"I'm really sorry I lost it," he was saying. "Even though there isn't a wireless phone system I can connect to here, there were a lot of other things I could do with it. I got quite a bit of use out of the calculator app." Realizing that the word "app" might not mean anything to her, he added, "Er, function, that is. It makes the phone into a hand-held adding machine."

Laurie frowned, trying to grasp the concept. She pantomimed holding something roughly like a pad in her left hand and working it with her right. She seemed to have it down as she dabbed at the imaginary buttons with her index finger, but went off the rails when she pulled an imaginary little crank to register the figure.

Matt had to laugh. "I'm sorry," he quickly apologized. "It's just that it's all electronic, not mechanical. We don't have cranks on calculators any more than we have cranks on cars now."

"You must be very lonely to be stranded on a strange world," Laurie said, her voice turning low and serious. "So far away from your family and friends..."

The sound of her voice, the way she looked at him, the mood of the moment... Matt may have spent a few too many years in the physics lab, but he knew something not unpleasant was starting to happen. He put his arm around her. She snuggled up close to him.

"You were very brave today," Laurie added. "Berserko could have killed you, but you tried to stop him anyway. You may have saved my life, and the way you protected that little girl... I knew you couldn't be evil." She looked up at him with an odd smile.

This was a moment to be cherished. Matt turned and slipped his other arm around her, drew her close, and pressed his lips against hers. For a moment, he no longer felt numb and cut off. For a moment, he had a girl in his arms and he was kissing her, and he held her tight...

Suddenly Laurie squirmed in his arms and tried to scream through the kiss.

Stunned, Matt broke off and drew back. Laurie looked up at him in shock. Her nose was bleeding. Her open mouth was a ring of blood and more was dribbling out and down her chin.

She started to say something, then grimaced and held her hands across her chest. "Oh God..." she moaned. "You hurt me..." Then she collapsed.

For a moment Matt sat there aghast. He felt sick, guilty. He had wanted to kiss the girl, not hurt her. But embracing her with hyper-strength, and one second's lapse in self-control... He had a passing thought of Laurie's story about Berserko killing a kitten he had tried to pet in all innocence, and wished he had remembered it in time before he just about did the same thing to a human being. Berserko was a dim-witted oaf who didn't know his own strength — what was Matt's excuse?

Then he rallied. Self-recriminations wouldn't help. He thought fast. Laurie's injuries were serious, beyond anything he could do in terms of first aid. He briefly considered calling for an ambulance, but was there something like a 911 number he should call? He couldn't waste time finding out. The safest assumption was that Chicago's older hospitals existed on this world. He decided to fly Laurie to the nearest one and let the emergency room staff take it from there.

She was all but unconscious now and probably never knew that Matt opened a window and launched himself with her in his arms into empty space. He realized a little late that he had left his coat behind and Edmond probably wouldn't appreciate it when he asked for a new one, but he didn't have time to go back. He flew over the lights of the city towards a high column of lighted windows he knew was the Northwestern University medical center. Carrying Laurie like this when she had internal injuries was doubtless a bad idea, but he couldn't think of anything better. His hope was that getting her to the hospital fast would make up for whatever he did to make her injuries worse on the way.

Matt landed by the Emergency Receiving door and walked in with Laurie in his arms. Mumbling something about a car wreck by way of explanation, he turned her over to the interns on duty. They immediately put her on a gurney and wheeled her into the depths of the hospital for examination and treatment.

A nurse handed him some forms. "You can fill these out while you wait." Then she looked at him quizzically. "You've got blood on your clothes. Are you sure you're all right?"

"Really, I'm fine."

He found a nearby restroom and took a look in the mirror. Any of Laurie's blood that had been on his face had apparently simply fallen off, but some had been smeared into his non-hyper shirt and he washed it out as best he could. Then, with a damp shirtfront, he went back out to find a chair in the waiting room.

His better judgment told him he should just head on back to Mac-Tavish Laboratories and escape further complications, but he felt responsible for what had happened to Laurie and he wanted to make sure she wasn't too badly hurt.

Besides, why did he have to go back to the lab? Because Dr. Mac-Tavish would be worried about him? As if anyone had to worry about a hyper-powered man on this world. Because MacTavish would be wondering where he had been today and what he had been doing? Turning on the TV would tell him that.

Matt looked over the forms he had been given. Mostly they asked for information he couldn't supply, like the names of Laurie's next of kin, along with her address, social security number, telephone number, blood type, and insurance plan.

"I don't even know her last name!" he exclaimed and pushed the forms aside.

While he waited, Matt passed the time by looking around. Not just up and down the hall but through the walls. He also tuned in on conversations around the hospital, although he still didn't have enough control over his hyper-hearing to pick up any doctors discussing Laurie's case. He ended up mainly being amazed by how low tech the hospital was, with bare linoleum floors, endless bleak green-painted walls, and the all-pervading odor of institutional disinfectant. This was health care stuck in a perpetual 1948.

After a while, Matt decided it might be a good idea in any event to let Dr. MacTavish know where he was. He found a pay phone with a telephone book hanging from it on a chain, and after fumbling with the rotary dial and working through the protocol of making a long-distance call with an operator, he used the last of his spare change to call the lab. An assistant answered and reported that Dr. MacTavish was unavailable at present. It sounded as though Matt's concern that MacTavish might be worrying about him was unnecessary. He left a message to tell him where he was anyway, and went back to the waiting room.

Finally, after about an hour, a doctor in a long white coat came out and spoke to him.

"I'm Dr. Shaw." He was tall and thin, perhaps about thirty-five. He was also black, for whatever that might say about the history of the civil rights movement and the state of racial relations on this world. "Your girlfriend was very badly injured. One of her broken ribs punctured a lung, but at least she's in stable condition and her prognosis is good. May I ask what happened? I'd guess a car accident, as she had a broken nose and several broken ribs, and a sprained back and neck."

"All I did was kiss her!" Matt exclaimed, horrified.

Dr. Shaw eyed him suspiciously. "I'd be more likely to believe you
if you told me you threw her against a brick wall." His tone of voice
turned serious. "By law, we're required to report obvious cases of battery—"

Matt sighed. "You might as well know the truth. I'm what you people call 'hyper.'" As grim as the situation was, just saying the word like
that struck him as absurd. "You know, like Astroman."

From the look on Dr. Shaw's face, Matt could see the wheels turning in his mind. "The fight at the Astroman museum this afternoon..."

"That was me, all right."

"I think I'll have to sit down for this one," Dr. Shaw said, and took a
seat in the chair next to Matt. "Can you prove you're hyper?"

Matt stood up, and kept on rising. He stopped several feet up and
drew his legs cross-legged beneath him, hovering like a levitating Bud-
dha.

Dr. Shaw nodded, not appearing particularly astonished. He did live
in a world where Astroman and Astrogirl were normal features in the
daily news. "I see... Are you from Helionn, too?"

"Not exactly," Matt answered, deciding to keep things simple.
"Let's leave it at saying another world." He floated back down and
resumed his seat in the chair. "I just got here yesterday... and no, I can't
explain why I can fly or why I have hyper-strength here. I certainly
didn't where I came from."

Dr. Shaw shook his head. "You don't waste any time, do you? Two
days on a new world and you found a girlfriend. Though whether you'll
still have one after this is another matter. Oh, she'll live, don't worry,
though no thanks to you. But she might prefer safer boyfriends when she
recovers. Let me give you a word of advice. Until you learn how to control your strength, lay off the romance. From what I heard on the news,
you fought Berserko to a standstill. If you're that powerful, you could
have killed this girl."

Before Matt could reply that he was well aware of that now, an
orderly came up from somewhere down the hall and stopped in front of
him. "Excuse me, but are you Mr. Matt Dawson?"

Matt nodded. "Why? Nothing's happened with Laurie, I hope—"

"No, it's not that," the orderly replied quickly. "We just got an
urgent call for you from a Dr. MacTavish. He wants you to get back to
his laboratory as soon as possible. Something about the lab being 'under
attack.' Does that make any sense?"

Bolton! shot through Matt's mind. "Perfect sense! I'm sorry to run,
Dr. Shaw, but I don't have a moment to lose. Thanks for everything." He
leaped to his feet and started down the hall.

"Wait!" Dr. Shaw called after him. "We need more information—!"

Matt didn't have time for that. He reached the door, then he was outside and arching his body upwards past the lights of the city and towards the stars in the blackness above.

Chapter Six: **Garth Bolton Strikes Again**

Matt could see the flashes of the guns in the darkness from miles away, then he heard the distance-delayed detonations. Even in the dark and from the air, it looked like a small war. No wonder Dr. MacTavish had called him. Unless the Batavia or Naperville police departments had an anti-terrorist strike force equipped with Army-level weaponry ready to deploy on an instant's notice, getting help to fight off something on this scale would take too much time to do any good.

As he approached, Matt saw that Bolton was attacking with a fleet of helicopters this time. Three gunships circled the perimeter of MacTavish Laboratories just outside the range of small arms and were laying down a heavy barrage from on-board machine guns. Return fire was coming from the windows of several buildings inside the compound, but without any noticeable effect. Meanwhile, a convoy of several armored vehicles rolled along the main road under the cover of the gunship barrage, approaching the outer chain-link fence that surrounded the former college campus, and a small party of night-camouflaged men was already at the gate and at work with wire cutters. Since Matt didn't see signs of any opposition to the invaders there, Dr. MacTavish's own men on guard duty had either been overwhelmed or had fled. The private security guards he had also hired may have decided that no contract could make them stick around for *this*.

The sheer size of the attacking force astonished Matt. How could a known criminal be allowed to operate a private army that from the look of things was just about large enough and well enough equipped to defeat the regular armies of small countries? Even if Bolton had bought off the local authorities and was now powerful enough to thumb his nose at the Feds, Astroman should have shut him down a long time ago.

Matt decided to take out the helicopters first, since they were pinning down the defenders while the ground forces were infiltrating. He flew down into the spinning rotor blades of the nearest gunship, snapping

80

them off as they hit his indestructible body. The helicopter lurched, then the gunfire it had been spewing broke off as it suddenly plummeted.

Perhaps it was lingering guilt over what he had accidentally done to Laurie, who certainly hadn't deserved it, but Matt realized he couldn't just let the crew of this helicopter die even if they were criminal mercenaries. He had a strong feeling that there was a line here that he must not cross, for the sake of looking at himself in the mirror every morning for the rest of his life if not for getting along in this world for however long he was here. Maybe Astroman had long ago realized much the same thing. Once he killed somebody, even in the line of duty, a door would close behind him that could never be opened again, and he would start down a dark path he would be better off not taking.

Matt slipped underneath the helicopter's body and slowed its fall, then let it drop the last few feet to let the occupants know they had been in a crash.

In the darkness and the scattered lights, neither the attackers nor the defenders could see what had happened, and probably assumed the helicopter had been hit by a lucky shot from the labs. The other two gunships continued their circling and firing. Then Matt knocked out the second helicopter the same way, smashing its rotor blades and letting it fall ten or so feet to the ground. This time, a spotlight from the roof of one of the buildings caught him in its beam as he flew away from the wreck, and he heard cheers break out from the defenders.

The pilot of the third helicopter saw what was going on and tried to break off the attack. Matt caught up with the gunship, shrugging off the streams of heavy machine gun bullets slamming into his body without effect, and snapped the rotor blades as he had the others. After grounding the wreck upside down in a cornfield, he flew back to the laboratory.

The commandos had cut through the fence and opened the gate, and the armored convoy was now rumbling along the main avenue of the campus. In the lead was some kind of enclosed jeep with armor plating and a heavy machine gun, followed by two armored cars and even what looked like a small tank. The defenders in the lab buildings were concentrating their fire on the leading jeep, but their bullets weren't penetrating the shielding and the jeep's machine gun was answering with heavier fire.

Matt hit the jeep and flipped it, sending it rolling over and over on its side until it came to a stop on the lawn upside down, its machine gun torn away from its mounting. The occupants would still be alive though badly shaken up.

He tore into the armored cars, ripping out their engines. Armed men poured out the back of the cars, brandishing assault rifles, but they were caught in the glare of spotlights and gunfire from the buildings kept them from advancing.

That left the tank. Matt wondered in passing why Bolton had sent a tank, of all things. It seemed a little heavy for a raid that should have been fast and light.

The turret gun swiveled to take aim at him as he approached. Did the men inside seriously expect to hurt him?

The cannon fired just before Matt hit the tank, but instead of a shell, an incandescent green ray shot out that crackled electrically as it stabbed into the night.

The bolt just barely grazed Matt's shoulder.

It hurt. For the first time since he had arrived on this world, something had hurt him badly. He suddenly felt weak, terribly weak.

Matt dropped to the pavement short of the tank. Somehow he knew that he was vulnerable and the first stray bullet in the hailstorm of lead flying all around him could kill him. He was horribly exposed in the spotlight glare, and there was nowhere to run. What he felt was beyond fear, somewhere between resignation to the inevitable and impotent panic. Fear had already done its job. He knew he was trapped and helpless, and there was nothing he could do to get out of this.

The men in the tank must have realized they had a sitting duck waiting for them to pick off. The turret swiveled, aiming the gun barrel towards Matt —

The turret exploded in an orange fireball. Dr. MacTavish's men had scored a bull's-eye with something more serious than rifle fire — a bazooka, maybe, or a small mortar.

Matt flattened himself against the pavement to protect his face from any flying shrapnel. As he lay there, his utter, infinite weakness caught up with him and his consciousness faded out.

Some indefinite amount of time later, he came to, slowly and tiredly. He was in his bed in his dorm room. Unfortunately for any pleasure he found in realizing that he was still alive, the first person he saw when he woke up was Edmond, sitting on a straightback wooden chair by the door and reading an advanced physics journal.

"It was high time you came round," Edmond complained, looking up. "I was starting to think I'd be confined here all morning listening to you snore. I've a lot of work to do but Dr. MacTavish wanted me to let him know as soon as you were awake. I'll go summon him."

Edmond left in a bustle of impatience and Matt relaxed, feeling too drained to do much more than enjoy the simple pleasure of not being dead. Not many minutes later, Dr. MacTavish came into the room.

"How do you feel, laddie?" he asked worriedly.

Matt groaned. "God, do I feel weak! That green ray just about knocked me flat. What was it, anyway?"

MacTavish sat down in the chair Edmond had left vacant. "I'll come to that, but first I wanted to thank you for your timely assistance. As a result, we sent Bolton's men packing like the dogs they are."

"Did they get away?" Matt asked.

"Not all of them. We pulled two out of that jeep you flipped. They were a bit bruised but they'll live. The police took them into custody and like as not their lawyer has already sprung them. They'll skip bail and no one will ever see them again. Bolton has extensive interests in Brazil, I understand, and there is always room for employees whose continued presence in North America is inconvenient. So much for getting any useful information out of them. As for the rest, they had escape routes planned and getaway vehicles stationed within easy reach. By the time the police arrived, the enemy had completely evacuated the field. Amazingly, there were no deaths, no thanks to all the bullets that were flying about, although several of my men were hurt by shrapnel and other debris."

"But what about that tank your men blew up? How could anyone live through that?"

"There wasn't anyone in it. Remote-controlled, it would seem. So Bolton gets off free again."

"Isn't there any way you can connect him to all this? Those helicopters must be registered to somebody."

MacTavish sighed. "Those helicopters mysteriously *stolen* from the factory just last week by parties unknown thanks to inexplicably lax security on one particular night, you mean? I'm sure we won't learn anything helpful from the rest of the vehicles, either. Oh, our Garth is a clever lad. He doesn't leave fingerprints or tracks if he can help it. Damn him, anyway! Here I am, trying to do important work, and I'm forever being distracted by these common thieves! My time is too valuable for this!"

"I've asked this before," Matt said, "but what *do* you do?"

"Some things are better shown than said," MacTavish replied. "I'll give you a tour of the plant when you're up to it. It's time you knew because I think it all ties in. How you came here, why Bolton is trying to rob me, what he hit you with, and what happened to Astroman."

He was interrupted by an assistant coming in with a breakfast tray. With an effort, Matt sat up in bed, his back against the pillow and the headboard. The assistant set the tray down across his lap, then left the room again. It was a breakfast to challenge the heartiest of appetites, with double portions of eggs, bacon, and toast, along with a quart of orange juice.

"I assumed you'd need to rebuild your depleted strength," MacTavish said, "so I ordered a fair amount."

"Great," Matt replied, slathering a slab of toast with butter and jelly. "The way I feel now, even this might not be enough."

"Hmmm... yes," MacTavish murmured. He took out his pipe from a pocket and lit it. ("You don't mind, do you, laddie?" "I think I can tune it out.") "It's no wonder you're exhausted. You certainly had a busy day yesterday. You go off to a museum, and the next thing I know you've wrecked the place in a dust-up with Berserko. What was that all about? And what were you doing in a hospital?"

Matt explained between bites of breakfast, and found himself wincing a little as he told what had happened with Laurie. He made a mental note to call the hospital as soon as he could get to a phone and find out how she was doing.

At the end of the story, MacTavish sat silently for a few moments, puffing reflectively on his pipe. "I can hardly blame you, lad," he said at length. "You're young, you're human, and you haven't realized all the dangers of being hyper yet. One thing's certain, though. It wasn't just because of his career that Astroman never married."

Matt put aside thoughts of his own lonely future for the moment. "But how could I jump-start Berserko by just touching him?"

"I suspect that being hyper has to do with energy," MacTavish answered. "Let's say you're charged with what we'll call hyper-energy. You provided the spark to activate his ignition, so to speak. He's an imperfect duplicate of Astroman, so he probably works much the same way. With only two hyper-powered people and one dog on Earth, none of them likely to go to the museum and touch Berserko, Astroman doubtless felt safe in letting the public shake hands with him. Someone such as yourself didn't figure in his calculations, obviously.

"And we know something else for certain. Hyper you may be, but Garth Bolton has a weapon that can hurt you."

"You're right about that," Matt said through a mouthful of toast. "It was pretty bad. That ray just barely touched me and it was like all my strength just drained away. I think I learned a lesson about overconfidence. Just when I thought I was invincible, I found out the hard way that I'm not."

"I don't want to alarm you," MacTavish said, "but two weeks ago, Garth Bolton's forces attacked the facility of one of my colleagues up by the Fox River. Normally, Astroman would have put in his customary appearance to stop it, but for some reason he didn't and has not been seen since, and Bolton's men got away unopposed with quite a lot of booty. Given that Bolton has such a weapon, I have a bad feeling that Astroman did in fact arrive on the scene to save the day, only to suffer dire consequences that the powers that be are desperately trying to cover up. You were very fortunate in that you were only grazed. The cannon was destroyed, however. Besides what our lucky shot did to it, there was also some sort of self-destruct mechanism on board the tank that finished the job so we wouldn't have any identifiable components to analyse. But how long will it take Bolton to build another such cannon, if he doesn't already have one or more? I'm just beginning to understand what makes you hyper, but I fear Bolton is far ahead of me. He knows how to take your hyper-power *away*."

"Well, what does make me hyper?" Matt asked. "You were able to make those razor blades sort of hyper, so you've been making some progress..."

MacTavish puffed on his pipe some more while he paused to assemble his thoughts. "I'm arbitrarily giving names to concepts that don't have names," he said, "but I think we can safely proceed on the assumption that the parallel universes are spaced along a continuum of increasing energy levels. You come from a universe higher up the energy scale, hence your effective invulnerability and hyper-strength. As I said before, you're in this world but not quite *of* it. Gravity doesn't affect you the same way, and you can see through matter."

Matt held up a piece of bacon. "All right, that sounds reasonable, but how can I eat the food here? How could Astroman live on this world for forty years without having to send out to wherever he really came from for his meals?" He popped the bacon in his mouth. "It tastes all right to me."

"My guess is that when you absorb nutrients into your system, they are somehow raised to your body's higher energy level. How that happens, I won't venture to guess, but you can be very glad that it does."

As Matt finished breakfast, MacTavish asked him if he felt like getting out of bed and taking a walk.

Matt took stock of himself. "I feel fine," he said, surprised by how quickly he had regained his strength. "The effects of the ray must have worn off. It was a good thing I was only grazed."

"Hmm... yes," MacTavish agreed. "A direct hit might have drained one hundred percent of your energy and... well, I'm not overly fond of funerals. But enough gloom. Now it's time you learned a wee bit about what we do here."

As they walked down the avenue, Matt saw work crews everywhere cleaning up the damage from last night's firefight. Mostly it was a matter of replacing shot-out windows and cleaning up shattered glass and spent shell casings littering the sidewalks and streets, but there were also bullet holes in the buildings' masonry that had to be patched.

"Sometimes I wonder if Bolton's actual long-term goal is to bankrupt me," MacTavish said gloomily. "I had hardly begun repairs of the damage from the last raid."

"Insurance doesn't cover it?" Matt asked.

"Hardly. Acts of war and terrorist attacks are explicitly excluded. It's hard for a master-scientist to get insurance at all because explosions and other lab accidents are a regular part of the trade, and as for something like *this*..." MacTavish shook his head.

From the outside, their destination was just another college building, if a little larger than most. A cast concrete sign embedded in the front wall just under the roof still read "Natatorium," which Matt dimly remembered from somewhere as a fancy word for an indoor swimming pool. Only this building had warning signs and guards. Newly added structures like large chemical tanks and piping had been erected along the sides as well, giving it the appearance of a small refinery.

Inside, the swimming pool was gone, replaced by a wildly complex array of pipes, cables, and machinery that Matt needed a moment to identify. The installation was a kind of particle accelerator, distantly related to the installation at Fermilab, yet confined to a space not much bigger than an Olympic-sized swimming pool instead of stretching for miles, some strangely primitive combination of a cyclotron evolving into a synchrotron. It struck Matt as a little crude even for 1967, maybe around 1950s Bevatron level.

MacTavish led him down a steel stairway into a narrow corridor fronting a basement laboratory. It looked as though some of the surrounding area had been dug out to extend the complex underground. The work area was behind a window of thick glass set in a concrete wall next to an airlock entrance. Matt looked through the window and saw workers in protective suits manipulating instruments at lab benches and tending the lower level of the reactor. Garth Bolton's men had worn suits like these during the raid on the night he arrived, he recalled. Warning signs with red radiation logos were posted prominently on the walls. Suddenly thoughtful, Matt watched the workers in what must have been a ferociously dangerous environment. No Occupational Safety and Health Act was in effect here, evidently.

"What are they doing in there?" he asked.

"This, lad," Dr. MacTavish answered with a note of pride in his voice, "is what Garth Bolton would dearly like to get his hands on. This is a production facility for transuranic elements."

"Oh." Matt was a little disappointed. All this build-up and acting mysterious, and that was all it was? "Like plutonium, you mean. Element 94," he added, in case the name was different here.

MacTavish smiled. "You do underestimate us primitive savages, don't you? No, I mean production of elements 114, 116, 120, 124, and even 126. Scotium, Caledonium, Glaswegium, Edinburgium, Glengarrium... They exist and I've produced them in quantity. I should imagine that you have much more sophisticated means of producing them on your world."

Matt gaped. They didn't have microchips but they had synthetic transuranic elements...?

"Not exactly," he admitted. "I know we're up to 118, but the higher ones aren't stable and decay too fast to be useful, and some have only been identified from individual atoms."

"Well, laddie, I'm glad to hear that we aren't complete dunces compared to your world. My assistants and I have managed to produce appreciable quantities of several transuranic elements and we are studying their properties now."

For all they seemed like a backwards 1967, they were still able to produce transuranic elements in bulk? Matt would need time to research things, but at the moment he didn't know whether Dr. MacTavish had stumbled onto something far more advanced than anything on his own world or if it was something possible only as a result of a very different physics in this universe. Either way, Matt couldn't argue with the results.

The fact was that transuranic elements — those with greater atomic numbers than uranium's 92 — were radioactive and unstable, and decayed rapidly into other elements and isotopes. They were so short-lived that they didn't occur in nature except as trace amounts, byproducts of natural nuclear reactions, but they could be created artificially. One such element was plutonium at 94. Its longevity varied by isotope, with half of a given quantity of plutonium-239 taking about 25,000 years to decay, which was long enough for it to be used for nuclear weapons and fuel in power plants. Higher elements had progressively shorter half-lives. Element 100, fermium, had a half-life of 80 days. Nobelium, at 102, was half decayed in three minutes, and element 103, lawrencium, was half gone in eight seconds.

Scientists trying to produce even higher elements had the problem of proving they had succeeded when the evidence changed to something else in an instant. As a further complication, some elements had longer-lived isotopes, like lawrencium with one that lasted several hours, but it wasn't enough for commercial applications even if they could be produced in significant amounts. Some theories contended that higher up the scale, islands of stability existed where certain super-heavy elements had properties allowing them to endure for some useful length of time, though science on Matt's world hadn't yet reached the point of confirming their existence.

But on a world fifty years behind, Dr. MacTavish had actually produced long-lived samples of several such elements. *Maybe it's like with the Russians*, Matt reflected. Soviet science had been behind the rest of the world in nearly everything, yet despite poor equipment and bureaucratic bungling it had managed to excel in certain fields by sheer concentration of effort. That might have been the way it was here. Dr. MacTavish had pulled off a major advance by pouring his time and effort into an area no one on Matt's world considered promising. Or maybe Dr. MacTavish's otherworld counterpart had thought it promising but his application for a grant had been turned down. Or maybe — and perhaps most likely — such elements could only exist in this universe with its different laws and not in Matt's.

"Transuranic elements are the key to power," MacTavish added. "Great power. I suspect the ray that weakened you was generated by a sample transuranic I created."

"But how could a *ray* weaken me?" Matt asked.

The answer was long, involved, and more than a little vague, based on this world's cockeyed theories of physics in general and energy levels in particular. Or at least they seemed cockeyed until Matt saw a connection with his world's conception of separate strong and weak nuclear forces. As MacTavish explained it, transuranic elements were *so* heavy on the atomic level that they strained the structure of space in their immediate neighborhood. Under normal circumstances, that was hardly more than the distance from the nucleus to the outer electron shell, but if a significant amount of a super-heavy transuranic element was stimulated by particle bombardment, tunnels through space might develop or the energy levels of nearby objects could be increased or decreased.

"I have been able to increase the energy level of inanimate objects," MacTavish concluded. "Unfortunately, living plants and animals are cooked in the process. I can make you a serviceable shaving kit, but it will be a while before we can make synthetic hypermen... if ever. Garth Bolton, on the other hand, seems to have gone in the opposite direction. He can *decrease* an object's energy level, even a living one, though it might not be living for long. That's what he did to you and what I fear he did to Astroman. His skill for original scientific work has deteriorated in the years since he took up criminal pursuits as his primary activity, so I suspect he acquired the de-energising device by fairly foul means from the master-savant who was testing it for Astroman as a means to neutralize Berserko. The device would work just as well on either Astroman or Berserko, but since Berserko is basically just animated rock, he wouldn't suffer any permanent damage and could recover. Astroman —and you — can't."

Matt considered that for a moment. "But wouldn't he need transuranics to power his ray machine? If you're the only one who makes them, how could he get any if he hasn't been able to succeed in robbing you yet?"

"I think I know," MacTavish admitted. "Some samples I lent to a scientific institution have gone missing, and I fear they fell into Bolton's hands. Shortly after they disappeared, his agents came here and offered to buy as much as I could make, but I turned them down. That's why he's trying to steal them instead. I'm sure he was quick to experiment with the samples he stole and determine their potential if he could obtain them in quantity. Since transuranics are so powerful, even the small quantity of samples would suffice to fill his needs for the time being. When we dig more thoroughly into the wreckage of his tank and ray weapon, I'm sure we'll find some wee dab of something that by all rights he should not have had in his possession."

MacTavish then explained some of the more technical details of the manufacturing process and showed Matt the security measures. Besides armed guards, heavy armored doors were ready to slide into place and block the entrances.

At the end of the tour, they came out of the Natatorium and started down the sidewalk towards the main office.

"You don't need me to stop Bolton's men," Matt said as they walked along. "They wouldn't stand a chance of getting through all that."

"Your optimism is not entirely justified," MacTavish sighed. "Bolton is a scientist himself, remember. Whatever security I install, he can circumvent one way or another. And much as I trust my men, he would only have to bribe or blackmail one or two of them and all my security would crumble. No, you were definitely in the right place at the right time."

"I'm starting to wonder if transuranics are worth all the trouble," Matt remarked. "If you stopped making them and switched to developing better fertilizer or something, wouldn't Bolton go away and stop bothering you?"

"I tend to agree with you," MacTavish replied, "but I've spent too many years on this project to stop now. The potential payoff of all my work is too great to just throw it away. Cheap energy, even eventual space travel... Transuranics are highly radioactive and dangerous to handle, but they have remarkable properties. Since such heavy elements weaken the fabric of space and time, my working hypothesis is that just when Bolton's men interrupted a test we were running on the largest sample of Glengarrium we've produced yet, your Fermilab was conducting an experiment of its own with accelerated subatomic particles in roughly the same physical location on both Earths, and somehow the net result was a series of brief manifestations of a tunnel between the universes persisting well beyond the initial triggering event. It was your bad luck to fall into possibly the last one."

"Great," Matt said. "Now you know how I got here. But can you send me home?"

MacTavish looked decidedly unhappy. "Difficult proposition. We would have to coordinate our transuranic stimulation with Fermilab's schedule for firing proton beams, which is not an easy task since we can't communicate with the people of your world. Even if we somehow managed it, and sent you through the tunnel, where would you emerge? On your world or some other? And when? These interdimensional holes seem to cut through time as well as space."

"It sounds hopeless," Matt had to admit.

MacTavish was no comfort. "It may well be. We don't even know how many alternate worlds there are. Are yours and ours the only ones, or are there several worlds, many, or an infinite number? Could we even find your world again without the coincidental Fermilab experiment? I agree that alternate worlds are a fabulous opportunity for scientific study and would open up whole new realms, but it would take years to develop just an adequate theory, and more years to experiment and develop the technology to find your world and send you back. Please don't misunderstand me. I appreciate your situation and I sympathise, but there isn't much at present that I can do to help. Perhaps with time there will come answers, if that's any consolation."

After that not very helpful remark, there was little left to say. MacTavish went off to his office to attend to the mounting paperwork related to what was now two nights of small-scale warfare, and Matt found himself at loose ends.

He found a phone in one of the other offices and had the switchboard operator put him through to the hospital to check on Laurie. Still in intensive care, he was told, but all signs were favorable. That cheered him a little, though she probably wouldn't want to see him again. Unless he could de-hyper himself, which he suddenly realized might actually be possible in the light of recent developments. He would have to be insane to do it, however, since he could probably never go back to his own world if he did, and there wasn't any future in the relationship anyway. Still, he had some feeling for her, however abstract it might be, and wished her well.

Then, for lack of anything better to do, he stopped in the library for a few things to read. After picking up some recent issues of the news magazines he found piled on the checkout desk, he went back to his room.

Chapter Seven: **The Friends of Astroman**

A little later that afternoon, Matt lay half-dozing on his bed. He had been skimming the magazines for useful information but tiredness had caught up with him. He might not have recovered completely from the effects of the green ray yet.

Just as he was about to nod off entirely, he was startled by a knock at the door. "Come in," he called, stifling a yawn.

The door opened and Edmond stepped in. "Somebody called asking for you." Giving every impression of reluctantly performing an unpleasant duty, he walked over to the bed and handed Matt a folded sheet of paper.

Who knows I'm here? Laurie was the only person who could have found him, but was she in any shape to call him? Would she even want to call him?

He unfolded the note and read: "Call Mr. Weiss, Stellar Sales Service. Important." With it was a phone number.

That was puzzling. Matt didn't know any Mr. Weisses on his own world, let alone this one, and the name of the firm was even more of a mystery. A used star salesman? ("Now here's a little beauty, right on the Main Sequence and never gone nova, with six planets standard and good mileage on the hydrogen-helium conversion!") Whatever it was, what did it have to do with him?

"Any idea what this is about?" Matt asked.

"None at all," Edmond replied coolly, sounding as though he didn't care, either. "Dr. MacTavish thinks you had better check it out, though, in case there is trouble brewing as a result of your little fracas at the museum." He turned and left.

Now thoroughly puzzled and his tiredness forgotten, Matt got up and went out into the hall. Using the pay phone on the wall at the end of the corridor, he called the number on the note. It was a long-distance call to Chicago from here, and since he didn't have any coins on him, he had to figure out the procedure for calling collect. The call was accepted by a secretary when the operator gave his name, and he was put through at once to Mr. Julius Weiss himself, an older-sounding gentleman with a hint of a New York accent.

"Are you the Matt Dawson who is acquainted with an Astroman Museum docent named Laurie Niven?" Mr. Weiss asked.

Matt wasn't sure that he should admit it after what happened, but what could anyone do to him? "I didn't know her last name, but yes—"

"Mr. Dawson, I can't say anything more on the phone, but please believe me when I say that this is an extremely serious matter. Can you meet me in my office in about half an hour for a conference?"

"I suppose... but who exactly are you?"

Mr. Weiss chuckled, if a little sadly. "How fleeting is fame. I used to be the editor of the Chicago *Daily News* before it was bought out. Now I just run a little literary agency. But this is much bigger than that. We *must* talk to you!"

So that was what "Stellar Sales Service" was. Matt was more baffled than he had been to start with since it was a little soon for him to be writing a book about his experiences in this world, but the urgent tone in Mr. Weiss' voice sounded sincere and he was curious to find out what was so important. Besides, it was something to do. He agreed and Mr. Weiss gave him his office address in the Loop.

As he hung up, Matt reflected that Mr. Weiss had a pretty good idea of whom he was talking to if he expected him to get from the distant western suburbs to the lakefront in less than half an hour.

Taking to the air on a warm July afternoon, what could be finer? He leveled off at a thousand feet or so and turned towards the east where the irregular building blocks of Chicago's skyline rose along the shore of Lake Michigan.

Soon he was soaring over the central city, using his augmented power of vision to read the street signs hundreds of feet below and find the neighborhood he wanted in the confusing welter of buildings and cross streets. Fortunately, the street layout hadn't changed very much since the Chicago Fire, so it was much the same on both worlds.

The buildings on this one were more what they had been circa 1948 on his, however, lower and older, lacking the starkly towering glass and steel modernistic monoliths. Matt did get a quick impression that postwar architecture had favored what was called *Tribune* Gothic, as the unfamiliar and presumably newer buildings he saw mostly had that office-building-designed-to-look-like-a-cathedral look with pinnacles and flying buttresses that was pioneered by the Chicago *Tribune* for its headquarters building in the '20s. If he looked more closely at some of them, he would probably even spot gargoyles.

Since he knew his way around the Loop, he soon found the drab, older office building at the address he had been given. He dropped down unseen into a handy back alley and walked out onto the sidewalk, merging with the crowd as just one more anonymous citizen. Unlike most of the men he saw, he was hatless, but he would be only briefly out in the open.

The wide avenue was thick with passing cars, Detroit behemoths gleaming with chrome, and a commuter train that looked as though it dated from the 1930s rumbled overhead along the elevated train track running down the middle of the street. The calendar may have read 1967, but once more this world didn't seem quite fully there yet.

When Matt went through the revolving door and came into the building's lobby, an almost stunning stench hit his hyper-sensitive nostrils. An awful lot of tobacco had been smoked in this lobby over the years.

The literary agency was on the fifth floor. Matt went up in an elevator that actually had a human operator, a little old man wearing a uniform something like a bellboy's. He came out in a narrow, dimly lit hallway with blank-looking doors on either side. Towards the end he found one with **STELLAR SALES SERVICE** lettered in faux gold on the frosted glass window. He opened the door and stepped into a small front office where a prim and sour-faced secretary of mature years sat behind a desk. He gave her his name and she ushered him into the inner office at once.

When Matt entered the cramped little room, he saw that he wasn't the only one who had been invited to the meeting. Several well-dressed men and women were sitting in folding chairs set up in front of a massive wooden desk at which a man in later middle age who was presumably Mr. Weiss himself sat. Everyone turned to look at Matt as he came in.

Since the three women were all wearing dresses and seated facing away from the door, Matt had a glimpse of the backs of their legs. He noticed that they were all wearing seamed stockings, something he had only seen in old movies and probably already out of style by this time on his own Earth. As with men's hats, there seemed to be some factor operating in this universe that was slowing new developments, even for something so trivial.

Mr. Weiss was just then on the phone. The editor turned literary agent was well into his sixties, bald with a fringe of white hair around his temples, heavyset and still vigorous, polluting the air with a cigar the size of a carrot. "I keep telling you, Howard, lay off the fancy-shmancy vocabulary! 'Eldritch' you can get away with, but words like 'rugose' and 'squamous'? Are you kidding? You're writing stories, not diction-aries!" He glanced up and saw Matt. "Look, I have to go. Just send me that story — yes, you have to type it, so stop bellyaching about it and get to work — and I'll shoot you a check as soon as they pay me for your last one. Love your stuff! 'Bye!" He hung up and shook his head. "Writers..." He stood up, came around the desk, and approached Matt.

"Ah, you must be Mr. Dawson," he said, holding out his hand. "Glad you could make it! I'm Julius Weiss, but since a name like 'Julius' is a little pretentious — makes it sound like I'm great Caesar's ghost or something — everyone calls me Julie."

A girl's name is better than an emperor's? Oh well, to each his own.

Still at a loss as to what this was all about, Matt stepped forward and gingerly shook hands with Mr. Weiss. As their hands touched, the old editor nodded faintly, as though something had just been confirmed in his own mind. Then he introduced the rest of the attendees.

The fortyish brunette was Ellen Loring, an investigative reporter formerly with the *Daily News* and now working for the *Tribune*. She was slim, immaculately groomed in a severe gray women's business outfit with gloves, skirt, and heels, and would have been extremely attractive if her features hadn't been so hard.

Next to her was Johnny Larsen, a red-haired reporter who looked enough younger than his likely thirty or so that he would probably still be carded if he ever went into a bar — maybe it was the bowtie that made him look like an eternal juvenile — who had followed Miss Loring from the *Daily News* to the *Tribune*. Matt remembered his name from the news story about the reporter who had slipped into Garth Bolton's lair to confront the renegade scientist about Astroman's disappearance. One of Johnny's arms was in a sling, the result, Matt guessed, of his less than gentle treatment by Bolton's private goon squad in expediting his exit from the premises.

Another redhead was Lisa Latham, a housewife of about forty just in from Centerburg, Ohio. She wore what was probably her Sunday best, but her dress looked a little dowdy compared to Ellen Loring's outfit. With her was a blond man of the same age, one Fred Rausch, also of Centerburg.

Finally, over by the wall sat a strikingly beautiful blonde woman around thirty, crisp in the blue uniform of an airline flight attendant (though in this world she was probably still called a stewardess). She was introduced as Olivia Loring-Larsen. The family resemblance to Ellen Loring was obvious in their faces, even if Olivia didn't have the hard-boiled, cynical look of her sister. Give her another ten years of serving cocktails to drunken businessmen asking for her phone number on the evening shuttle to New York, however, and Olivia might surpass Ellen in that respect. If she had been married to Johnny Larsen, the fact that they weren't sitting together and the absence of wedding rings on their fingers suggested that it hadn't lasted.

They all seemed worried about something, and looked at Matt as though he was some new and unexpected part of the mystery. As he carefully took a seat in the remaining empty chair, Mr. Weiss sat down again behind the desk and resumed the meeting.

"Mr. Dawson, I hope you will regard everything we say here today as strictly confidential. Our little group doesn't have any name or recognized existence. You might call us the Friends of Astroman, and that sums us up as well as anything. We are meeting today in what amounts to an emergency session because something is terribly wrong and unless we can find some answers to our questions fast..." He paused for a moment, then sighed heavily. "Well, I don't know what will happen, but it probably won't be good. The lives, property, freedom, and happiness of millions of people may depend on what we can find out."

"All right," Matt said, "but what do I have to do with it?"

"A great deal, evidently," Mr. Weiss replied. "Garth Bolton's men have attacked MacTavish Laboratories twice and both times they were stopped in their tracks by a hyper-powered man in civilian clothes. Yesterday, a hyper-powered man in civilian clothes fought a battle with Berserko at the Astroman Museum." He held up a newspaper that had been lying on his desk. The enormous headline read: **MUSEUM MELEE**. "I think you have to have more than two people involved for a fight to be a 'melee,' but never mind the copy editing." He set the newspaper down. "As it happens, I'm on the Board of Directors for the Astroman Museum, and the curator told me one of his guides is in the hospital. Apparently she got a little too friendly with a hyper-powered man last night. She was able to communicate some today, and by adding things up, I seem to have found... well, *you*, Mr. Dawson. I'll put the most important question to you bluntly. Do you know where Astroman is?"

"No," Matt replied in some relief. For a moment, he had wondered if Mr. Weiss was going to try to pin the damage to the museum on him, but that issue, at least, didn't seem to be on his mind at the moment. "I've never met him and I have no idea where he is."

Ellen Loring reacted with a stricken gasp. "Then who fought with Berserko and broke up Bolton's attacks?"

"I did," Matt admitted.

"But how?" Johnny Larsen demanded. "I covered the MacTavish-Lab story. Bolton's helicopters were wrecked so there weren't any casualties, just the way Astroman would have done it!"

Mr. Weiss broke in before Matt could say anything. "Mr. Dawson, I've shaken hands with Astroman enough times to know what a hyper-powered man's skin feels like. It's hard and unyielding, and I felt the same with you. You're hyper, aren't you?"

I've got to stop thinking that's funny every time I hear it put that way! The word 'hyper' doesn't have that meaning here!

Matt nodded. "Yes, I am."

That brought everyone in the room to their feet and blurting astonished questions. "But how—?" "Who are you?" "Where are you from?" "Then where's Astroman?" Finally, Mr. Weiss had everyone quieted down and back in their seats, and Matt was allowed to tell his story. Since he saw no point in keeping any secrets, he told them everything he knew, which was not a great deal as it related to what they were most concerned about.

Where he came from, talk of parallel worlds and alternate universes would have been meaningless techno-babble to the lay public, if it didn't bring the men with butterfly nets running. Here, Mr. Weiss merely nodded grimly. They believed Matt because they had no choice. That is, most of them believed him.

"Parallel worlds?" Ellen Loring demanded shrilly. "Alternate universes? What kind of nonsense is that? I'm not believing a word of it until I see him do something hyper. Bend a chair leg or something."

Well, she was a cynical, hard-bitten reporter. Even so, bending a chair leg didn't seem like much of a stunt. Matt got up, walked over to her, bent down, wrapped his hand around one of the chair legs, and stood up straight, holding the chair aloft with her in it with just one hand.

Unfortunately, he misjudged her center of gravity and nearly tipped her out of the chair. She screamed, scrambling in mid-air to grab the back of the chair for support, and he quickly set her down again.

"All right," Ellen snapped, glaring at Matt. "I'll believe you. For the time being, at least."

Mr. Weiss then turned to the matter at hand. "After all these years," he said heavily, "we finally know some of the truth. All the unanswered questions, all the details that didn't add up... now we know. Probably too late to do any good, though."

"Excuse me," Matt spoke up, sitting back down in his own chair, "but I'm still in the dark here. Exactly what is going on?"

Mr. Weiss exhaled audibly and kneaded his hands on the desktop for a moment. "There's no reason to hide from you what we all know," he replied wearily. "Astroman is missing. Since there are rumors that Garth Bolton has some new hyper-weapon, we fear it could have been used on him and he could be dead or badly hurt."

"Bolton's men hit me with it last night and I barely got away alive," Matt said, "so I'd say that's a possibility." He explained about the green ray and how it had worked.

Mr. Weiss nodded grim-faced. "So that's what Bolton has. We are all hoping fervently, of course, that there is some other explanation for Astroman's disappearance. At the same time, a newspaper columnist named Kirk Collier has also been missing." He gestured to the others in the room. "We're all friends and colleagues of both men, and we've come to the conclusion that they must be one and the same."

Fred Rausch interrupted. "There's no doubt about it. I grew up with Kirk and I saw him change into Astrolad one night when he didn't know I was watching him. He was my buddy and I never told anyone what I knew. I didn't even tell *him* I knew, but there's no reason to keep it secret anymore."

"Fred's right," Lisa Latham, the redhead from Centerburg, added. "I never actually saw Kirk change into Astrolad the way he did, but I grew up with Kirk, too, and... well, you can't keep something like that secret from people as close to you as he was to me." She glanced significantly at Ellen Loring, who pointedly looked the other way. "I knew how important the secret identity was, so I never said anything, either."

"I'm not doubting either of you," Mr. Weiss said. "It's just that we never had solid *proof* before. It does confirm what we've long suspected, however. Now," he went on, looking at Matt, "Kirk was a columnist for the Chicago *Daily News* when I was editor there. When a consortium controlled by Garth Bolton bought the paper and forced me out, Kirk quit and went to the *Tribune* even though the Bolton forces tried to hold him to his *Daily News* contract. It would have amused Bolton to have his worst enemy work for him, had he known. It's also a little strange to realize that I was Astroman's editor for years."

Ellen Loring had been growing increasingly uneasy while Mr. Weiss explained matters for Matt's benefit. She suddenly interrupted with an impatient, "All this background story isn't getting us anywhere! Astroman's still missing and Garth Bolton's out there taking advantage of it! If this keeps up for very long, nobody will be able to stop him! What are we going to do, Julie?"

Mr. Weiss remained unruffled. "I don't think we can do anything until we find out what happened to Astroman. But I do believe our guest from another dimension can help us a great deal in solving that mystery."

"Me?" Matt exclaimed, astonished. "What can I do? I'm not even from this world. I wouldn't know where to start looking. I'm just a minimum-wage lab assistant!"

"But a hyper-powered one," Mr. Weiss pointed out. "You can go where the rest of us can't. And the first place to go if you're looking for Astroman would be the Secret Citadel."

"The... *what?*" Matt asked blankly.

Johnny Larsen jumped in to explain. "That's Astroman's private retreat in the Rocky Mountains. He needed a place where he could relax and be himself. That's where he'd be if he's anywhere, I'll bet. I know pretty much where it is since he took me there a few times, but you'd have to be hyper to get in very easily."

"You want me to break into a man's house?" Matt asked.

"It's a little more complicated than that," Larsen said, and proceeded to fill in the picture.

During a particularly hot phase of the Cold War, the management of a large corporation concluded that nuclear war was inevitable. Believing firmly in the principle of *"Après le déluge, nous!,"* the executives had a bomb and radiation-proof hideaway constructed in the Rockies as a place to sit out Armageddon, hollowing out a sizeable portion of a mountain and furnishing it with all the amenities.

Not long after it was finished, however, the company went through a series of buy-outs and mergers, and the members of the former executive team who had supported the idea of a luxurious bomb shelter were dispersed, retired, laid off, and otherwise lost in the shuffle. Meanwhile, American and Soviet leaders pulled their countries back from the brink in a series of summit conferences, and the nuclear threat receded. Some beancounter soon noticed a white elephant on the books that was costing a small fortune to maintain with little likelihood of it ever being used, and the new Board of Directors, astonished to discover that the company actually owned such a thing, decided to sell it off even if at an enormous loss. The winning bid came from an obscure company that was actually a front for the Astroman Foundation.

Astroman had been looking for a little hideaway of his own, and the mountain redoubt filled the bill. He moved in with all his memorabilia and remodeled the place to suit his taste. Some hint of it reached the general public, and while no one knew much about it or exactly where it was, newspapers started referring to it as Astroman's "Secret Citadel." The name stuck.

He was just one man occupying a complex intended for hundreds, so many rooms remained unused. Johnny Larsen mentioned a dusty nursery in particular, with cribs and toys that had never been touched, since the executives who had built the place had planned to bring their families as well. When Astrogirl came along, she was allotted a suite of her own.

"I still don't like the idea," Matt said. "What if he likes it even less? I could barely hold my own against Berserko, and I don't think Astroman would make the mistake of breaking off the fight too soon."

"This is an emergency," Mr. Weiss reminded him. "Besides, what if he's hurt or needs help? Even if there's some other reason for his silence, somebody has to find out what it is and talk to him, or failing that, Astrogirl. You're the only one who can do that."

"You can't just ask Astrogirl yourself?" Matt wondered. "Don't you have some way of contacting her?"

"We do," Mr. Weiss replied, "but she hasn't been returning our calls. She's been seen, so she hasn't gone missing, too, and the fact that she suddenly won't talk to us is one reason why we're convinced something must be terribly wrong."

"All right, if I go there, how am I supposed to get in?" Matt asked. "Smash through the walls? The Astros would really like *that*..."

Johnny Larsen reached into his jacket and produced an oddly shaped metal key about six inches long with what looked a conical drill bit at the end. "You can use this. It'll open a steel door in the cliff face about halfway up the mountain. Astroman gave this to me once, telling me I could use it to get inside the Citadel if anything ever happened to him. That was easy for him to say since I'd have to find the mountain again and then climb up a sheer cliff to get to the door, but I thought I'd be able to figure something out if it came to that. Later, Astrogirl showed up, which made it all unnecessary since she could take care of things as executor of his estate or whatever, but he never asked for the key back, either. Forgot I had it, I guess. Now it looks like it'll come in handy. I can't do it—" He glanced ruefully down at his injured arm "—so you'll have to."

Matt took the key from him, looked at it without learning much, and put it in his pocket. He was a little uncertain about what to do next and when to do it, and felt he could use a little advice rather than just blindly agreeing to what these people were asking.

"Can I use your phone?" he asked Mr. Weiss.

While the others discussed among themselves what they had just now learned, rather loudly in Ellen Loring's case, Matt called Dr. Mac-Tavish and explained the situation.

"It may not be a bad idea," MacTavish told him. "Astroman's the pivot on which this mystery turns. Along with everything else, he can certainly tell you more than I ever could about being hyper in a normal world. It might be best for you not to come back here for a day or two, anyway. The lab is swarming at the moment with police, detectives, and reporters asking questions and snooping around in response to the last attack, and I'd rather not have to explain you just yet. Bolton also isn't likely to attack me again for a while now that there's such a concentration of constabulary on the premises, so I can spare you for a couple of days. Do what you think best, laddie."

That was certainly a nice way of telling me to get lost for a while, Matt thought as he hung up.

He then announced to Mr. Weiss and the others that he was willing to break into the Secret Citadel and see if he could roust Astroman. There was a problem, however. He had absolutely no money. This was a project that could take two or three days and he was expected to start out immediately without being able to return to the one place that he could call something like home on this world, with only the clothes he was wearing right then and no prospects for his next meal or a place to stay.

"I think we can help you with that," Mr. Weiss said with a slight smile. "I keep something on hand for starving writers, and in the circumstances, I can't think of a better use for it."

As he explained it, he kept cash in his office safe since desperate writers between payments would occasionally appear in his office and beg for something to tide them over. He probably had petty cash there for incidental office expenses as well, as Matt had the impression that much of the business on this world was still conducted on an old-fashioned cash and carry basis.

"Here's a couple hundred," Mr. Weiss said, counting off the bills. "You shouldn't need even half of it, so bring me back what's left."

What could I spend it on? Matt had to wonder. Alcohol probably didn't have any effect on him, and as recent events had shown, women were out of the question. Once his basic needs were met, there wasn't much *to* spend money on. What was really startling was that Mr. Weiss seemed to regard $200 as a near fortune, when in Matt's time after fifty years of inflation it was hardly more than pocket change.

Some further consultation followed about what to look for and what to ask if he found Astroman, or failing that, Astrogirl. Mr. Weiss was also curious to find out how Berserko could have been reactivated just by touching a hyper-being. While he wasn't blaming Matt for what had happened, reports had to be filed to satisfy the police and various other authorities, not to mention the insurance company. Matt couldn't explain it very well, either, and could only repeat Dr. MacTavish's speculations on the subject.

Finally, he was able to get away and left the building through a handy window. He tucked a folded sheet of paper with Johnny Larsen's scribbled directions in his shirt pocket, then flew off towards the west and Colorado.

Chapter Eight: **The Secret of the Citadel**

Matt didn't expect to have any problems finding the Citadel. He had Johnny Larsen's directions and knew that the retreat was somewhere near the town of Ouray in southwestern Colorado. In addition, Johnny had included a rough map with some of the local landmarks so Matt could find the mountain itself. It was drawn from memory, however, and a little vague in spots.

Denver was around a thousand miles from Chicago, Matt recalled. He hadn't tested himself to see how fast he could fly yet, but the museum exhibits had made it sound as though Astroman could get to a trouble spot anywhere in the world in a fairly short time. If he flew all out, Matt could probably reach Colorado in a matter of minutes. But what about sonic booms? Would he blow out every window down below as he passed overhead? He decided to keep his speed moderate until he got the hang of things.

While it was hard to estimate how fast he was flying, he guessed it was in the four hundred mph range. He was running into considerable air resistance, but since he was hyper, it didn't bother him any more than plowing through a brick wall had. He didn't need goggles, either. Any strain he felt was mostly in keeping his body rigidly horizontal for the better part of three hours. As the afternoon wore on, the sinking sun directly in front of him became a nuisance, though more of a distraction than anything painful or harmful. He could have stared at the sun and counted sunspots if he wanted to.

Navigation was simple. Just fly west until he saw mountains, then find the right mountain.

When he did spot mountains ahead, he used his extended vision on road signs a mile below to see where he was. Wyoming, it looked like. Too far north. He made a left turn and struck south.

By the time he was over the southwest corner of Colorado and pre-sumably not very far from the Citadel, it was getting on towards evening.

He was also worn out from the flight, perhaps still feeling the lingering effects of Garth Bolton's green ray. He decided he wouldn't be good for very much serious effort today and started looking for a place to stay.

Seeing a little mountain town, he angled down towards its only motel. He checked in, picked up some extra clothes at a store that was fortunately still open, then had dinner at a diner that was conveniently close. He had to marvel at how incredibly cheap everything was at 1967 prices compared to his own world. Even treating himself to the most expensive item on the menu, a T-bone steak dinner with all the trimmings, with the idea that it was justifiable as a needed restorative after the day's exertions, only set him back $4.50. With the motel costing him less than ten dollars a night, his two hundred-dollar advance on expenses would last him a good long while at that rate, though he didn't expect this mission to take long enough to make a very big dent in his available funds.

After that, there wasn't much else to do but see a movie in the one local theater, hoping that Mr. Weiss wouldn't begrudge him the $1.25 ticket price for a little entertainment. The film interested him because it was a fair to middling adaptation of Jules Verne's science-fiction novel *Off on a Comet*, which as far as he knew had never been made on the Earth he had left. Unfortunately, it had been made instead on an Earth without CGI, and special effects were still obvious models and visible wires. Watching a movie was also a pain because of his extended senses. For most people, a projection speed of twenty-four frames per second blended into the illusion of continuous motion, but he kept seeing the film as a succession of individual still pictures. After some experimentation, he found that simply relaxing and letting the movie flow over him without concentrating too much on what he was seeing helped, though it was still not a perfect viewing experience.

After it was over, he went back to the motel and tried watching TV for a few minutes. With a somewhat faster rate of thirty frames per second, it wasn't quite the annoyance the movie had been, although scanlines were all too obvious, but he couldn't find much of interest in black and white sitcoms with laughtracks. This world didn't have a continuous news network on cable, so he ended up going to bed early. Tomorrow he would crack the Citadel.

The next morning, as the sun rose over yet another bright and clear day (*Does it ever rain on this world?*), Matt started out fresh and took to the air to look for Astroman's private retreat. Johnny Larsen's directions lost their precision at this point, however. Even though Johnny had known the Citadel was near Ouray, and the original intent had been for him to be able to find it and get inside if anything ever happened to Astroman, he wasn't clear on the exact location.

If he had ever had to find it, Johnny could have used his talents as an investigative reporter to track down the records of a massive construction project hollowing out and furnishing a mountain years before, but he had told Matt that he felt it would betray Astroman's trust to go looking for it until the time came when he actually needed to know where it was. One of the reasons for having a secret citadel was that it *was* secret, and Astroman preferred for it to stay that way.

While it was known among the public at large that Astroman had a home away from home somewhere, the prevailing idea was that it was located at the North Pole, which seemed to be confusing his legend with that of Santa Claus. Possibly Astroman had started the rumor himself as a tactic to divert enemies like Garth Bolton away from his actual base, despite the fact that there was no solid ground anywhere near the North Pole where he could build such a fortress.

On the other hand, even knowing that the place did exist and approximately where it was, finding it wouldn't be easy. There were a lot of mountains in Colorado, even in as small a defined area as near Ouray, and from the air they were all a confusing mass of rocky peaks, valleys, and steep slopes bedecked with pine trees. The one clue was the fact that the original builders had needed an access road to reach the mountain with supplies and equipment. Since the roads were not well-marked, Matt spent hours looking for possible candidates and following them to their ultimate dead ends.

Finally, somewhat past noon, he found a road that cut through a dense pine forest without any obvious reason for existing. It was wide and paved but apparently hadn't been used or maintained for some years, with weeds and grass sprouting through the cracks. It also went nowhere. Five miles into an uninhabited mountain wilderness without a turn-off, it came to an abrupt stop at a sheer cliff face.

Even years later, the ruts made by the tires of numerous heavy trucks were still visible in a wide unpaved turn-around space in front of the cliff. Along the road and at the base of the cliff were piles of rocky debris mixed with occasional rusting scrap metal like pipes. They were overgrown with grass and weeds as nature reclaimed them, but nature hadn't put them there to start with. At the end of the road and to one side still stood the empty shell of an old house trailer that may have been the guard shack during construction. This was looking promising. Hollowing out a small mountain and fitting the interior for human habitation would have taken an army of workers and endless truckloads of supplies and equipment. It couldn't have been very secret at the time it was built, and as simply a private bomb shelter it wouldn't have had to be. Since it was out of sight and out of mind in a remote corner of the mountains, memories had probably faded as the years passed.

Matt flew in for a closer look and stared at the mountain until his vision began to penetrate it. He hadn't fully mastered the technique of seeing through objects as yet, and that much solid rock still presented a problem, but he got an impression of cube-shaped empty spaces within the mountain. Bingo — this had to be it.

Matt didn't want to smash his way inside since Astroman certainly wouldn't be pleased by a hole punched through his wall, but the original front entrance used by the construction crews had long been sealed and convincingly covered by an artificial rock face of concrete and stone. The mountain was to serve as a shelter for several hundred people who would have to be able to get inside with a minimum of trouble, so there was probably some hidden entrance at ground level somewhere, but a relatively fresh-looking rockslide off to one side may have been Astroman's doing to block it. That left Astroman's own private entrance, high up on the mountain side and accessible only to people who could fly.

Hundreds of feet above the ground was a ledge jutting out over a sheer cliff face, Astroman's front porch. A simple steel door was set above the ledge and several feet back in a niche in the rock wall. Carved into the rock above the door was a shield about a foot high and emblazoned with a winged A. *Give it away, why don't you?* If Garth Bolton or his minions had ever gotten this far, say by rappelling down a rope from a hovering helicopter, any doubts they had found the right place would have been eliminated and they could have proceeded at once to planting explosives around the frame. Fortunately, Matt wouldn't have to go to all that trouble thanks to Johnny Larsen's key.

Towards the right-hand edge of the smooth, featureless face of the door was a small hole at about waist-level. Matt inserted the key and the heavy door opened easily enough, although a man without hyper-strength never could have budged it. One thing was obvious: Johnny Larsen would have been stymied at this point unless he had brought some dynamite along.

Beyond the doorway, a normal human being would have seen only a tunnel leading into utter blackness. Since Matt's extended perception made use of every last stray photon, he could dimly see the metal-lined walls of a long corridor that went deep into the heart of the mountain, with a very faint light at the far end. He closed the door behind him and launched himself into lateral flight, speeding down the corridor.

He came out into a dimly lit central chamber that reminded him a little of the sixteen-story high atrium at Fermilab, though this wasn't quite as large. It was large enough, though. Five levels of balconies ringed the open area, like the lobbies of some hotels Matt had been in. Adding to the hotel look were finished interior walls as opposed to just raw rock surfaces. The lighting was a bare minimum, perhaps just the emergency lights, left on because even an Astroman needed at least a few photons to work with to keep from stumbling around in an artificial cave buried under hundreds of feet of rock. There had to be a switch somewhere that turned on the rest of the lights for a more natural level of illumination, but Matt couldn't tell where it would be. Since he could do just fine with the dim lighting, he didn't go out of his way to look for it.

The vast hall was deserted with no living beings in sight, Astroman or otherwise. The silence was nearly total, and all Matt could hear was the faint background hum of an air circulating system.

He had been wondering what souvenirs and trophies Astroman would keep in his private retreat. The first aircraft carrier he had ever lifted, perhaps?

There weren't any aircraft carriers, but in the center of the hall was a bulbous object about the size of Laurie's VW. A large sign in front of it read:

SPACESHIP IN WHICH KARSTEN (ASTROMAN) THEL-NARR CAME TO EARTH FROM THE PLANET HELIONN.

While the depictions in the Astroman Museum displays had shown a small torpedo with flame spewing from the tail, the real thing looked more like a life-support capsule that had been launched by something else much larger. What basic on-board propulsion system the craft had was probably just for guidance and braking. The capsule also had a solidity that gave it every indication of being the actual spaceship and not just a mock-up, as though whoever had found it and the baby inside had kept it hidden in a barn or shed somewhere for years afterwards until Karsten himself was old enough to take possession of it.

Matt found it cheering to see that travel between star systems was possible and practical. In his universe, anyway, the speed of light was an absolute limit for any theoretically feasible spaceship, which meant trips to even the closest stars would take years — unless there were more nooks and crannies in the time-space continuum than were dreamt of in anyone's philosophy, and there was some way around the problem, whether worm-holes or space warps or hyperspace or whatever. He had to wonder how it was done, but he'd have to put off satisfying his curiosity until more urgent issues were resolved.

The spacecraft display didn't strike Matt as peculiar. It would be only natural for someone to preserve the last remaining link to his lost home and parents. Still, a lot of scientists would have been eager to examine the spacecraft for what it could tell them about the science and technology of an advanced civilization on another planet, but Astroman had apparently never allowed it. Not if that naive conception in the museum of Karsten's spaceship as a miniature version of the V-2 was anything to go by.

What did bother Matt was the excessively detailed sign in front of the spacecraft. It was the first indication of a syndrome he would discover endlessly repeated as he searched the Citadel. Anyone else would have put newspaper clippings in a scrapbook and small souvenirs in a display case, but Astroman kept all his memorabilia in his Citadel. He had not only carefully saved the relics of his life, he had meticulously labeled each item with an exhaustively detailed description. It was an Astroman museum far more complete than the one in Chicago, but who besides Astrogirl had he ever expected to see it?

Matt looked into one of the rooms fronting the first level of the central hall, and was startled to find Julius Weiss sitting at a desk, smoking a cigar, and talking on the telephone. The room was a duplicate of Mr. Weiss's office in Chicago, so exact that for a moment Matt wondered if he had stepped through some kind of teleportation gate and really was back in Illinois. Then he realized that this Mr. Weiss was not moving or saying anything, and there was no cigar smoke or odor in the room. Matt's hyper-senses failed to pick up any heartbeat or breathing, and the figure's body heat was strictly room temperature. It was a lifelike wax dummy posed in a natural setting.

As he looked around the room, Matt found some things that weren't in Mr. Weiss's real office. On the walls were framed photographs and newspaper front pages, and in a display case was an assortment of relics including a half-smoked cigar, a faded **PRESS** card probably once worn in a hat band, a necktie with holes in it eaten by droplets of acid, and a pistol with a barrel twisted to one side. Together, they were a collection of artifacts illustrating the life and times of Julius Weiss. A typed card by each item explained its significance. Mr. Weiss had been lucky Astroman was nearby on the day the mobsters he was exposing in a series of articles for the newspaper tried to throw acid in his face, for example, or he would have suffered much worse than a ruined necktie. Each of the other display items had a similar story behind it. It reminded Matt of the Astroman Museum again, except that this was more personal. While the Museum generally had to make do with replicas and reconstructions, Astroman had stocked the Citadel's display cases with the genuine artifacts.

Matt checked the adjoining rooms and discovered that each was dedicated to one of Astroman's friends. Ellen Loring had a room where her wax double stood forever with a portable reel-to-reel tape recorder strapped over her shoulder and a microphone in her outstretched hand. In Johnny Larsen's room, the cub reporter turned investigative journalist was caught in the act of pounding out a hot scoop on the keys of his manual typewriter. Lisa Latham's room was a little strange in that her wax double depicted her as she was in her teens, not as she was as an adult. In her girlishly furnished bedroom in probably her parents' house, she was immortalized in a pose of sitting at her desk and chewing on her pencil while pondering a particularly knotty problem in her geometry homework. Perhaps that was how Astroman remembered her, and he hadn't seen much of her after leaving Centerburg.

Even Kirk Collier had his own room, probably a replica of his office at the *Tribune*. His wax double sat at his desk typing with one hand and holding a telephone receiver to his ear with the other, as though taking down the details of a tip being called in by an informant. Without the mask, Collier was the dark-haired and craggily handsome fellow Matt had guessed, his rugged features somewhat softened by a pair of glasses. Around him were the framed photographs and the display cases with artifacts of his reporting career that a casual visitor would have been expecting after seeing the other rooms. It seemed a little odd to Matt, though. Had Astroman taken his split identity to the point that he regarded his alter ego as not just a pose but a real and separate person? Someone stumbling into the Citadel by accident and seeing this room would have assumed that Astroman and Kirk Collier were two entirely different people. Or was *that* the whole idea? Come to think of it, Johnny Larsen had been here more than once, so Astroman did have occasional guests who would have required him to keep up the façade.

Astroman's friends had said that he had always been somewhat cool and aloof towards them, friendly enough but somehow unapproachable past a certain point, almost godlike in his remoteness. They would have been amazed to have known about these rooms and the evidence of his actual feeling. Ellen Loring and Lisa Latham in particular might have been gratified to realize how Astroman felt about them.

Perhaps, Matt thought with a slight chill, these rooms and the devotion lavished on his friends in what must have been very time-consuming hobby projects (how could one man, even a hyperman, *do* all this?) were less signs of obsession and more an attempt by a man doomed to be a perpetual outsider to make up for the human contact he could never have.

This could be me in a year...

After looking through the exhibit rooms, Matt went on to explore other parts of the Citadel. Going down a ramp into a lower level, he found the original builders' recreation rooms with a handball court, a gym with exercise equipment, and since the facilities were intended for business executives, even several putting greens with artificial turf. None of them showed any signs of use. One room was a workshop for hobby projects, again with the tools and benches untouched for the most part. In one corner, however, it looked as though Astroman had spent some leisure time here.

I've heard of building a ship *in a bottle*, Matt thought in amazement, *but this is ridiculous!*

On the workbench stood a large clear glass bottle, in the six or seven gallon range. A neighbor down the street had been a home brewer when Matt was a teenager, and the word "carboy" for that kind of bottle came to mind. Probably using very long tweezers, Astroman had been building a model of a city in the bottle. It was only half-finished, but with architecture based on pointed spires and buildings like cut-glass perfume bottles, Matt could tell it was not a city on Earth. Several tiny buildings in various stages of completion lay scattered on the bench, waiting to be finished and placed in the bottle, and propped against the wall was a book open to several color photos of an otherworldly cityscape that had evidently been used as reference. The pictures had an inherent three-dimensional effect that just wasn't possible with 1967-era — or even 21st Century — printing technology.

Was this a city on his home planet? If he had been sent to Earth as a baby, he wouldn't be able to remember it, so was this model the outward expression of a longing for the world he had never known? It was one more piece in the puzzle that was Astroman.

All this was interesting enough in its own right, but it wasn't really telling him what he needed to know. Matt went back up to the main level to see what else was there.

After some cursory inspection of the dining hall and an auditorium for meetings and showing films, he eventually came into a large room that had been designed as a chapel. The pews, altar, and backlit simulated stained glass windows had been left as originally installed, but the spotlit cross on the wall above and behind the altar was different. It had two crossbars arranged as an X near the top of an upright beam, rather than one perpendicular crossbar. It looked like a railroad crossing sign, but it may have been the sort of cross preferred by orthodox Helionnians.

In front of the altar, on a bier, was a black-draped casket. Puzzled, Matt stepped up to it and pulled the cloth back from the end. The lid was transparent and he could plainly see the figure lying in state within.

The costume told the story, and Matt recognized the face from the photographs and exhibits he had seen.

Astroman would not be coming back to Chicago.

Ever.

Matt turned away, sad and depressed even though he had never met the man. He had certainly heard enough about him in the last few days, almost enough to feel as though he had known him. Now the mystery of why Astroman hadn't been seen lately was solved. It just wouldn't be easy telling Mr. Weiss and the rest of Kirk Collier's friends...

Then it sank in. Astroman's disappearance dated to an attack by Garth Bolton's men. The green ray that had knocked Matt out by merely grazing him must have hit Astroman squarely. Nothing had ever been able to hurt him before, so maybe he hadn't realized the danger. Bolton might not have known just what he had, either. But the bottom line was that Bolton had killed Astroman, and he could kill Matt the same way.

The realization was sobering. Matt still had no idea what his future was on this world, but if he wanted to go home eventually, he would probably have to hang around Dr. MacTavish and encourage him to work on that particular problem. Which in turn would mean being called into service to help defend the lab if Bolton attacked again, and that would mean facing the green ray. He could easily enough avoid Garth Bolton and his green ray by disappearing into anonymity, but it would leave Dr. MacTavish in the lurch and he would never get home that way.

That was all something he could figure out later. Right now, Matt suddenly had a thought. How had Astroman's body been removed from the scene of the battle and brought to the Citadel? He would have thought of the answer in another second, but he was suddenly interrupted by the only possible suspect.

"Who are you?"

Matt whirled. In the doorway at the other end of the chapel stood a woman of about twenty, wearing a modified green and white Astroman costume. With the short skirt, knee-high boots, shoulder-length blonde hair, and a slim, tautly muscled body of about medium height, she looked like a skater — if skaters wore domino masks, anyway. It was Astrogirl, said to be Astroman's cousin, and obviously angry.

"Er... Julius Weiss sent me," Matt explained. "He wanted me to find out what happened to Astroman."

Astrogirl stepped into the chapel and strode briskly towards Matt. "How did you get in?"

"The front door. Johnny Larsen gave me the key—"

Astrogirl came to a stop just in front of Matt, arms akimbo and cape hanging loosely down her back. She looked as though she was only barely repressing the urge to splatter him against the wall.

"I don't believe it!" she exclaimed, and Matt noticed just the slightest hint of a foreign accent that he couldn't identify in her otherwise pitch-perfect American pronunciation. "No one has ever been able to get in before this. No one has ever been able to even *find* this place! Johnny Larsen must be insane if he told you where it was and how to get in. How do I know you aren't one of Garth Bolton's men?"

"You can call Julius Weiss," Matt said quickly. "He sent me, so he'll vouch for me."

Astrogirl clearly wasn't in the mood for anything so reasonable. "Get out of here — *now!*"

She reached out with one hand and shoved him for emphasis, her palm against his shoulder. She was holding back and Matt barely felt it, though a native would have been knocked across the room. She looked startled, shoved again, harder, and still nothing happened. Then she raised her fist to hit him outright, and he parried it. She was still testing him, he sensed, since it had been at only a fraction of her full strength.

She stepped back as realization dawned on her face and her anger faded. "You're hyper, aren't you?"

There was that question again. Would he ever get used to the lack of a figurative meaning for "hyper" on this world.

"Yes," he replied. "Could you stop hitting me now?"

With an effort, she relaxed and no longer seemed quite so hostile. "All right, truce," she said, still a little guarded. "I'd heard somebody who might be hyper had just turned up, so I'm not too surprised to see you. Were you the one who fought with Berserko in the museum?"

"That would be me, yes. Sorry about the damage."

"We're insured, but the premiums will probably go way up after that. And you were also the one who fought off two of Garth Bolton's attacks on MacTavishLab?"

"Yes, though only barely the second time."

"You've still got a lot of explaining to do, whoever you are."

"I'll be glad to. Is there anything to drink in this place, by the way? I'm a little thirsty."

"Certainly." She turned to lead him out of the chapel. "Come with me. I still don't know who you are, so it might be a good idea to start with an introduction. You do have a name, don't you?"

"Matt Dawson. How about you? Or do I just call you Astrogirl?"

"That's a little formal. I do have a name for my private life, but we'll have to be a lot better acquainted before I can tell you that. I'm sure you understand. And thank goodness I talked Karsten out of doing one of those exhibit rooms about me or you'd know by now. But my Helionnian name is no secret. I grew up with it and it's the name I feel is me more than the other names will ever be. Call me Lynestra."

Dwight R. Decker

To emphasize her sincerity, perhaps, or help de-escalate hostilities, she pulled her mask back over her head. The mask hadn't really disguised very much, and she just looked all the more like a very pretty girl. She reminded Matt of a young Olivia Newton-John he had seen in an old music video — but there was something else. Her large blue eyes had sharp outer corners pointing slightly upwards, giving them a subtly cat-like look. While it wasn't so pronounced that it would attract attention as something freakish, it was there. She may have been human otherwise, but if her ancestors had spent a long time on another planet, they had evidently begun to deviate from the Earthly norm. Perhaps the reason she wore the mask was to hide that unusual distinguishing feature since people would recognize it from her civilian guise.

She took him to the Citadel's commissary. It was obviously little-used but its refrigerator was stocked with some food and drinks.

"What do you do about supplies?" Matt asked as she peered into the fridge to see what was there.

"They're delivered," she replied. "The Astroman Foundation has an arrangement with local vendors through one of its companies. There's a drop-off point a few miles away, and we pick everything up from there. The people around here are well aware that some kind of bomb shelter was built in the area some years ago even if no one remembers quite where it is anymore, and no one knows that it was sold a while back. The original owners maintained a small permanent staff of caretakers to keep an eye on the place, and we've encouraged the idea that things haven't changed to justify the need for occasional supplies."

She finally selected a couple of bottles of soft drinks, then went to a cupboard to look for glasses.

"That isn't Karsten Kola, is it?" Matt asked.

Lynestra shivered. "Brrr. I'd rather drink battery acid. The Foundation actually wanted to supply us with the stuff —they got a deal on it for the Museum — but I insisted on Pepsi."

They retired to a wood-paneled lounge that had been furnished to resemble the smoking room of a private businessmen's club of the late 19th Century. Years before, some corporate executives had planned to sit out a nuclear war in that room, sitting on the overstuffed couches and chairs and dozing by the fire in the open fireplace or swapping golfing stories over their drinks, but it had never happened that way. Now it was just Matt and Lynestra, him in a chair and her with her boots off and curled up on a couch, sipping their drinks and contemplating the fire.

It was a cozy moment that Matt wished could last for a while, but as she had informed him rather bluntly, he had some explaining to do.

112

"So who *are* you?" she asked. "Where do you come from? I don't remember you from Eristhar and you don't sound Helionnian."

"I'm not," Matt replied. "I'm from Earth. Just not *this* Earth." He then told her his story.

"Good grief!" Lynestra exclaimed when he had finished. "If you're telling the truth... I'm even further from home than I thought! Ten thousand years, twenty light-years... and a whole universe! We never knew what made people from Helionn hyper on Earth, but this explains it! Helionn must have been in *your* universe!"

"I'm surprised to find out Helionn was real and not some kind of cover story," Matt said. "It was a little hard to believe that a duplicate human race could evolve independently on another planet—"

"Oh, Helionn was real, all right," Lynestra assured him, "or I dreamed the first fifteen years of my life. We didn't evolve on Helionn, though. We evolved on Earth just like you did. About two hundred years from now, a Swedish group will land on a planet in the Delta Pavonis system and establish a colony there, and ten thousand years after that, that planet will explode. I can't explain it, but there's a loop in time connected with faster than light travel. The Thelnarr brothers knew this and when they sent both Karsten and me to Earth, they calculated it so we would arrive ten thousand years in the past. Contact with Earth had long since been lost and no one knew what conditions were like there. Civilization might have fallen, people might have been wiped out by an epidemic... nobody knew. So we were sent to a time when civilization was known to exist on Earth, and even a couple of centuries before the last contact so we could live out our full lifetimes well before whatever happened happened."

The pieces of the puzzle were fitting together. "So that's why Jarn Thelnarr's letter to his son was in Swedish," Matt said.

"Or Old High Helionnian. After ten thousand years, Modern Helionnian was different from Twentieth Century Swedish, but the texts of old documents from the earliest years of settlement had been preserved in one form or another, and scholars could read Swedish and even write in it. Even if English or some other language was spoken wherever Karsten happened to land, he could eventually have something written in contemporary Swedish translated. The reason why he didn't release the whole letter was that he didn't want it to be known that time travel was involved and he came from the distant future. Since he didn't know this Earth was in another universe, he thought too much knowledge about the more immediate future could change history and prevent some Swedish cult leader from taking his flock to another star two centuries from now. Helionn would never come to be, and neither would he. But if Helionn was in a different universe, then he'd never had to worry about changing history at all. How ironic..."

Matt had come to the Secret Citadel for a reason — to find out what had happened to Astroman — and it was time he got on with it.

"You must have brought Astroman here, then," he ventured after a minute or two of silence.

Lynestra nodded, still looking at the fire rather than at him. She seemed more relaxed now, or at least less suspicious of him after they had been talking for a while. "He asked me to back him up that night. He had gotten a tip that Garth Bolton's men were going to raid a master-scientist's lab for some specialized equipment Bolton needed. Karsten had also heard a rumor that Bolton had something that might be able to hurt him and suspected that the tip was planted to lead him into a trap, so he wanted me to stand by in case he needed help..." She choked back a sob. "Instead, he died in my arms. Bolton's green ray hit him and... he was gone." She paused for a moment to recover, then continued, her voice heavy. "Bolton never knew I was there. It was dark and I stayed hidden. If he could kill Astroman, what could I do? I had to get away, hide until I could find out more about it. I brought Karsten's body here so Bolton wouldn't know he had succeeded. If he knew he had killed Astroman, nothing would stop him, and he would be after me next. I haven't told Julie Weiss or Karsten's other friends what happened so Bolton can't accidentally find out through them even though they obviously suspect the worst. For the public, I've put out the story that Astroman is away on a mission, but I don't know how much longer people will believe it. Once they realize that Astroman is no longer there to stop them, every crook and criminal mastermind in the country will come out of the woodwork and go wild. I'm just afraid everything Karsten spent his life trying to accomplish is about to fall apart, and there isn't anything I can do to stop it..." Lynestra trailed off, sounding as though she was about to break down entirely.

The sudden silence stretched on a little painfully and Matt jumped in. "Bolton got me with that ray, too. It barely grazed me but it knocked me flat for hours."

"It drains hyper-energy," Lynestra said. "Karsten didn't have a mark on him, but he was dead, as if he had never been alive at all. When I brought him back here, I still had some slight hope that the ray might not have really killed him. It might have drained his energy but left him simply dormant and maybe he could be revived... but no... dead was dead..." She came close to sobbing again.

"But how could Bolton invent something like that?" Matt asked. "As I understood it, nobody knew what made us hyper before now."

Lynestra dabbed her eyes and her tone turned a little grim. "Unfortunately, Karsten made it himself, or at least had it made according to his specifications. He needed something to stop Berserko, so he came up with a device based on something they had on Helionn called a Deactivator that he thought could drain hyper-energy. My ship came with a library in its databank that included a lot about Helionn's technology, and he also borrowed a few specks of left-over hyper-fuel from the ship to power the machine."

"Oh, right," Matt said. "The guide at the Astroman Museum mentioned the Deactivator. They only had a model of it on display, so I couldn't use it on Berserko myself. The guide said she thought Astroman still had the real one—"

"It was loaned out to a master-scientist who wanted it to test some technique he thought the authorities could use if Berserko was ever reactivated and Astroman wasn't available. The scientist never did come up with anything useful, but he did discover that it could probably drain Astroman's energy, too, and not just Berserko's. You can imagine that Karsten wanted it returned fast when he found that out, but somewhere in the transport between here and there and back again, it was stolen some time ago and never found. That's partly why Karsten was anxious to train me as a backup. He thought Garth Bolton might have ended up with the Deactivator and could use it to destroy us, but he could never be sure. Bolton got to be very good with screens and shields that prevented even Karsten from seeing what he was up to. So now I'm guessing Bolton did get hold of the Deactivator and managed to figure out how it worked and produce larger versions of it..."

She swallowed hard, then continued.

"Well, now we know a little more about ourselves. That still doesn't solve the problem of what to do about Garth Bolton."

"That's easy," Matt said. "An all-out assault on his headquarters. We take it apart and whichever one of us gets to Bolton first can do whatever seems like a good idea."

Lynestra glared at Matt as though he had said something especially cretinous. "I'm sure his headquarters is now defended by hyper-cannons. His tank may have been destroyed but he was probably smart enough to fortify his estate first." She turned back to staring into the fire again. "Still..." she said reflectively, "that hyper-cannon reminds me of something they taught us in school. The Deactivator was used in Helionn's last war, as a sort of energy-drainer to disable the enemy's weapons. There was also a defense against it, something called the Neutralizer. Its design was secret and there wasn't anything more about it than a brief mention in Karsten's database."

"That doesn't do us a whole lot of good here," Matt pointed out.

Lynestra continued to think. "After the war, most of Helionn's weapons were destroyed, but samples of some of the more advanced ones were stored away in case they were ever needed again. No one outside of the Peace Commission knew exactly where the weapons were stockpiled, but there was a legend that called it the Arsenal of Wonders. That's where the Neutralizer would be. If we could just get our hands on that, Garth Bolton couldn't touch us and I could bring him to justice."

"Hold on a second," Matt said as he realized where she was going with this. "You're saying that what we need to fight Garth Bolton is on another planet in another universe, twenty light-years away and ten thousand years in the future? We can't get there from here, so what's the use in even thinking about it?"

Lynestra looked off into space. "I'm not so sure we *can't* get there from here," she murmured.

The Citadel's builders had anticipated that World War III would not start on a moment's notice. There would be a deteriorating international crisis, ominous troop and naval movements, and high-level threats and ultimatums between the nuclear powers, so they would have some warning that things were about to go bad. That would give the executives time to round up their families and hop company planes to Colorado. The access road that had served for constructing the mountain shelter had a long straight stretch that was designed to double as a landing strip, and near where the road dead-ended at the mountain face was a camouflaged hangar.

It had been built large enough to accommodate several corporate jets in the hope there would be someplace worth flying to after the dust settled outside. That scenario had never played out, and what the hangar did end up housing was certainly never dreamed of by its planners.

The starship stood on extended landing gear with wheels. It was designed to take off, land, and rest horizontally, like a medium-sized airliner, rather than stand vertically like a rocket, and it took up most of the large hangar. At the forward end was a crew quarters and cockpit in a pointed, wedge-shaped head with stubby wings. Back of it was a long cylinder like a neck, narrower than the crew compartment, stretching to a bulky section with engines, propulsion ports, and delta wings that were folded up against the sides.

Looking up at the ship from the concrete floor of the hangar, Matt flashed back to a childhood memory of seeing a mounted flying dinosaur skeleton at a museum. It had been a pterodactyl or something along that line, with perhaps somewhat the same proportions as this ship, at least in respect to a pointed head at the end of a tubular neck sprouting from a winged body, and it had seemed about as gigantic to the toddler-sized Matt.

The ship even had a name, lettered on the side in a strange jagged script: **DE SIST HOPP**.

"It means *The Last Hope*," Lynestra said in response to Matt's puzzled look. "In today's Swedish it would be something like *det sista hoppet*, but the language changed some in ten thousand years."

"Why that name?" Matt asked.

"Because that's what it was," she replied. "We knew the colony on Eristhar couldn't go on for very much longer. The ship was designed and built to scout nearby solar systems for habitable planets where we might be able to migrate. We knew of several likely planets that had been colonized from historical records, but like with Earth, there hadn't been any contact with them in ten thousand years so we didn't know what current conditions were like. Had they been destroyed in some interstellar war, did people still live on them, would there be enough room for us to settle, would we be welcomed? Unfortunately, the end came for Eristhar before anyone expected it, and the ship never set out on its original mission. I used it instead when I came to Earth."

Lynestra led him around the ship and pointed out various features. Finally, they stopped just under the forward command and crew module. The crew quarters and cockpit were just large enough to accommodate three men somewhat comfortably and four not so comfortably.

Matt glanced up and down the length of the ship. "Is that all of it?" he asked.

Lynestra looked blank. "What do you mean? Isn't it enough?"

"I mean, is this just the landing craft and there's a bigger section in orbit?"

"No, this is the whole ship. What makes you think there would be more to it?"

"For one thing, Astroman's spaceship in the Citadel is a lot smaller, like it's just an escape pod."

"That's about what it was. It was a one-way trip with just a baby on board. It only had to land once and never take off again, so it could be launched from Helionn on a preprogrammed flight. My ship was designed for interstellar scouting and carrying several crewmembers, and it had to be larger and more complex."

"But even this ship is on the small side, I'd think. We're talking about twenty light-years here. I always imagined interstellar spacecraft being the size of battleships or aircraft carriers. It would take a lot of energy to travel across light-years."

"Oh, I see what you're getting at. It doesn't work that way. The main thing is getting out of the atmosphere and clear of the planet, then accelerating to near light-speed. You find the mathematically determined point in higher dimensional space that will take you to the intersection of time and space where you want to go, you *jump*, and there you are. Think of it like going through a hole in space and coming out somewhere else. It isn't how much energy you use but how you apply it."

"If you say so..." Matt said hopelessly.

"This ship brought me here," Lynestra added a little dreamily, looking up at the crew compartment. "Across twenty light-years, ten thousand years... and a universe. There's nothing wrong with it. It could take me back. Since there's a recurring loop in time, my arrival could be timed to before Helionn exploded."

"So why haven't you gone back before now?" Matt asked.

Lynestra sighed. "Karsten felt our home was on Earth now and we had responsibilities. He came from Helionn as a baby and grew up here, so there was nothing familiar there that he could really go back to. He talked about making a return to Helionn a few times, just to visit and see where he had been born, not to stay, but he never got around to it. There have been times I've been homesick and wanted to go back, but then I had to ask myself back to what. I grew up in a dying little colony on Eristhar and I escaped just before it was destroyed, so while I miss my parents, it's not a place I could go back to, either. If I changed history too much by going there before I left, I might not even be born. It would be nice to see Helionn before it exploded, but if I went too far back into the past, I'd be marooned there."

"How come?"

"Because there's only just enough fuel left for a one-way trip. I could go back to Helionn, but I couldn't return to Earth without refueling. The ship was intended for a round-trip scouting expedition to another star system, and I've already used nearly half the fuel on board coming to Earth. I'd have to refuel on Helionn, which would be really difficult. The fuel was something that wasn't made on Helionn until late in its history, and there was only a small amount stored on Eristhar. Karsten told me it's something Earth science won't be able to make for a long time. There should be some at the Arsenal since it was used for other things, like exotic weapons, but we'd be running a risk going there hoping we could find enough so we could come back."

"Fuel is just an energy source," Matt said. "If one thing doesn't work, something else might. Did Astroman say what it was, exactly?"

"Oh, I don't know. It didn't have a name, just a number. Does Element 126 mean anything to you?"

Matt gave a start. The coincidences were mounting, as though Fate itself was conducting the orchestra. Astroman had underestimated Earth science in general and Dr. MacTavish in particular. "It means a lot. In a way, it brought me to this world, too. And it does have a name — Glengarrium."

"You know about it?" Lynestra asked excitedly.

"Not only that, I know the man who makes it."

Impetuously, Lynestra suddenly threw her arms around his neck and pressed her lips against his. The kiss lasted a few moments, and even though he was astonished, he went along with it. After what had happened to Laurie, it was a relief to be able to embrace a woman without having to worry about breaking her back. Their hyper-bodies weren't as supple as they would have been on Earth, so the kiss was a little stiff and wooden, but Matt wasn't complaining. Then, just as suddenly, Lynestra broke off.

"Don't get me wrong..." she said quickly, turning away, nervous, flustered, reddening. "Just excitement... heat of the moment... oh, I just wanted to know what it *felt* like for once!"

After that, they went back inside the Citadel to start formulating their plans. This time they sat at a table in the elegant, wood-paneled formal dining room so Lynestra could make notes and lists and do quick figuring on various sheets of paper spread out in front of her.

Now the scale of it all was setting in on Matt. "You're really serious about this? Going back to Helionn for a secret weapon?"

"Very serious," she told him. "*Garth Bolton killed Karsten!* I will *not* let him get away with it!" She was suddenly vehement, trembling with anger. With an effort, she calmed herself down, but she was still seething under the surface as she went on. "Everything else in my life is on hold until I've put Garth Bolton away. If what I need to do that is located twenty light-years away in another universe and ten thousand years in the future, and I have a way to go there, then I'll go there and get it. Simple as that."

You call that simple? It was the most roundabout way of accomplishing something that Matt had ever heard of.

She continued, regaining more of her composure as she spoke. "So how do I do it... The exact location of the Arsenal of Wonders was supposed to be a secret, but since my great-grandfather was High Councilor of the Peace Commission that established it and the knowledge was passed down in my family, I heard it discussed. After Helionn was destroyed, there was no point in keeping it a secret anymore. I'm pretty sure I can get in because it was a hereditary thing and the security system was programmed to recognize members of the family. As Tharn Thel-narr's great-granddaughter, I should be authorized. Quick in, grab the Neutralizer, quick out, nobody will ever know I was there. I think it's our only option. I can't do it all by myself, so you'll have to come along."

Matt gave a start. *I do?* "Er... I appreciate the trust, but we just met and..."

"It's true I barely know you," Lynestra said, "but I'll trust you for now. If Julie Weiss and Johnny Larsen felt they could trust you, you must have something going for you. Besides, you're hyper, too, so this concerns you as much as it does me."

It was stunning, suddenly talking about taking an interstellar trip like it was just a Sunday drive. Matt had idly daydreamed of going to other planets since his earliest boyhood, but it had been purest fantasy on his own Earth. Now that the opportunity had been dropped in his lap, he wasn't about to pass it up.

I'm not doing anything else at the moment, so I might as well take a twenty light-year round-trip through space.

"I'm just a little sorry that I won't have a chance to see the sights," he remarked. "It isn't every day I go to another planet. At least one that's more different from my own world than this one is," he added, realizing that he *had* gone to another planet.

"Helionn is my world," she replied, "and I've never even been there, so I'd like to do a little looking around myself. But like I said, quick in, quick out. We don't dare spend very much time there or the authorities might notice us, and then things would get *really* complicated. The last thing I want to do is accidentally change history somehow. Figure a week in total if we're lucky, a week and a half or even two weeks if we get hung up somewhere. If we're there very long, we'll have to wait for the cycle to come around again so we don't come back to Earth at the wrong time. Arriving thousands of years in the past or future wouldn't exactly accomplish our mission."

Meanwhile, Matt had been thinking. "You know, once we're in the other universe, I'm halfway home. You couldn't take a little detour through time and drop me off on my Earth on the way back, could you?"

Lynestra glowered at him for a moment, as though she suddenly wasn't entirely sure of his dedication to the mission. "I'm sorry, but all I have to go by are my father's notes and Karsten's calculations, and they had no idea they even were dealing with two different universes. They just thought it was just a regular cycle in normal time. So let's not com-plicate things and run that much more risk of something going wrong. Besides, I *need* you. I know it isn't your fight and it isn't your world, but you're hyper and I'm going to need all the help I can get to take on Garth Bolton. Help me with that and then we can see about sending you home."

It's always something... "So when do we start?" And with that, he had signed up for the duration.

Lynestra thought for a moment. "I'll have to do some research first to find out when we should take off. Like I said, Karsten had played with the idea of going back and I'm fairly sure he did the calculations for the trip. I can check his notes and see how far he got with it. Besides, the ship's computer has the programming and data for figuring trips to Earth and other planets, so I can work it out... just give me a few days. The calculation's really intricate because we have to enter the contact point in space at just the right time, at just the right speed, and at just the right angle so we come out the other side where and when we want to. Depending on where we are in the recurring cycle of relative times in the two universes, we could be leaving next week or next month. We'll have to keep our eye on Garth Bolton until then, of course, and hope he doesn't decide to make a move."

"All right," Matt said, "I'll wait by the phone for your call. In the meantime, Julius Weiss and the others sent me here to find out what happened to Astroman. Now I know, but what do I tell Mr. Weiss when I go back?"

Lynestra sighed. "I wish we could just come out and tell him the truth, but even if we swore him and the rest of Karsten's friends to secrecy, there'd still be a risk of it getting out to Bolton. One indiscreet remark by Johnny Larsen that makes it sound like he knows something and he'd be kidnapped by Bolton's men and worked over until he talked. No, I think it's better for both us and them if we keep them in the dark for now. They can't reveal what they don't know."

"So what *do* I tell Mr. Weiss, then?"

"Let me be the villain," Lynestra suggested. "Say that you found the Citadel all right, but there was no sign of Astroman, then Astrogirl showed up and refused to answer your questions."

"I hate to lie to Mr. Weiss..." Matt said uncomfortably. "He did trust me on this mission and provide me with some money..."

"Do you want Garth Bolton to kill us both?" Lynestra demanded a little shrilly. "Use some common sense! You're starting to sound like Karsten. He even felt guilty about having a secret identity because it wasn't quite honest although it made everything else possible."

In the end, Matt agreed to maintain the fiction that he didn't know what happened to Astroman.

Dwight R. Decker

He had to grab his spare clothes and check out of the motel first, then they flew back to Illinois together. He had rather hoped she would kiss him goodbye when they split up, but no such luck. Apparently the kiss in the Citadel had been a spur of the moment thing she was now too embarrassed to repeat. Lynestra just waved to him as she turned away to head downstate to wherever she lived, and Matt continued on to Chicago.

He found Mr. Weiss alone at his desk in the Stellar Sales Service office.

"So how did it go?" Mr. Weiss asked, outwardly calm but with an underlying hint of both eagerness and anxiety. "What did you find out?"

"Not much," Matt replied. "I located the Citadel all right, but I must have set off every alarm in the place getting in even with the key Johnny Larsen gave me. Astrogirl showed up within a few minutes, before I had a chance to look around much. She wasn't happy about me being there."

"To be expected, I suppose..." Mr. Weiss muttered, starting to look as though he knew he wasn't going to like the rest of Matt's story. "I had hoped she would open up to a fellow hyper-being. Still, you must have had the presence of mind to ask Astrogirl the obvious questions, right?"

"I did but she wasn't talking. All she cared about was getting me out of there. The fact that I'm hyper didn't help matters. She even seemed to have the idea that I might be some kind of experiment Garth Bolton did to create synthetic hyper-people. So I left."

"I see... You have hyper-senses, though. Did you catch a glimpse of anything that might seem important, hear anything...?"

Hating having to lie like this, Matt shook his head. "I didn't get past the central hall. All that rock made it hard to get a good read on the interior of the mountain even with X-ray vision. There seemed to be a lot of hollow spaces, though, and I'd guess there were living quarters further in, but I couldn't tell if anybody was in them. I didn't want to get into a fight with Astrogirl, so when she told me to get out, I got out."

Mr. Weiss sighed heavily. Matt wasn't sure he quite believed his story, suspecting that the shrewd old newspaperman had detected a certain hint of prevarication. This was somebody who had spent his life interviewing Chicago politicians and had probably developed a keen sense for someone not telling the whole truth, but he apparently decided not to press the matter.

"All right, I guess you did what you could," Mr. Weiss said, then asked, "You didn't spend all the money I gave you, I trust?"

As the air turned a little chilly, Matt returned the unspent portion.

"And you did remember to keep the receipts?"

Matt dug into his shirt pocket. "Right here."

Then he left and flew back to MacTavishLab.

Part Two

The Gathering Storm

Chapter Nine: **The Noose Tightens**

It was not a joyous homecoming there, either. For the first time since Matt had arrived on this world, Dr. MacTavish was unhappy with him about something and took him to his office to explain.

He waved an official-looking paper. "This is from a lawyer representing that girl you put into hospital with your clumsy lovemaking. Her medical bills will be considerable and she doesn't have any money. Because you're to blame for her problems, it seems to the barrister as though you're the one who should pay."

"I don't have any money, either!" Matt protested. "How can they sue me, anyway? I don't even have a legal existence."

"But I do," MacTavish snapped, "and they figured out from things you told the girl and her doctor that you work for me in some way. Somehow that makes me responsible, maybe because they think I made you hyper. It will probably cost me quite a lot of money and tie me up in court for years proving I don't have a thing to do with this."

"She works for the Astroman Museum," Matt said, "and isn't it owned by the Astroman Foundation? Don't they have health and accident insurance for their employees?"

"I gather that enquiries were made in that direction," MacTavish replied, frowning, "since she did meet you in the course of her official duties for the Museum. It would have been a different story had she been hurt as a result of your fight there, but what happened was after she was off the clock and on her own time. I don't know how employee health plans work on your world, but here she has to pay her own hospital bills if she wasn't injured specifically at work. So the lawyer is looking around for somebody, anybody, with a pocket he can pick, which seems to be me. You're a good lad, Matt, and I like you, and I'm grateful for what you've done to help out around here, but I really don't need this to worry about along with everything else. So, if you could think of some way to make this particular unpleasantness go away, I'd be much obliged."

Matt considered. Unless he could pull off the squeezing coal into diamonds stunt, which he doubted, there seemed to be only one solution. "The Astroman Foundation must have a lot of money, right?"

"So I understand, but they already turned the lawyer down flat with this. Part of the reason why the Foundation exists is to take care of nuisance lawsuits arising from collateral damage resulting from Astroman's crime-fighting battles, and they don't want to set precedents making it too easy to extract money from them. I'm just fortunate they're not coming after me to pay for the damage you did to the museum, but since they're the ones who put Berserko on display like that, any court would rule it was their own bloody fault."

"But the Foundation would listen to Astrogirl, wouldn't it?"

"Probably. It's her foundation, too. I take it you met her when you went out West? If you think you can convince her to help, by all means."

The prospect that the problem might have an early solution took the edge off Dr. MacTavish's displeasure, and Matt could turn the conversation to other matters, like what he had learned at the Citadel.

"So Astroman really is dead..." MacTavish said when Matt told him about the body in the casket. "It's sad news indeed, especially with Garth Bolton on the loose, but I'm not surprised. Being missing for so long, Astrogirl being less than forthcoming about where he is... It doesn't bode well for the future of this world since he's been such a prominent figure for so long, and his absence as a force for good will be keenly felt. Astroman only barely kept Bolton in check as it was, and now that he's gone, there is nothing to hold our lad Garth back if he has some greater mischief on his mind. It doesn't bode well for *your* future, either. We now know for certain that Bolton's ray really can kill you."

"Believe me," Matt replied, "having already been hit with it once, I didn't need any convincing."

He then described what else he had seen.

MacTavish shook his head at the end of it. "I feel as though I'm rolling in catnip. You're telling me wonderful things one after another that have been mysteries for years. And Astroman not only came from another planet but from the future, so his ancestors originated on Earth! It restores my faith in evolution because a species physically identical to ours could not possibly evolve independently. Funny thing about that bottled city you spoke of, by the by. I recall that Johnny Larsen wrote an article called 'Secrets of the Citadel,' or some such thing. Judging from what you've told me just now, he didn't really reveal very many secrets at all, not even where the Citadel is, but he did mention the bottle.

Though he made it clear enough in the article that the miniature city was just a model Astroman was building, these things get exaggerated in the telling and retelling. Half the people out there in the world now believe that the model really is a city from Astroman's home planet that had somehow been reduced in size, and it even has actual wee people living in it."

"Shrinking people like that wouldn't be possible!" Matt exclaimed, then remembered where he was and added, "In my universe, anyway."

"Nor in this one, but our less scientifically informed fellow citizens do love their myths and legends."

Matt finished up by informing Dr. MacTavish of his plans for the immediate future.

"A voyage to another star..." the old scientist mused. "I envy you, lad. If I didn't have more pressing problems, I'd be tempted to invite myself along. I appreciate that you have a job to do, but I hope you can find the odd moment to make some observations. You will be going places where no one from our world has ever been and seeing things no one has ever seen. This is something that wouldn't normally be possible for centuries, if even then, so I hope you make the most of the opportunity. You are a scientist yourself, and our calling is to explore the unknown, then report back on what we have discovered."

"I'll do what I can," Matt replied, "but Astrogirl did say it would be quick in and quick out. When she calls to tell me she has our departure date set, I'll be taking off. Uhm... about that..."

He explained about the need to borrow a cup of Element 126.

MacTavish brightened. "If you think that super-weapon will do any good in fighting Garth Bolton, you're welcome to all the Glengarrium you like. How much did you have in mind?"

"Astrogirl said about four and a half kilograms," Matt said. "Call it ten pounds."

MacTavish's eyes nearly popped out of his skull. "Good Lord!" he exclaimed in horror. "We don't have nearly that much on hand! We normally deal in fractions of a gramme. A quantity that large could flip a galaxy on its back. But give me a few days and we'll make up a batch. Let's see... we should have enough thorium in stock to get started..."

Because Lynestra preferred to keep her secret identity secret even from Matt for the time being, she had given him the number for an answering service the Astroman Foundation maintained in case he needed to reach her. An operator would take the message, relay it to Astrogirl through an answering machine at the Citadel, and she would call him back.

Which she did within an hour after he called the Foundation. She actually seemed glad, even eager, to talk to him. Until he explained what he wanted. Then her voice lost all of its warmth.

"You want the Foundation to pay the hospital bills of a girl you injured while trying to make love to her?" Matt could practically hear the icicles forming.

"I just kissed her," he protested. "That's all. I didn't mean to hurt her."

"Is that how you do things on your world? Go around kissing every girl you meet?"

Now Matt understood what had brought this on. He was about to point out that Lynestra had actually kissed *him*, not the other way around, but realized in time that there was no way he could win an argument like that.

The amazing thing was that in the end, Lynestra actually did agree to have the Foundation pick up Laurie's hospital bills, and somehow passed along instructions to that effect even though she wasn't currently in direct communication with Julius Weiss or other members of the board because she was dodging questions about Astroman. She had more important things to worry about with preparations for the trip to Helionn, and she and Matt didn't need threats of lawsuits and court appearances hanging over their heads. In effect, Laurie would be bought off. Her injuries would be ruled to be directly related to her employment by the Astroman Museum, since she wouldn't have met a visiting hyperman otherwise, a unique set of circumstances that would set no precedents or affect any other present or future claims, and a mutually satisfactory settlement could be reached without the need for judges and courtrooms.

But whatever initial warmth Lynestra had seemed to feel for Matt... that had cooled considerably as a result of the incident. He got a very definite sense that relations between them would be strictly business for some time to come.

Laurie was still in the hospital at last report. Feeling a need to make some kind of amends, Matt took flowers to her one afternoon.

With all the various medicinal and disinfectant odors in the air, he just about had to turn his nose off as he walked down the dimly-lit corridors. When he came into the bleakly barren if functional room — the calendar for this world may have read the 1960s but a lot of things were having trouble getting out of the '40s — he found her reading a magazine while half-sitting in her bed with a tray table over her middle and leaning back against the pillow. Her head and neck were encased in some medieval-looking contraption with metal rods, struts, and headband, the local low-tech version of a neck and back brace. He felt a twinge of guilt realizing that he was the one who had put her in it. Lower down was some sort of chest support that may have been for the broken ribs.

When she saw who it was, she tried to look away though her range of head movement was somewhat limited in that cage. "I'm not sure I want to see you," she muttered.

Matt set the vase of flowers down on a small table next to some other flowers and several cards, and went to her bedside.

"I came to apologize," he said. "I'm really sorry about what happened, and…" He trailed off, not sure what else to say after that of if she was even listening. This was getting awkward. Might as well cut to the finish. "Anyway, I managed to get the Astroman Foundation to cover your medical expenses."

She looked back at him, if reluctantly, setting the magazine down on the tray. "So they told me. Well, thanks for that. That's a big worry off my mind."

"I'm kind of new here, didn't know my own strength—"

"Never mind. I figured it out. Another lesson learned, I guess. Don't get mixed up with hypermen."

Ouch. "So how are you doing?"

"Not too badly, considering you almost broke my back. I'm already walking a little every day now. They tell me I can go home in a couple of days, though I'll still have to take it easy for a few weeks. I just hope they have the Museum rebuilt by the time I'm fully recovered so I have a job to go back to."

After that, the conversation was strained and halting. She wasn't inclined to chat with the author of her misery and he couldn't think of much to say. They had been getting along so well, at least up until *that* happened, that perhaps in other circumstances, in some other world, they might have gotten together. Here, the difference in "energy levels" would keep them apart forever even if she did forgive him eventually. Now Matt understood more than ever the predicament Astroman had been in with the two women in his life. A hyperman without a hyperwoman would be lonely indeed. Not that Matt's prospects looked all that much cheerier unless he found a way back to his own world. Failing that, he and Lynestra would have to come to some kind of terms.

Before very long, Matt had completely run out of things to say and there didn't seem to be any point in apologizing for the third or fourth time. It was also clear that Laurie didn't want to talk. He repeated his apologies anyway for the sake of at least trying to do the right thing, said goodbye, and left. The last he saw of her, Laurie was staring up at the ceiling, perhaps relieved that he had finally gone.

Alarmingly, Lynestra didn't call Matt at the next agreed-upon time. His calls to the Astroman Foundation's answering service went unreturned, and he spent two days wondering if she had changed her mind about including him in her return to Helionn. She wasn't still mad at him about having to pay Laurie's hospital bills, was she? Both Edmond and Dr. MacTavish noticed his edginess and commented on it, snippily in Edmond's case, with concern in MacTavish's.

He had every right to be worried, he thought. With no way of getting in touch with Lynestra otherwise, of course his worst fears would gnaw at him. Something must have happened to her, but what could happen to an Astrogirl? He had nightmares of Garth Bolton and electric green rays...

Then, on the third day, as he was helping the technicians in the laboratory where the Glengarrium was being produced, he was summoned to the telephone. He answered and the switchboard operator transferred the call to him. To his relief, it was Lynestra, but she sounded terrible with a hoarse voice and a stuffed-up nose.

"What happened?" Matt asked, both astonished and worried to hear her like that. "Did Garth Bolton get you?"

"No... *you* got me," she croaked.

"What...?"

Lynestra explained between coughs, although she was weak and woozy and had to force herself to make the effort. Disease was all but extinct in the super-scientific utopias of Helionn and Eristhar, and she had been routinely treated as a baby to be immune to whatever few bugs were still loose in her largely antiseptic colony. On the Earth of this universe, the local viruses couldn't do anything to her. Then enter Matt, infested with the germs of her own universe and ten thousand years before her time, probably including a few extinct ancient varieties that Helionnian medical science had forgotten about. Matt's body had a built-in resistance to them, but Lynestra's was wide open. And when she kissed him... It sounded as though she had caught the flu.

"I've never been sick before in my life!" she exclaimed, though a little weakly and setting off more coughing. "I don't like it one bit. I was tossing and turning for two days, half out of my mind, I lost all track of time... I'm better now, but I still don't feel very good."

"I'm really sorry!" Matt said earnestly, feeling somewhat mortified himself. He wasn't accumulating a very good track record as a lover. After all but breaking one girl's back by kissing her, he had kissed a second girl who was physically invulnerable, only to make her sick. He wondered if any monasteries were taking applications.

"Don't worry about it," Lynestra said quickly. "It was probably inevitable, and I'm just glad it wasn't something worse. The universal treatment I had when I was a baby should have covered everything serious, but this was something that I guess slipped through the cracks. I ought to be all right in a couple of days. I hope I'm immune to you by the time we take off!"

"So, you talked to the lassie?" Dr. MacTavish asked, looking up from the paperwork on his desk when Matt came in to his office to report on the latest development. "What's been keeping her incommunicado?"

"She's sick," Matt replied. "The flu or something like that."

MacTavish looked astonished. "How can Astrogirl take ill? She's... well, hyper!"

"Er..." Matt paused, not certain how much he should say. Then he decided he might as well come out with it. "I probably gave it to her when she kissed me."

MacTavish's jaw dropped for a moment, then he burst out laughing.

"What's so funny?" Matt wondered, puzzled by the reaction.

"You do work fast, laddie!" MacTavish exclaimed. "Besides the lass who wanted to sue us, you also managed to kiss the single most desirable young woman on the planet! You've no idea how many boys and men dream about Astrogirl, to put it mildly. Just to kiss her — it's never been done, so far as I know. You must have been quite the ladies' man on your own world!"

"Hardly," Matt said. "I've only had two serious girlfriends in my life and both dumped me because I was spending too much time in the lab."

There was a sudden faraway look in MacTavish's eyes. "Aye, lad, it's an oft-told tale..."

The next time Lynestra called, Matt could report that production of the required amount of Glengarrium had been completed.

"That's wonderful," she said. "Once you've loaded it on the ship, we can take off as soon as the cycle comes around again. All we have to worry about is what to pack."

Even that problem solved itself when they realized that anything they took with them from the lower-energy universe would probably collapse or shrivel in the higher. Lynestra could wear the clothes she had brought with her from Eristhar, assuming she hadn't grown too much since then and they still fit, but Matt was limited to what he had been wearing when he translated from his Earth to this one and the few items that had been processed in MacTavish's facilities.

Those clothes were in need of laundering, Matt realized. For Lynestra's sake if not his own, since they would be in close quarters for days during the trip, he tried washing them. Unfortunately, local water had little effect. Dirt acquired on this Earth hardly even adhered in the first place, but dirt from his own world, not to mention his sweat, seemed permanently bound in with the fabric. Clothes could be washed in high-energy water, of course, but there wasn't enough on hand for laundry. He ended up putting the clothes in MacTavish's industrial furnace for a few hours at a temperature hot enough to melt a number of metals, then rinsed them out in ordinary water. The results weren't perfect, but the heat treatment did at least loosen the dirt and sweat enough that the water could wash the particles away. The shirt came out wrinkled, though, but Matt decided he would just have to live with it. Trying to iron it this side of Helionn would have been futile.

Out in the world, developments were taking an ominous turn. The most obvious one was summed up in a TV news report one afternoon showing film footage of a ceremony in the Rose Garden of the White House in which the young President presented Garth Bolton with an official pardon for any and all alleged crimes he might have allegedly committed in the past.

Feeling that this was something everyone needed to know about, MacTavish had called the senior staff together in the lab administration building's lounge to watch the program on a small black and white TV set.

"Good God!" MacTavish exploded halfway through from where he sat between Edmond and Matt. "People are dead because of him! He should be serving life in Joliet at the least, not getting a medal at the White House!"

Everyone else just watched in grim silence. Matt wasn't as well informed about what it all meant, but he was starting to get an idea.

Looking uncomfortable, the President made some remarks woodenly read from a prepared speech written out for him on a sheet of paper he held in trembling hands. In a monotone, he stated that since Bolton was now lending his valuable talents to the government for the benefit of the American people, this far outweighed any alleged harm he may or may not have done in the past...

"Did you see the look on the President's face?" MacTavish said to Matt. "He looked like he had the worst job in the world. You could almost hear him thinking: *I'm supposed to be the leader of my country and have all this power, but I still have to follow orders and recite lies I don't believe from the script they gave me.*"

"What are you saying?" Matt asked. "That Bolton has enough clout to make the President of the United States do what he tells him to?"

"That's exactly what I think," MacTavish said. "And it's got to be more than buying off one Congressman or Senator after another until he reached critical mass. I'm sure he's been doing that, too, but there's something more to this, and that's what worries me."

After the ceremony, a clip followed of a reporter interviewing Bolton. "I'm not admitting I've ever done anything wrong, of course," the allegedly redeemed master criminal said, his grin a mile wide. "I may have made a few mistakes in my younger days that gave a wrong impression of my true aims, and I've been badly misunderstood by the press as a result, but I hope to rectify that through public service."

"What does Astroman have to say about it?" the reporter asked.

Bolton scowled for a second, as though that question hadn't been in the script and he was caught unprepared for it. Then he recovered his broad grin and gestured expansively to the broad, blue, and very empty sky above him. "That's a very good question. I'd like to hear the answer to it myself. So when you see Astroman, just ask him!"

With that he turned away to mingle with the crowd, abruptly ending the interview and leaving the reporter with a follow-up question only half-asked.

The news went to something else and MacTavish motioned for Edmond to turn the TV set off. The rest of the staff began drifting away, still stunned, no one saying anything

"All right," Matt said to MacTavish as they started back to the office, "so what does this pardon mean in practical terms? Bolton wasn't in jail up to now, and he seems to have a powerful organization that isn't being prosecuted. What's the difference?"

The old scientist looked gloomily down the hallway ahead. "Freedom of movement, for one thing. He had the local politicians bought off, so he could live on his estate in Kenilworth and operate his laboratory, but he couldn't leave the immediate Chicago area. Too many outstanding arrest warrants all over the rest of the country where he didn't have influence. This effectively quashes every last one of them, even the parking tickets. Now he can go anywhere he likes, such as Washington as we just saw. Maybe he just got tired of the inconvenience of being a wanted master criminal in most of the country, but I have a grave suspicion that it's just the first step in a much bigger plan. When the President dances to your tune, all manner of possibilities open up."

Just after noon the following day, Dr. MacTavish was having Matt lift some steel beams to clear the damage in a building that had taken a hit in one of the attacks, when Edmond came rushing up. He was pale and out of breath, and for once, he had lost his petty arrogance.

"Sir! We have trouble! At the front gate!"

"Not another raid!" MacTavish exclaimed tiredly.

"In broad daylight?" Matt asked. Without thinking, he let the beam he was holding drop, and it hit the ground with a thump.

"Careful, laddie!" MacTavish admonished as he turned to go see what the problem was.

Followed by Matt, Edmond, and several of the assistants, the old scientist went out to the front gate.

A raid was exactly what it was, only this time with all the proper papers. On the other side of the fence, filling the road and crowding into the surrounding fields, were US Army vehicles, columns of soldiers, and trucks from the local TV stations. Technicians were setting up TV cameras by the side of the road near the gate, presumably so they could catch the drama of the convoy rolling on through.

A uniformed officer of some high rank stood at the gate, flanked by several troops with drawn weapons and some civilians in suits who had the look of politicians and lawyers about them. In back of them was a scattering of reporters and cameramen. Lounging nearby and keeping their eyes on the sky were several men with gorilla-like physiques stuffed into civilian suits, resembling the sort of hired muscle a gangster would have in his retinue. Alarmingly, they wore backpacks that resembled the Deactivator mock-up Matt had seen at the Museum. Bolton had apparently developed portable models now, not just cannon.

"What's all this?" MacTavish demanded of the officer at the gate.

"You'll have to ask him, sir," the officer said, stepping aside.

A portly middle-aged man with meticulously combed white hair and sporting an expensive-looking suit all but pushed his way past the officer. He stopped just in front of Dr. MacTavish, arms crossed and a self-confident smirk on his flabby face.

"And who might you be?" the scientist asked in a tone that suggested he already thought the answer should be "nobody worth wasting my time on."

"Don't you watch the news?" the man sputtered, genuinely astonished. "I'm Senator William Ruttle. I represent the State of Illinois."

"Do you always take the Army with you to visit your constituents?" MacTavish countered.

The smirk reappeared on Ruttle's face, even broader than before. "That's actually not a bad idea when I'm touring war zones like this one."

"War zone...?"

"Have there not been all-out battles between two private armies in precisely this location?" Ruttle asked, gesturing sweepingly to the buildings inside the compound, many still showing damage and provisional repairs like boarded windows.

"I was defending myself from attempted robbery," MacTavish snapped in mounting irritation. "So what's your point? And be quick about it. I'm a busy man."

Ruttle's smirk widened still more. "Oh, you'll have plenty of free time now. The gist of it is that effective immediately, this facility stands under the protection of the United States Government. For reasons of public safety, we obviously cannot permit small wars being fought in close proximity to surrounding towns, farms, and residential areas."

MacTavish's mouth twitched. "I'd like to think you're offering to protect me from any further attacks so I can go on about my work in peace, but I have a feeling you're up to something. What else?"

Unperturbed, Senator Ruttle continued, more for the benefit of the cameras behind them than of MacTavish. "Also effective immediately, this facility will be occupied by the United States Government and its designated representatives until such time as the relevant authorities decide otherwise. You and your employees will vacate the premises at once. If you wish to claim compensation, you can fill out the appropriate forms when they're printed."

Now MacTavish realized the seriousness of the situation. "But this is private property! You don't have any right—"

"Oh, yes, we do." Ruttle held up a sheet of paper and waved it aloft for the cameras. "It's all right here. The National Defense Resources Security Act. Just passed late last night. These... er, substances you manufacture are too important for national defense for any one man to have a monopoly on them. Not to mention the fact that they are dangerously radioactive, and I doubt if your safety precautions are adequate for what is, after all, a populated area near a large city."

"But you can't just kick us out like this!" MacTavish sputtered, as though unable to quite believe this was really happening. "There are processes in operation we can't just leave be! You don't have the trained men to operate the equipment or—"

"On the contrary," Ruttle assured him. "Bolton Laboratories has generously offered to provide trained personnel who I'm sure will be up to the task."

Dr. MacTavish looked as though he was about to pop several arteries. "So that's it! You're in Bolton's pocket!"

Ruttle shrugged, then added in a mutter that the microphones behind him wouldn't pick up, "If you have any proof that will stand up in court,

I suggest you call my good friend Dave, the Attorney General, once you're situated in your new quarters, wherever they might happen to be. In the meantime, you and your, er, associates have fifteen minutes to get out of here." He continued in a louder voice, addressing the officer beside him. "Colonel, assign troops to watch each and every one of these men as they pack, and search their bags and anything else they try to take with them. Make sure nobody leaves with anything like plans, diagrams, or other material relating to whatever it is they do here. You also have full authorization to shoot if anyone attempts to sabotage the equipment on the way out."

"Very well," MacTavish said, still managing to contain his anger but only just. "You have the upper hand for now. Just be sure you report Garth Bolton's bribes on your income tax forms." Senator Ruttle ignored the remark and MacTavish turned to his men. "I'm afraid it's time to execute Evacuation Plan C, lads!"

That was also the cue for Senator Ruttle to call to the soldiers in back of him. "All right, boys, move in!"

The soldiers started forward through the open gate to begin the occupation of the laboratory, and the MacTavishLab staff scattered to carry out the roles they had been assigned in the plan.

"The Glengarrium!" Matt whispered urgently to the old scientist as they headed down the street towards the main office. "We've got to get it or there won't be a trip to Helionn!"

MacTavish rested a hand on his shoulder. "Easy, lad. It's already too late. If you try to get it now, you'll be seen, and there are men with Deactivators to stop you. You can't fight the government in front of all these cameras when they're taking over legally. I have enough trouble as it is and I can't have it look like I'm putting up any resistance. Give it a few days until their guard is down, then come back some dark night."

"Oh, all right... I still don't like doing nothing. What if Bolton finds the Glengarrium and takes it somewhere else in the meantime?"

"That's a possibility but not a probability. I do have some security and the Glengarrium is not precisely marked with a nice clear label saying what it is. He'll be weeks figuring out what we were doing here and what's on hand. Now let's get to my office while we can. There are some things we can still do."

In the office, MacTavish had Edmond call other master scientists around the country to see if they were experiencing anything similar. It quickly became clear that the National Defense Resources Security Act wasn't written with just him in mind. One after another, other private laboratory complexes were being occupied by soldiers on the same pretext used to seize MacTavishLab. Too important for national security to be allowed to remain in private hands, or so the official explanation went. Only Bolton's own laboratory had been spared.

"He's eliminating the competition, making sure no one can threaten him," MacTavish said to Matt. "They claim it will make science more efficient and coordinated by putting it under centralised control, but going about it like this will just throttle science in the crib for the next twenty years. You've told me how your lot does science on your world. That may be all right for you, but innovative loners are the ones who do science here. Put us on the street and scientific advancement stops cold. I can't believe they justified this on the basis of national defence. There's no better way to let the Russians get the jump on us than to do what they just did."

"Hurry up in there!" yelled a soldier from out in the hallway. "You've got ten minutes to vacate the premises!"

"I could have cleared all those troops out," Matt muttered. He was sitting with some of the refugees from Dr. MacTavish's lab watching TV in the lounge of the hotel in Batavia where Edmond had arranged temporary quarters for the key members of the staff. Others had dispersed to other hotels in the area or to the homes of friends or relatives. Nothing of much interest was on the black and white screen at the moment, and several of the men were talking lowly among themselves. Matt sat next to MacTavish, pondering recent events and the changes in fortune that had brought them here.

"It wouldn't have done any good," MacTavish replied. "You can't fight the Army and the Government, and it would have just made you an outlaw. As it is, they hardly even know you exist. Best to keep it that way until we get a better idea of how things are sorting out."

"So what do we do now?" Matt wondered.

"Bolton's won this round," MacTavish admitted wearily. "It's enough to make me tear out what little hair I have left. He's a known criminal yet he gets away scot free, to use a highly inappropriate expression. I'd noticed he'd been trying very hard these past few years to go 'legal,' but until recently, I just assumed he was tired of crime and was simply planning a peaceful retirement so he could enjoy his ill-gotten gains on some country estate without having to worry about being arrested. And not even all his gains have been ill-gotten. He's actually invented advanced technology with practical applications that he's licensed to industrial concerns, and he's probably made far more money that way than through outright crime. But money by itself was never what he really wanted. It was just means to an end, and the end was power. Now I see that he was actually planning a masterstroke. He wasn't just buying respectability, he was spreading all that money around to buy influence, not to mention a few politicians. So when he can't get what he wants by armed robbery, he gets it anyway by legal chicanery. He must have called in every favour he was owed to organise this take-over. And that Senator had the bloody cheek to justify confiscating my laboratory because it had been attacked by criminals — the same criminals he just gave it to!"

"Can Bolton do much with your lab?"

"He certainly knows the general theory of transuranics. Master scientists have their trade secrets, of course, but what you called 'the state of the art' on your world does apply to some extent here, too. Even so, it'll take him some time to figure out just what we were doing. Running us out like that with hardly even a chance to grab our hats was intended to prevent us from sabotaging the place, but without anyone to show them the ropes, Bolton and his men will have to try to make sense of the equipment and the plans, notes, and other paperwork. There are things he needs to be doing right now to keep the operation running smoothly, and he doesn't know the least bit about them. By tomorrow morning, he will probably have some massive breakdowns on his hands, and he'll be lucky if he doesn't have a radiation leak to contend with. He'll be weeks getting the lab back in full operation, if that's even his plan."

"If that isn't it, then what?"

"He probably wants the stocks of transuranics we've already produced, plus whatever equipment he can nick for his own lab or at least copy."

A murmur from the other staff members announced that something was happening on TV. Matt looked up and saw Senator Ruttle giving a speech. It had been filmed in front of the gate at MacTavish Laboratories, though some time after the rightful occupants had been hustled out.

"...in order, therefore, to protect the citizens of DuPage and Kane Counties from further outbreaks of violence by armies of unidentified criminals, and to ensure that this shockingly primitive facility can no longer endanger the inhabitants of the surrounding area with an alarming potential for radiation leakages due to inadequate safety measures, the Government has seized the property until further notice. Everyone living for miles around can sleep easily tonight knowing that soldiers are on duty patrolling these premises so that no attacks or accidents will occur..."

"Turn him off!" MacTavish snapped disgustedly.

At least things can't get any worse, Matt thought.

Chapter Ten: **Sounds in the Silence**

The next day, they got worse.

The TV newsreaders announced that in addition to the recently passed National Defense Resources Security Act, Congress had just voted to approve the Dangerous Persons Restriction and Accountability Act. Scraping away the legalese, the Act basically stated that individuals with hyper-powers were a potential threat to the nation because they could not be restrained by normal means such as arrest, prison, or in extreme cases, shoot-to-kill orders. No matter what public services certain hyper-powered individuals may have allegedly performed in the past, they could not be trusted not to turn rogue at any moment. Rather than allow the future of the nation to rely on the continued good will of several persons who hitherto had not been subject to any legal accountability, such individuals were requested to present themselves to federal authorities. They would then submit to questioning, examination, and if deemed advisable or feasible, possible removal of their hyper-powers, at which point they would be allowed to return to their ordinary lives as citizens. Three individuals were specifically named:

1. Kirk Collier, aka "Astroman"
2. Jane Doe, aka "Astrogirl"
3. Richard Roe, reported third hyper-powered person at large

Matt drew several conclusions from the news.

One. Garth Bolton still wasn't entirely sure Astroman was dead.

Two. Astroman's secret identity was no longer secret, but then Matt had suspected that a little detective work could have revealed it just by following the Centerburg/Ohio State/Chicago leads. Sadly, it didn't matter anymore.

Three. Unless she really was calling herself "Jane Doe," which seemed unlikely, Astrogirl's secret identity still hadn't been cracked. With a public career of only about three years behind her, she probably just hadn't had time to leave an obvious trail. If she wanted to, she could stop appearing as Astrogirl and revert to her private life full-time, and no one would ever find her. Whether the country would be a good place to live in as a regular citizen the way things were going was another matter.

Four. Matt's whereabouts were still unknown on the higher levels. That meant nobody on Dr. MacTavish's team had spilled the beans to the authorities, which spoke well of the men's loyalty to the old boy. Other possible weak links included Laurie, her lawyer, and the hospital staff, but apparently the hostile powers hadn't found out about them yet. Even so, they were probably all too aware that "Richard Roe" had some connection with Dr. MacTavish, and it wouldn't be long before they came looking for him.

Five. With the mention of possible removal of hyper-powers, Bolton had just about admitted that he had the means to do it. He seemed to be promising that the subject would survive the treatment and could go on to live a normal life, but Matt had his doubts.

All in all, things were getting hot, and Dr. MacTavish had enough problems without Matt drawing additional fire. Besides, with the lab pulled out from under him, MacTavish no longer needed his services as a hyper-powered guardian. It was time to relocate and spend the last few days before leaving for Helionn somewhere else.

Matt came to a decision and went to Dr. MacTavish's room that evening to announce it.

The old man was sitting in a chair and had been reading a newspaper. He put it down as Matt came in. "Ah, Mr. Roe. I see you haven't turned rogue yet."

"Believe me, I'm tempted," Matt said. "About all that... I think I've outlasted my usefulness here and I'd just cause you more problems if I stayed."

Dr. MacTavish nodded gravely. "As matters stand, I suspect you're right. Do you have a place to go?"

"I think so, but I won't say any more. When the Feds come knocking and ask where Richard Roe is, you'll probably want to be able to give them an honest answer when you say you don't know."

"True enough," MacTavish replied, then sighed. "I'm just sorry I wasn't able to hand over the Glengarrium you needed for your space voyage before the soldiers booted me out."

"Well, you couldn't have known this would happen."

"Now you'll have to make a midnight raid. Don't put it off much longer or Garth Bolton might finally get around to inspecting the vault and realise what's in there. If he moves the Glengarrium, you'll have a devil of a time locating it and his own vault will be much better guarded. I have a little something for you, by the way."

He reached over to the lamp table next to him and fished through a pile of papers on top, then handed a sealed envelope to Matt.

"What's this?" Matt asked.

"A diagram showing where the Glengarrium is," MacTavish explained, "with instructions on how to open the vault. It might be helpful if you want to be subtle about this smash and grab. In fact, I wish you would be since I cherish some hope that I might get the lab back sooner or later, and I'd rather it wasn't demolished. Do it with enough finesse and Bolton will never know you were there, let alone notice that something important is missing. Just be careful with the Glengarrium when you remove it, and above all, don't drop it. It can be unstable when it's knocked about and might cause all manner of unfortunate effects."

"I'll be careful," Matt promised and started to make a move to leave.

MacTavish touched his arm. "Oh, and one more thing. If you don't mind a little more skullduggery, there's a sheet in the envelope with some code words I devised. I don't know what the landscape will look like by the time you return, or even where I might be by then. I might have to go into hiding if a certain Mr. Bolton decides he needs me after all to answer questions about my production methods and such. Any road, I don't think I'll be in this hotel much longer. I'll call the Astroman Foundation answering service now and then as events play out and plans are made, and keep you informed as to what I'm about by using the code. Even if our lad Garth has the phones tapped or the switchboard operator is on his payroll, all he'll be able to make out from the messages is that I'm trying to reach you but it won't be clear why. If need be, you can leave messages for me using the same code."

Matt nodded. "Got it. Then it's goodbye for now. Thank you for all your help."

"And thank you for *your* help, laddie! If nothing else, thanks to you I now know a bit more about what makes a hyperman tick, which I'd always wondered about. When this is all over, I hope we can take up the problem of sending you back to your own world."

"I appreciate it."

They shook hands and Matt left to go back to his own room. He packed his few clothes in a valise he had been given, then opened the window and took off into the night. MacTavish would have to explain to the desk clerk downstairs that one of the guests had made a sudden exit, and cover the bill.

Spotting a phone booth from the air some miles away, he dropped down and called the answering service to leave a cryptic message for Lynestra.

The Secret Citadel

"If you've been watching the news, you know things have boiled over. Meet me where we first met."

From there it was off to Colorado.

With whole floors of furnished if somewhat dusty suites at the Citadel, Lynestra let Matt have his pick.

He now had nothing to do but wait until it was time to take off for Helionn according to her calculations, so he was facing an enforced five days of leisure. He was stuck around the Citadel for lack of anywhere else to go, while Lynestra was in and out. She did have a private life somewhere that she felt was important enough to keep up. All Matt knew was that she was a college student but it was summer and she was between terms. Exactly where she went and what she did, she didn't say and he didn't pry. If she wanted to have her secrets, she was welcome to them, and getting nosey would violate the trust they needed to have between them to accomplish their mission.

Shaving wasn't a problem even away from MacTavishLab's high-energy conversion facilities. *The Last Hope* had been outfitted for a crew of three men, and the supplies on board included shaving kits made in Helionn's universe. Matt just had to run a powered hand-held unit over his face and his beard stubble disappeared almost magically. That would keep him presentable until they took off. It was the first really good shave he'd had since arriving on this world. Lynestra remarked that he would take some getting used to without a dark tinge on his face.

You should have seen me with the beard.

Then Lynestra added that she used her own Helionn-razor for her legs, which struck him as TMI. She mostly wore jeans around the Citadel, so it may not have been strictly necessary, but she did appear in public as Astrogirl with a short skirt and would have worn skirts in her civilian identity.

To get some exercise and keep his muscles toned in a world where nothing offered any resistance or required any effort, Matt took daily jogs around the mountain. When he was bored with that, he occupied his time reading history books he found in the Citadel's library to learn more about this world. Since they had mostly been acquired by the original builders, the books were all at least a few years old, but they did tell him something.

He also watched the TV news to stay abreast of events. It was a little surprising that the Citadel had television reception, but cable TV for remote and isolated areas existed in this world. In order to keep up on the news out in the world for as long as they could, the tycoons had run a line from some distant town to the mountain at no doubt enormous expense even though in their worst-case scenario there wouldn't be any-one left on the outside to broadcast at all after a few days.

Garth Bolton was consolidating his control over things. The media outlets weren't even trying to be objective in denouncing master-scien-tists as traitors, and some scientists had already been rounded up for allegedly resisting the bans on their research or stealing valuable files and equipment from their former labs. Matt was relieved that Dr. Mac-Tavish wasn't among them, at least so far.

Meanwhile, the announcement that the Dangerous Persons Restric-tion and Accountability Act had named Kirk Collier as Astroman had caused a sensation. Astroman's secret identity was known on the highest level — if you can't trust the President, who can you trust? — but it had been closely guarded before this. Now that it was revealed that Astroman had spent his off-hours as Kirk Collier, a well-known reporter, the news broadcasts were filled with special reports covering Collier's personal history and interviewing as many of his friends as they could find about his connection with Astroman. Sound bites with Johnny Larsen, Ellen Loring, and the other Friends of Astroman were run repeatedly, though they were mostly non-committal and obviously unhappy that the secret had come out. They were all asked where Astroman was now, and none could provide a good answer.

Matt thought he could detect some snideness on the part of the inter-viewers, as though instructions had come down from upper management to make Kirk Collier seem like a shady character with an oversized ego. After all, who else had a museum dedicated to touting his own glory? Doubt was insinuated about his story of coming from another planet, and maybe his hyper-powers really were the result of some outlawed biology experiment by renegade scientists as the conspiracy theories claimed. There was also a suggestion that having hyper-powers wasn't enough to satisfy him, and it was out of spite and envy that he had continually tried to prevent Garth Bolton from performing noble deeds for the benefit of humanity.

With all that going on, it was no surprise a couple of days later when a message from Dr. MacTavish was forwarded from the answering service.

"The time has come for some roamin' in the gloamin'. Don't worry about me, laddie. I'll be fine. Good luck in all your future endeavours!"

Translated, that meant MacTavish and whatever remained of his staff had checked out of the hotel and left for parts unknown. If Matt wanted to get in touch with the old scientist again after coming back from Helionn, he'd have to play a little telephone tag with the answering service to make contact with him and find out where he was. The "future endeavours" referred to the upcoming trip, making it not so obvious that somebody was going somewhere.

For anyone with normal hearing, the interior of the Citadel would have been as quiet as a Pharaoh's burial chamber deep inside an Egyptian pyramid with masses of stone between it and the outside. No sound could penetrate and the utter silence was on the hear-your-own-heartbeat level of a sensory deprivation tank.

For Matt, however, with extended hearing, he was aware of faint and distant background noises, like the crackle of electricity through the wires in the walls and the low rumble of the air circulation system. It was somehow reassuring since it made him feel less like a disembodied mind with no connection to the world. At the same time, he was used to it and mostly didn't notice it.

Then one night, as he was lying asleep in the bed in his room, some indistinct hint of a sound woke him. It was barely this side of total inaudibility, but it had been different enough to stand out and attract his subconscious attention.

It sounded like a whimper.

As Matt woke up more completely, he realized what he was hearing. Had some injured animal somehow gotten into the Citadel? Now he was curious and knew he wouldn't get back to sleep before he had solved the mystery of what it was.

He had been sleeping in his shorts. Even though he was certain that he was the only human being for miles around, he pulled on a pair of pants before leaving the room. Force of habit, perhaps, or in case Lynestra showed up unexpectedly.

He followed the sound of the whimper, tracking it to a part of the Citadel he hadn't been in before. In a small room in the maintenance and storage section, he found what had been whimpering.

What everyone had forgotten was that there was still another member of the Astroman Family at large.

In the room, furnished as a comfortable little den, a badly hurt dog lay huddled and trembling in a large basket filled with blankets. Not just any dog, but one wearing the tattered remnants of an Astroman cape still attached to its collar. It was definitely Helio, but depowered, injured, and possibly dying.

Helio had his own private entrance to the Citadel, an actual doggie door that evidently opened automatically when it sensed an electronic signaling device on his collar. Matt guessed that the entrance was disguised on the outside, and the winding tunnel that led inside was sized for Helio and too small for any human intruders. A second doggie door

Dwight R. Decker

led into the main part of the Citadel so Helio could come and go as he pleased, but the room was his own private den.

Matt did what he could for the whimpering dog, which wasn't much beyond putting down a pan of fresh water within easy reach of the basket, then went out into the Citadel complex to find a phone and leave Lynestra a message.

By the time she arrived at the Citadel the next morning, it was too late for her to do anything. Helio had died during the night. Matt's one encounter with the dog in the sky near Chicago hadn't been particularly pleasant and Helio hadn't been exactly friendly, but he still felt a little depressed.

All they could do was find a child-sized casket in a storeroom (the Citadel's builders had prepared even for some sad possibilities), put Helio in it, and place him next to his master in the chapel. While Matt stood silently by, Lynestra murmured a few words of a funeral service for beloved pets she remembered from her childhood on Eristhar. She felt the loss even though she had never been close to Helio. He had been Astroman's dog all his life and wasn't inclined to bond with strangers, but he was one of the last survivors of Helionn and she felt at least some kinship. She might have liked a hypercat of her own, but unfortunately a cat hadn't been sent from Helionn and no conceivable contrived circumstances could give an Earth-born cat hyper-powers.

Now the question was, *what* could kill a hyperdog?

"I can only guess that Helio flew a little too close to Garth Bolton's estate," Lynestra said over lunch in the commissary. She was still saddened by the loss of the dog, but since something that could kill hyper-beings was a threat to her as well, her more practical side had come to the fore. "Bolton or his men must have spotted Helio flying overhead and decided to take advantage of the unexpected opportunity to test the Deactivator again. It may not have been a direct hit, so it didn't kill Helio outright and he was able to make his way here. Since Bolton's men didn't find him, the irony of all this is that Bolton *still* doesn't know how effecttive the Deactivator ray is, but he's wreaking havoc with it just the same."

"How old was Helio, anyway?" Matt asked. "If Astroman had him since he was a boy, wouldn't he have been at least twenty-five? That's pretty old for a dog. Just about impossible, actually."

"Jarn Thelnarr sent Helio to Earth first, as a test," Lynestra replied, "but with the constantly shifting relation of time periods, he arrived about fifteen years after Karsten. So you're right, Helio has been around for over twenty-five years. That would be impossible for Earth dogs, but

144

dogs on Helionn were bred over the centuries for longer lifespans. It's such a shame that family pets like cats and dogs only live for about fifteen years here. I think they had dogs on Helionn living for up to fifty years or so. Their intelligence was increased, too, though not to human-level because there are limits on what you can do with a dog-sized brain in a dog-sized head. Helio was smarter than the average dog, but not by a lot. Fortunately, he was 'altered' before he was sent to Earth, or some horrible things could have happened to the female dogs here. He lived with Karsten most of the time but he sometimes went off on his own for long periods, though he always came back sooner or later."

Now Helio had come back for the last time, and would be with his master forever after.

When they loaded supplies on the *Last Hope*, Matt had a look at the crew compartment. It probably made the average submarine look roomy, but at least there had been some effort to make life on an extended space mission somewhat tolerable for a crew of three or four. At the rear was what on Helionn was termed a "sanitation cell," designed for function rather than comfort, with a separate "personal cleansing unit" next to it that could handle both human bodies and laundry. A narrow aisle led from there with two small cabins on either side. Each cabin had only enough room for a bunk and storage for personal effects, but it did allow for privacy. Past the cabins, the aisle opened onto a small compartment for recreation and eating, with a tiny galley and food storage and preparation units to one side. Beyond that, at the forward end, was the cockpit with two seats facing an instrument and control panel and a blank curving wall that Lynestra said would turn transparent in flight.

Once again, Matt was reminded of his cherished childhood dreams of becoming an astronaut and going to the Moon or maybe even Mars. As he grew older, he had learned that the space program had actually peaked at Apollo, well before he was born. Its vision had steadily narrowed over the years as its budgets contracted, so those dreams had been regretfully put aside. Now, he was about to take off for another star twenty light-years away. His boyhood fantasies of space travel had not only come true but far more spectacularly than he ever could have imagined. Even better, he would be going into space with a pretty girl. He remembered reading somewhere that the Apollo capsule, with three astronauts in close quarters for several days, had been called "the flying men's room." Neil, Buzz, and Mike would have choked on their envy if they could have seen the *Last Hope*.

When Lynestra was in the Citadel, she spent some time over Pepsi's in the commissary giving Matt a crash course about the basics of life on Helionn so he'd have a better idea of where he was going, and teaching him a few useful phrases of the language. In addition, she showed him a book about Helionn that Karsten's father had sent along in his spacecraft so the little refugee would know something about his origin story. Matt recognized it as the book Astroman had been using as a reference for his city in a bottle model.

He noticed that the views of Helionn from space didn't look quite like Earth. The surface of the Earth was roughly three-quarters ocean and only about one-quarter land, and he remembered playing with a globe as a boy and noticing that it could be turned to show the Pacific Ocean and not much else. On Helionn the proportions were more nearly half and half, with several nearly circular seas in the Mediterranean size-range and a couple of respectable oceans, though nothing comparable to the Pacific. The seacoasts looked almost unnaturally round, rather than the result of continents being torn apart by plate tectonics, and there were quite a few suspiciously circular lakes. Underneath the white streaks of clouds, it reminded Matt of artists' conceptions of what a terraformed Moon might look like, with seas in the larger craters and oceans in the impact basins.

"It looks like Helionn's been hit by meteors a lot," he said.

"What else would you expect?" Lynestra asked. She pointed to a page in the book. "Look at this diagram of Helionn's solar system."

The view was from above the local ecliptic, depicting one planet in its orbit around the star and six elliptical bands at various distances.

"Oh, I get it," Matt said. "The diagram just shows Helionn as a planet. Those circles are the orbits of the other planets, right?"

"No, there *aren't* any other planets. Those aren't orbits, they're asteroid belts."

"One planet and six asteroid belts? What kept the other planets from forming?"

"Nothing. They did form, but they exploded a long time ago. Six planets have blown up in that solar system, so there are an awful lot of rocks flying around. That's why there are so many crater lakes on Helionn."

"And your ancestors still went ahead and settled the planet? It sounds like everything that forms in that system is inherently unstable. It may be a nice place to visit, but I wouldn't want to settle down and raise a family there."

Lynestra winced at his lack of reverence and respect, then launched into an explanation of how Helionn had been colonized.

Sometime in the next two centuries, the secret of faster than light travel would be discovered and humanity would begin exploring and then settling the planets of other stars. One interesting planet orbited the Sun-like star Delta Pavonis just twenty light-years away. At first glance, Helionn was a highly desirable Earthlike planet, perhaps the most Earth-like of any planets known and relatively close by. It was about the same size as Earth with nearly the same gravity and an almost identical atmosphere and environment. With conditions so similar, evolution of the native lifeforms had proceeded along much the same path as on Earth, though with some minor differences. The important thing was that there had never been an intelligent species comparable to human beings on Helionn, and none of the current species seemed to be evolving in that direction, so there were no natives to displace and no moral objections to colonization. As a whole, the planet was almost better than Earth, with double the land area, and it was all wide open and welcoming as a new home for humanity — with one serious drawback.

The fact that it was the last surviving planet in its system gave the authorities pause. Settlement was delayed until scientists figured out what was going on, and soon they had the answer.

As Matt had guessed, it was determined that as a result of whatever quirk in the particular mixture of elements making up the primordial cloud of matter surrounding the parent sun, every planet in the Delta Pavonis system had formed with a slow nuclear reaction at its center that would sooner or later go critical. Helionn was no different, the last intact planet remaining in the system but no less doomed. When this would happen was unknown, but since it could as easily be tomorrow as a century or a millennium from now, it was declared off-limits for colonization. Enough suitable planets with far longer potential lifespans had been found around other stars that they could be settled by colonists from Earth representing every national, political, racial, ethnic, and religious group or mixture thereof that chose to seek its destiny in the distant reaches of space, so one planet with a fatal flaw could be eliminated from consideration.

Even so, a planet that attractive and that close was hard to pass up. The probability that Helionn would explode in the near future on a geological time scale, which could be a million years or more, didn't count for much in human terms with lifespans of less than a hundred years. After all, looked at from a standpoint of billions of years, Earth itself wouldn't last forever.

Little was known about how it had been arranged, but the few surviving records showed that a charismatic Swedish religious leader known to history only as the *Kyrkoherde* ("pastor") made an under the table deal with an interstellar shipping company. His flock of several thousand followers had been long in exile from its native country and had established a community in a remote part of North America where it could maintain its traditions and language, like a Swedish version of the Amish. Northern Manitoba wasn't quite the Promised Land, however, and the members weren't happy there. The larger society outside was encroaching ever closer and the group's youth were too exposed to the temptations of the bright lights. The obvious answer was to relocate to another planet where there *was* no larger society outside and probably never would be because no one else would ever move there.

Although it was no secret that Helionn was ultimately doomed, the Kyrkoherde assured his parishioners that it was all a hoax by the government for some reason. The group didn't believe in evolution, either, so with such an extreme distrust of science when it contradicted their faith's doctrines, it was easy to believe that wicked scientists had concocted this story, too. Even if it was true and the planet really was a bomb that could go off at any time, the Kyrkoherde was convinced that the Second Coming was imminent or at least no more than a couple of generations away, and the faithful would be raptured to Heaven long before anything else happened.

Further authority was found in the Bible. Besides the example of Moses leading the children of Israel out of Egypt to a new homeland, there was John 14:2: *I min Faders hus äro många boningar; om så icke voro, skulle jag nu säga eder att jag går bort för att bereda eder rum.* The Kyrkoherde interpreted the statement that "in my Father's house are many mansions" as referring to habitable planets, and that one world in particular — Helionn — was the place that Jesus had prepared for His followers. It was a stretch, but it was believed and gave everyone confidence that what became known as the Second Exodus was truly justified and approved on the highest level.

Since the planet had scientific interest, a few research stations were located on Helionn, similar to the Antarctic bases on Earth in Matt's time, but when an uninhabited planet had twice the land area of Earth, it wasn't hard to set a few thousand colonists down without detection. By the time anyone discovered their settlement, they were too well entrenched to move them very easily. With no obvious place to move them *to*, no one cared to expend the resources necessary for a compulsory evacuation. Faced with a *fait accompli*, the official attitude was just about literally, "Well, it's your funeral," and the colonists were left alone just as they wished.

After a decade or two, exploring settlers came across the sites of the research stations and discovered that they had long been abandoned. The scientists and their staffs had apparently been recalled, but the reasons why were never learned. With that, all contact with Earth was lost. As far as anyone knew, no ships from Earth or any other settled planet ever dropped by in the centuries that followed. Interstellar space was strangely silent as well, with no signs of active radio communication either directed at Helionn itself or intercepted in passing. The suspicion was that some massive collapse of civilization had affected not only Earth but all its associated colonies, which led to some self-congratulation that isolated Helionn had been spared whatever had happened. The planet's inhabitants may have settled on a dormant volcano, but at least its slopes were higher than the surrounding floodwaters.

As the years passed, the Helionnian population increased. The doctrinal fervor of the founding colonists faded away as successive generations grew up with this world as the only home they had ever known. Earth became a distant legend known only from books and videos, and people forgot what had brought their ancestors to Helionn to begin with. Factional disputes tore the community apart time and time again, and dissenters broke away to start their own communities. Remote settlements became the cores around which nations formed. The original religion mutated into forms that the old visionary who had led his people to a new star would not have recognized, and later generations had no particular prejudice against science. Quite the contrary. If it made life easier, people healthier, and crops more abundant, they were all for it.

When Helionnian civilization was up to it, radio signals were broadcast to Earth and the neighboring star systems known to have been colonized to see if anybody was home and answering the phone, but no one ever replied.

"Can you really blame my ancestors?" Lynestra asked in summing up. "Since Helionn was such a wonderful planet otherwise, settling it must have seemed worthwhile. Even if it was fated to destruction in the end, it could be thousands or millions of years in the future. They probably figured that by the time the planet showed signs of breaking up, their descendants would be so advanced that they could easily solve the problem. They didn't know that Helionn would lose touch with Earth early on and spend most of the next ten thousand years trying to increase the population and build a civilization, with wars and collapses and dark ages hampering progress and slowing things down. I don't know how you'd stop a planet from exploding or if the technology for it could even be developed, but maybe it would have been possible if we had been able to advance steadily without any interruptions and having to start over again very nearly from scratch at least twice in our history."

She then went on to the object of their expedition, finding the Arsenal of Wonders. Although its location was officially a secret, the story that had been passed down in Lynestra's family was that it was somewhere in the northern part of a vast nature preserve off-limits to anyone from outside and deliberately maintained as a primeval wilderness like that which had covered the entire planet when the first settlers came. Matt was surprised that any wilderness was left after ten thousand years of settlement, but the total population of the planet had never been very large and vast areas had never been settled in the first place. The area around the Arsenal was roughly equivalent to northern Canada, though south of the tree line and densely forested to the point of being a cold-climate version of a jungle.

"If it's where I think it is," Lynestra told Matt, "we shouldn't have any trouble finding the Arsenal with the *Last Hope*'s scanning equipment. It was designed for surveying other planets, but it will work just as well for Helionn."

Then she showed him a view of Eristhar, Helionn's one large moon among several small ones not much larger than flying mountains. It was so distant from the planet that gravitation barely held it in its orbit, and it rotated slowly instead of being tidally locked. Larger than Earth's moon and between Mercury and Mars in size, it even had a scant atmosphere. Astronomers thought it was possibly a small planet that had once been in an independent orbit around Delta Pavonis but Helionn had captured it at some point in the past. Aside from some relatively large asteroids, it was the only place for Helionn's space program to go since faster than light travel wasn't reinvented until just before the planet's end, and a colony had been established there. After Helionn's destruction, it was once more independent and the largest planetary body left in the solar system. About fifteen years later, however, it was slagged by a meteor storm, dooming the colony.

When she turned to scenes of life in the mostly underground colony, which to Matt resembled an upscale, multi-level indoor shopping mall, Lynestra had a faraway look. "I never knew Helionn except as scenes in movies and pictures in books. Eristhar was my real home."

Lynestra also began teaching him how to fly the *Last Hope*. She would do most if not all of the piloting, but she felt it would be a good idea to have him on hand as a back-up or relief pilot. Fortunately, the ship had been designed for largely automatic operation with semi-autonomous control systems, so for most of the flight the pilot would have little to do other than keep an eye on things. Matt picked up the principles fairly quickly.

Almost without realizing it, he also picked up a lot about starship construction. Lynestra could fly the ship without having to know very much about what was under the hood, but she had grown up in the designer's household and had overheard years of discussions about the ship's construction. She knew a great deal about the nuts and bolts as a result, even though her field of interest was more biology than technology, and could explain how it was all put together. Matt absorbed even more from learning how the ship's various systems functioned so he could monitor them from the control panel. While he couldn't read the text of the displayed pilot's manual, the numbers made some kind of sense, particularly several key equations.

When Lynestra mentioned that her father and uncle had picked up the principles of faster than light travel from some fragments of ancient science texts that had survived through the ages, Matt got the idea that they had not completely understood the fundamentals that had been worked out ten thousand years before, but they had gleaned enough to be able to build working starships. Gradually, Matt started to get a vague inkling of what lay behind the technology and what the Thelnarr brothers had missed.

What that meant didn't hit him until he remembered that the *Last Hope* had been constructed in his own universe. Its faster than light capability didn't depend on the different and somewhat wacky physics of the Astroman universe to be feasible. Which meant... *I could just about build a faster than light ship myself!* Well, maybe, if he was given several hundred billion dollars for development. If he suddenly found himself back on his own Earth, he'd have to spend a few years fleshing out the theory from his now still sketchy grasp of it while getting a background in engineering. Then he'd have to invent the technology and the machinery for the reactionless drive that pushed the ship to near light-speed as well as the inertial compensator that kept the ship's occupants from being flattened by the acceleration, along with the time/space disruptor that opened up the hole in space so the ship could leap across the light-years in hardly any time at all. There was also the matter of making the exotic materials he'd need for the engines and power cells, not to mention the fuel for those cells. It wasn't just star travel — he'd revolutionize Earth's technology and industry about four times over along the way, but if he took it step by step, each step could finance the next one. It would be a project for decades, but maybe, just maybe, it could be done. He could put the human race on the road to the stars centuries before it might have otherwise been accomplished. It gave him a dizzy feeling just thinking about it, and suddenly he realized that he had found his purpose in life. He'd have to find a way back home first, however, before he could even get started.

One evening, Matt and Lynestra settled in the den for drinks and a fireplace chat. He sat in what was becoming his favorite chair while she was curled up on the couch facing him across a low table. As they discussed their plans and how things were going, they both relaxed a little and the conversation turned in a more personal direction. In particular, Lynestra was curious about Matt's life, what his Earth was like and how it was different from the Earth she had been living on.

He didn't think his life story was all that interesting, but she seemed to find it fascinating, perhaps because it had been so much different from hers. His parents had been academics who believed in a well-rounded life and taught their children that there was more in the world than just books and studying, and he had been that odd combination of a science geek who was fairly good at sports as well as other interests and hobbies. His boyhood and teenage years in the upper Midwest were mostly uneventful, more or less Norman Rockwell meets Tom Swift. The highlight had been the high-school science fair where he had built a homemade cloud chamber for showing the trails left by charged atomic particles, using scrap parts and incidentally working out a new wrinkle that not only made it much cheaper than commercially made units but had a better display. He had nearly been disqualified by the judges, who refused to believe that a sixteen-year-old could have independently come up with such a radical new design and hadn't had professional help. After it was determined that he really had done it on his own, the judges gave him a blue ribbon and one passed the word along to a science supply house. The company saw some possibilities and offered to license his design for the science-fair market since it made relatively sophisticated cloud chambers affordable for kids who might otherwise have to make projects out of clay volcanoes and baking soda. He didn't make a fortune out of the deal, but it would help put him through college. He then followed his scientific bent to CalTech, majoring in physics and minoring in astronomy. There, he had managed to make top grades while getting a degree, though at the cost of a couple of failed romances.

Lynestra seemed oddly curious about that last and asked a few questions. Just for reference or something. Perhaps it was to assure herself that he really didn't go around kissing girls all the time, or more likely because she simply wondered how such things were done on Earth. There weren't many boys her age on Eristhar since births had been low in the crisis years immediately following the loss of Helionn, and she had left at fifteen before she had really started dating. Then, on Earth, the idea of romance with non-hyper boys never got any traction. Besides the obvious physical problems, boys her own age didn't seem *serious* when she was training to be Astroman's assistant fighting crime and saving lives, and few interested her even as casual friends.

"But we were talking about you, not about me," she hurriedly added when she realized what she had been saying, "so go on."

He had been about done with his autobiography anyway. There may have been more to life than books and studying, but no one had informed his professors of that and most of his outside interests had been sidelined for the time being. Then he had started a degree program that had led him to Fermilab with the hope of a successful career — only to take a highly unexpected detour.

"Someday I'd like to live a normal life for a change," he finished, "but right now, I'm not even sure what normal *is* anymore."

Lynestra nodded. "I grew up in an underground colony on the nearly airless moon of a planet that was destroyed before I was born. I'll let you know what normal is when *I* find out."

Following Matt's example, she then opened up a little more about her own life than she had before. "The real reason Karsten didn't announce me for two years," she told him when he asked her about it, "was because I didn't speak English when I came here. All Karsten remembered of Helionnian was baby talk like 'me want candy,' so communication between us was a little... interesting... at first."

"'Me want candy'?" Matt echoed. "Did he actually talk like that?"

"Yes, he did. It sounds a little strange in English, like something no real baby ever said, but it makes sense if you know Helionnian grammar. Anyway, I needed time to learn English and lose my accent. I could be passed off in school as a Swedish orphan, but if Astrogirl had appeared in public talking exactly the same way, people would have noticed. While I still use the accent in my private life since it's now part of my secret identity's character, Astrogirl had to speak perfect American English from the start. Besides that, there was so much more that I had to learn about Earth and how I could be Karsten's stand-in or substitute when he needed one, or even his successor if something happened... like now... " She trailed off, as though she didn't want to break down right then and there.

"So Astroman was something like your teacher when you came to Earth," Matt ventured, to fill the sudden pause.

Lynestra swallowed, then composed herself. "You might say that. Karsten was a good man," she added a little defensively, "even a great one. My respect for him, even my love, are more than I can express. Now, I know what you're thinking—"

"I didn't say a word!" Matt protested, although he actually had been thinking what she thought he had been thinking.

"Maybe not," Lynestra conceded, though still not sounding convinced that she hadn't accurately read his mind, "but it *is* the elephant in the living room, and it's something that occurs to everyone sooner or later. We were male and female, both of reproductive age, the last of the Helionnians, and we could never mate with Earthpeople for various reasons."

Tell me about it!

"Ellen Loring was after him for years, even trying desperate stunts to trick him into marrying her. I think the reason for that was because she heard the clock ticking. She was actually a little older than he was — I mean, she was already a big-name reporter at the newspaper the day Karsten started work there. I wish he had told her the cold, hard facts from the start so she didn't waste years of her life waiting for him, but he seemed to think he was being a gentleman by not discussing such matters with a lady. People from this Earth and Helionn *can't* have babies together. Even if Karsten trained himself to be very gentle with Ellen, there were some things he couldn't control and they'd have to have a platonic marriage. See me after class if you haven't figured it out yet because you'll need to know if you have to stay on this world. I'm majoring in biology so I can give you all the gory details — which they would be. If they tried artificial insemination, hyper-sperm would tear a normal egg apart, and even if they got around that somehow, normal and hyper-chromosomes wouldn't join together."

Meanwhile, Matt figured it out, and realized with a chilly feeling that he could have killed Laurie even if he had held his hyper-strength back.

"As for Karsten and me," Lynestra went on, "there were a lot of problems. We were first cousins and we have something of an instinctive aversion to matches that close. It may have come from the early days of Helionn's settlement, with such a small founding population and maybe a little too much inbreeding in the following generations even though it was unavoidable. In the circumstances, we might have eventually gotten around our inner resistance to the idea even so. The biggest problem, I think, was that Karsten was so much older than I was, by about twenty years. He was old enough to be my father, really. He looked at me as something like an adopted daughter, and I came to feel about him as more than an uncle, though not quite a father, since I remembered my own too well. I loved Karsten, but not as a potential husband or lover. For his part, he was in his late thirties and had never been able to get close to a woman, so he may have just put that part of life aside. He never pressed the issue and we never even discussed it, really, except once or twice in very theoretical terms. It wasn't out of personal desire but whether it was our duty as the last of our people to have babies. The difficult question was what would happen in the next generation. Who would our children mate with when there were no other Helionnians on Earth? It was an uncomfortable subject and we mainly decided to put it off until I was older, but we never got back to it to make any decisions one way or the other."

Now, Astroman may have been gone but there was another hyper-powered pachyderm in the parlor. Matt was close to her in age and not the least bit related. He had a sense, though, that Lynestra was reluctant to bring the matter to the floor, at least before the mission to Helionn was behind them, and decided to change the subject.

"You mentioned your father," he said, "What was he like? And your mother?" Then, remembering some of the odder ideas he had read about, he added, "Helionn's super-science aside, it doesn't sound like you were an embryo grown in a vat."

Lynestra had just then been taking a drink and nearly choked as she spluttered. "A *vat*? Where do people get this stuff? Wait, I think I know. Karsten never said much publicly about what life on Helionn was like, so people imagined all kinds of crazy things. I think they were trying to outdo each other by being as weird and science-fictiony as possible. Like Helionn was some cold technological nightmare where people were more electronic than human. Actually Helionn wasn't really that much more advanced than Earth. As I told you, we had to start over a couple of times with our civilization, so it wasn't ten thousand years of continuous development. I'd estimate that our civilization was maybe about two centuries ahead of Earth's at the time of its destruction. It was advanced but still recognizable as something human and not *too* different from modern Earth. We didn't live inside of icebergs, either — I've seen artists' conceptions that put us in these horrible ice caves — no, we lived in regular cities, and I was born the normal way and had perfectly natural parents."

She paused, as though to collect her memories and perhaps blink back a tear, then continued.

"I remember my real mother and father like I just left them yesterday. It's only been about five years since I last saw them, and I still miss them. My foster parents have been lovely but I was already fifteen when they adopted me. Oh — you should have seen that awful orphanage Karsten wanted to put me in at first. I mean, what was he *thinking* trying to drop me off in some old county children's home that was practically out of Dickens even if it was in downstate Illinois? (Yes, I know about Dickens. I went to high school on Earth, remember?) You wouldn't believe somebody would do that to their own cousin in a story some writer made up, let alone in real life, but it probably just goes to show that he sometimes didn't quite get how ordinary people lived. I wasn't about to live with six other kids in an attic dorm room with a leaky roof and I insisted that he find a real family to take me in."

She then told Matt her story. Her parents were supposed to come with her to Earth, but events had taken a tragic turn in a perfect storm of bad luck and malign coincidences.

Much of the colony on Eristhar was underground, with only a few domes and other installations on the surface. With such a thin atmosphere and next to no protection from radiation and ultraviolet light, and so much meteoric debris frequently coming down, an above-ground colony could not have survived for long. Decades of growth had expanded the sub-surface network of tunnels between the habitation complexes, laboratories, factories, and food production facilities until the various far-flung sectors had to be connected by a light-rail transportation system.

Even underground, the lack of resources on an uninhabitable little moon forever cut off from supplies from the mother world meant that the colony was unsustainable over the long term. Within ten years, twenty years at most with severe rationing, the entire population would have to be relocated to a more hospitable planet. Since none existed in this solar system, Project Last Hope had been initiated with her father at its head, the construction of a faster than light starship for scouting nearby star systems for habitable planets. It was underway in an underground hangar complex at the furthest end of the subway line, as far from the inhabited parts of the colony as possible since dangerous materials like Element 126 were involved. The *Last Hope* was also a prototype, the first full-scale starship ever built by Helionnian civilization not counting the small test models that sent Karsten Thelnarr and Helio to Earth. If it proved successful, work could begin on the first of the planned much larger ships that would ferry the population to a new home... if one could be found. Evacuating a billion people from Helionn never would have been possible, but the 15,000 people of Eristhar were a much more manageable number, especially if given a few years to work with. In the end, however, time was the one thing they did not have.

Lynestra and her parents, Rhynn and Velyra Thelnarr, lived in an apartment at the outer edge of the colony only a few kilometers from the hangar. Because her father needed to finish some calculations, the family had stayed home while everyone was off work for the big Year End Day celebration in the colony's distant central gallery.

Then the worst meteor storm in decades hit. A cloud of debris from Helionn's explosion years before had finally caught up with Eristhar.

While the communication systems were still functioning, Lynestra's father heard the news go from bad to much grimmer. The central habitat area was mostly destroyed and the death toll was probably 98 percent of the colony and climbing. A few people had managed to find temporary safety in sealed shelters, but their air would not last much longer.

For the Thelnarr family, the choice was only too clear. *The Last Hope* was ready for its maiden voyage, fueled and provisioned, and it was large enough to hold all three of them. With the rail line to the rest of the colony cut off by tunnel collapses, no one else could reach it.

Lynestra was sent on ahead to start the power-up and launch procedure. Her mother and father stayed behind to pack some essentials, then came after her on a second rail speeder. About five kilometers from the hangar, a large meteor strike caused a tunnel cave-in, blocking the track ahead. Rhynn and Velyra would never be able to reach the hangar, and retraced their path to the previous station on the line, now in ruins from a meteor strike and open to the near-vacuum outside. Although it had lost its air, they could call Lynestra from there. They were wearing space suits but the air would only last a few more minutes, so they would never make it overland, especially in the middle of a meteor storm. She could not come back and get them in the *Last Hope* because they would be dead by the time the ship was ready to take off.

Lynestra sobbed. "What should I do?"

"Head for Earth," her father told her. "It's one of the destinations I've already programmed into the course computer. I've done some rough calculations and if you leave now and go through the time loop, you'll get there about thirty-five years after your cousin. He'll be a grown man by then, and if you can find him, he'll be able to help you."

They said their tearful goodbyes, and her parents wished her good luck on Earth. Then another meteor apparently hit somewhere and the line went dead. Lynestra was on her own.

She was almost too grief-stricken to go on, but she managed to complete the launch sequence. It was down to her now, the last survivor of Eristhar, the last daughter of Helionn. Giving up and just waiting to die wouldn't do anyone any good. Going through the procedures helped take her mind off what was happening to her parents. When she finished half an hour later and the *Last Hope* started rolling towards the opening hangar doors and into the launch tunnel that led up to the surface, she realized that her parents must be dead by then. Her tears flowed all over again and she nearly broke down right there, but the ship's automatic systems had taken over and she was on her way.

The *Last Hope* burst out of the launch tunnel and into a storm of blazing dust and rocks pelting down from the sky. The meteor shields were up and Lynestra sailed on through, sad and lonely, grieving for her parents, her people, her home, her world, and she set course for Earth.

By the end of her story, Lynestra was close to breaking down in tears. Trying to comfort her by holding her in his arms seemed like a reasonable thing for Matt to do, but he was in a chair and she was on the couch with a table between them, and the logistics of crossing over to her would have been obvious and clumsy. All he could think to do was express his sympathy for her loss and what she had gone through, even though he'd never experienced any tragedy in his life that remotely compared to hers.

"Thanks…" she murmured bleakly, then they went their separate ways to their rooms.

Chapter Eleven: **The Great Glengarrium Robbery**

Matt and Lynestra sat at a table in the Citadel commissary and looked over Dr. MacTavish's notes and diagrams to plan the Glengarrium raid. With the trip coming up soon, they couldn't put off the operation any longer. There was just too much risk that Bolton would soon discover that a relatively enormous quantity of insanely rare and valuable Element 126 was sitting there in the vault, and grab it for himself.

"I'm sure Bolton will have a suspicion that you or Astroman might try something like this," Matt said, "and he'll have his hypercannon installed and ready by now. Maybe I should go alone since I know my way around the place pretty well. That way, if something happens, it'll just be to me and you'll still be able to go ahead with your plans."

Lynestra shook her head. "If something happens to you, there's no Element 126 and no trip to Helionn to get the Neutralizer. That means I wouldn't be able to do much even if I was free. No, you'll need me to give you cover. I found that out the night Karsten died. He had me keep back too far, and then... Well, I'm coming along, so get used to it."

Matt still didn't like the idea of putting both of them at risk, but left it at merely shrugging. "All right, then. Your world, your rules."

"So we'll have to sneak in," Lynestra went on, "maybe wearing all black so we can hide in the dark and keep to the shadows. It'll be a little strange, not wearing my Astrogirl costume when I'm on a mission..."

Matt had a sudden thought. "Wait a sec. Astroman trained you in secret for two years before you went public. Surely you didn't wear your costume then, did you?"

"Actually, I did. It was part of the training."

"But your existence was supposed to be secret! The first accidental glimpse anybody got of you in an Astrogirl costume would have given it away."

Lynestra shrugged. "What can I say? That was how Karsten wanted it, so I didn't argue. Besides, the costume was made from clothes I brought with me from Eristhar, so I could fly through forest fires or whatever."

Even at three in the morning on a warm and clear starlit night, Mac-TavishLab was a brightly shining island of light in the darkness of the Illinois farmland. Off in the distance were the lights of small towns and the glow of Chicago to the northeast.

It didn't escape Matt that after fighting to keep someone from robbing the place on two separate occasions, he was now here to rob it himself.

As one of the risks of the master-scientist trade, Dr. MacTavish had realized that raiders working for less scrupulous competitors might force him out of his own laboratory at some point, and made a few plans for just that contingency. In the few minutes he and his men had been given to clear out of the facility, they had managed some small acts of sabotage to make life a little harder for the occupying forces. Since he would eventually want his lab back in some kind of order, the damage was minor and more to impede any worthwhile work being done than outright destruction. One item in the emergency plan was disabling the alarms, both to cause the occupiers more headaches and to allow possible counterforces to infiltrate the grounds without being detected.

Tonight, the counterforces were here and ready to infiltrate, though Matt and Lynestra were probably a long way away from what MacTavish had originally had in mind.

The occupiers would have to deploy human patrols to keep the facility under surveillance, which would be easier to avoid or neutralize than TV cameras or trip wires or door alarms. They might be expecting an attack from the air by Astroman or Astrogirl, so they would keep their eyes on the sky. Matt decided to sneak in overland, thinking the complex would be more lightly defended from that direction. Dr. MacTavish didn't have a private army like Bolton's and couldn't have reconquered the facility even if he wanted to try. The government had already given Bolton the right to occupy the laboratory, so MacTavish would have just been ousted again, probably with much less gentle treatment the second time. A commando raid to get vital papers or equipment might have been the most Bolton would be expecting, but two hyper-beings who could fly at a low altitude ought to be able to slip in.

Matt and Lynestra kept to treetop level on their approach, then dropped to just above the cornstalks as they came to the fields, hoping to be lost in the ground clutter. To keep from being spotted in the night, they wore black pullover sweaters and slacks, and had blackened their faces. Lynestra even wore a black wig to hide her naturally blonde hair, which was why the Ellen Loring dummy back at the Citadel was temporarily bald at the moment. Matt had teasingly told Lynestra that she looked like a ninja, but while such an ancient concept surely existed in this world's Japan, she had never heard the word before.

About a quarter of a mile from the lab complex, Matt gestured for Lynestra to stop. They hovered over the cornstalks and used their extended vision to scout the terrain.

The lights mounted on poles and buildings did not illuminate the entire grounds and there were large stretches of pure black shadow between pools of light, but Matt could see that as he had hoped, not much activity was going on inside the compound at that hour. A few guards made their rounds along the fence, while inside he caught glimpses of other guards with flashlights patrolling the grounds and the streets of the former college campus. He saw a couple wearing backpacks that were most likely portable Deactivators. At least two high-tech cannons had recently been installed on the roofs of the tallest buildings, and next to them stood men scanning the skies with binoculars.

"It's like they're expecting us," Lynestra said in a voice too low for non-hyper eavesdroppers to perceive.

"They pretty much *are*," Matt replied, also keeping his voice down to near-inaudibility. "They know *somebody* who's hyper has been working for MacTavish, and who knows what he might do to help his old boss out. Of course they'd plan with that in mind."

"Let's just hope they don't expect us to do what we're planning on doing," Lynestra said.

They came in just over the fence in a particularly dark corner where a light on a high pole had burned out, which Dr. MacTavish had helpfully mentioned as the weakest point in the perimeter and something he had been meaning to attend to for a while. Being able to fly, they weren't confined to the ground, and could make their way across rooftops or even along the sides of buildings, wherever the shadows gave them cover. They could see in the dark, so the complex looked to them as though lit in bright moonlight with colors washed out almost to tones of gray, and they didn't need any lights of their own. Matt was tempted to yank the power cables leading into the facility, hampering the opposition with near-total darkness while he and Lynestra wouldn't even be slowed up, but it would be too much of a signal to Bolton's men that something was afoot. The best outcome was no one knowing they had even been there until they were gone with what they had come for.

One building they passed showed signs of a recent fire in a few rooms, with smoke residue on the outer wall around the windows, charred wooden frames, and broken glass panes. It had happened since the hostile takeover, hinting that Dr. MacTavish was right and Bolton's men would find themselves confronted with on-going processes they didn't understand and couldn't control when they occupied the lab.

The objective was the Natatorium. Since its conversion into a small-scale nuclear reactor had been ad hoc, adding pipes, tanks, and machinery to an existing building rather than designing it from scratch, it had some weak points in its security. Among them were additional entrances along the sides and in the rear as well as the well-guarded one in front. Bolton probably hadn't had time to give the building a careful inspection and fill in the holes, and in particular, MacTavish had recommended a rear door that led directly into the lab. The door was in a suitably dark corner and lost in the shadows, and easily missed if a would-be intruder didn't already know it was there. It wasn't even locked, and Matt wondered if MacTavish had ever seriously considered that he might be a target for a break-in, or had just assumed that any attack would be an all-out assault he would see coming. Then again, he might have just overlooked it.

While Matt hated to admit it, he was starting to think Senator Ruttle may have had a point about what a safety hazard a facility as improvised and even primitive as MacTavishLab was.

Once inside, they went down a steep, steel stairway that led well below ground level, and came out into a narrow corridor, eerily lit with dim emergency lighting. No guards were in sight anywhere. Following Dr. MacTavish's written instructions, Matt led Lynestra along the maze of corridors and through several empty rooms, then came into a control room with consoles filled with glowing indicator lights in various colors, hissing video screens showing only snow and interference, and cabinet-sized computers with tape reels whizzing as they spun. In the background, a low background rumble could be heard as unidentified machinery behind the walls ran automatically, with a slight accompanying vibration. At least three low-level alarms beeped faintly but rhythmically, suggesting that Bolton still hadn't fixed all the problems from his abrupt takeover of the lab yet. A large window of thick, heavy glass looked into an adjoining room that was a radiation containment chamber. The control room was deserted now, but when it was in use, technicians would stand in front of the window and manipulate remotely controlled mechanical arms on the other side to perform various operations or industrial processes involving radioactive materials.

From there, they went down a short corridor that ended with a heavily reinforced door. It wasn't locked, and led into a small, windowless room. Built into the opposite wall was an armored vault door, something like a small version of what might be found in a bank. Using the combination Dr. MacTavish had given him, Matt opened it.

Inside the vault, in an unmarked drawer, he found what he was looking for: an otherwise non-descript foot-long bar of dull gray lead that could have been mistaken for an unusually heavy ruler. He took it out and hefted it. It felt warm to the touch.

"That's *it*?" Lynestra murmured. "I expected something a little more spectacular."

"You'd be even less impressed if you could see the Glengarrium itself," Matt said. "The lead's just to hold it and so you don't lose it. What's inside is barely visible to the naked eye, but it weighs ten pounds. It's just about dense enough to ooze out of the solid lead holder and sink through the floor."

No one would know from looking at the dull gray bar what power it contained. Sealed inside was a tiny but super-heavy and ultra-dense droplet of the rarest element in the Universe. If a relatively stable isotope of Element 126 ever appeared naturally, it would be as a few atoms forged in the heart of a supernova — and this was ten pounds' worth, probably the largest concentration of Glengarrium anywhere in the Galaxy.

"Okay, I'm impressed," Lynestra conceded. "Now that we've got it, let's get out of here before somebody notices us."

It was already too late for that. As they came into the control room, they froze as they realized they weren't alone. Two thugs were waiting for them. Matt and Lynestra should have heard them even out in the hallway, but their attention had relaxed a little too much once they thought their mission was accomplished. Also, the telltale signs of the thugs' presence, like their breathing and heartbeats, had been masked by the background rumble of the machinery.

One man wore a backpack that resembled a leaf-blower, connected by a heavy cable to a metal rod that he held pointed at Matt and Lynestra. Just behind him and to one side was another thug, holding an ordinary pistol at ready. They were hired muscle in ordinary streetclothes and the inevitable hats, not even rating security guard uniforms.

"Come on in, kids," the goon with the backpack said with a smirk, "and get those mitts up!"

Hesitantly, Matt put his hands up and stepped into the room. He wasn't worried yet, just wondering if he was fast enough to move before the goon could react and pull the trigger on the Deactivator. Lynestra followed behind him.

The goon snorted. "You thought you could just waltz in here? Like it wouldn't be guarded? The boss thought somebody might try some-

thing. Now hand that thing over! Any funny business and *zap!* Then let's
see how you can handle my pal's rod when you don't have any powers!"

Despite their best efforts, they had still been caught. Shrugging,
Matt started to hand the bar to the hired thug.

*He doesn't know how heavy it really is. He'll drop it and that's
when I make my move—*

The goon reached out with his free hand to take the bar. As Matt
suspected, he didn't realize how much heavier it was than it looked. The
man grasped the bar — and it slipped through his fingers, falling to the
floor with a thunk.

Matt started to move forward but the man jerked the rod up and
fired. A livid green burst of energy shot out with a sharp electric crack.
Matt ducked — more by sheer instinct than any rational thought — just
barely dodging the sizzling beam. It went by harmlessly over his shoulder and next to his cheek, and blistered and blackened the paint on the
wall behind him. The man stepped back, still pointing the rod at Matt.

"Stay back! I told you don't get cute! I oughtta fry you anyway!"

It was a standoff. Matt had hyper-powers, the thug didn't, so that
ought to count for something, but could he move faster than the crook's
trigger finger—

Suddenly, the air above the bar on the floor began to whirl, like a
rapidly expanding, nearly transparent tornado six feet high, howling as it
spun.

"What th—?" the thug choked.

The howling crescendoed into a scream of space itself being torn
apart, the tornado darkened as it whirled ever faster, blurring into utter
blackness that was a gaping hole in space with only emptiness beyond.
Every loose object in the room suddenly started flying towards it, as
though carried along with air being sucked into a vacuum beyond the
hole. Matt seized the edge of a control console with one hand to keep
from being swept into the hole himself, then threw out the other to grab
Lynestra's arm as she was pulled past him. The two thugs were closer to
the tornado and had nothing to hang onto. They were engulfed by it even
as they struggled to get away—

And then nothing. Only silence. The hole in space, the tornado and
the thugs were gone. Dangling wires swung back and forth while loose
sheets of paper fluttered to the floor.

"Thanks for holding on to me, but... what happened?" Lynestra
murmured in astonishment as Matt let go of her.

"Dr. MacTavish warned me about this," he replied, feeling a little
shaky about what he had just seen. "I think when the Glengarrium hit the
floor, it was jarred into a brief state of instability. It ripped a hole in

space and those guys were pulled into it. I don't know where they ended up, but I doubt if there was any air there."

Lynestra shuddered. "What a horrible way to go…"

"Just be glad we didn't go with them," Matt said, bending down to pick up the Glengarrium bar and affecting a nonchalance he didn't really feel. He hadn't wanted to kill anybody, not even men who were ready to kill him and Lynestra. Maybe it wasn't really his fault, but it was still disturbing that two men were dead because of him. This would take some getting used to — and he didn't *want* to get used to it. "We got what we came for, so let's get out of here before more of those guys with leaf-blowers show up."

With any luck at all, Garth Bolton would never know they had even been there. He apparently hadn't done an inventory yet and was unaware of the Glengarrium in the vault, and so wouldn't realize something was missing. He would wonder about the sudden disappearance of two of his men, of course, but probably assume the men had simply deserted with a valuable piece of equipment — a Deactivator — and were even now trying to sell it to some other renegade scientist or crime lord. If Bolton wasted a lot of time trying to track them down, Matt thought as he and Lynestra flew back through the star-glittering night to Colorado, so much the better.

Chapter Twelve: **Journey Through Space and Time**

X minus three hours.

It was about noon and Matt and Lynestra were sitting at their usual table in the commissary, eating one last meal on Earth and reviewing their plans a final time.

He still had a feeling of unreality about it. Today, they would be taking off for another star. He tried to remind himself that he was about to travel twenty light-years, but it somehow refused to sink in. He kept thinking of a family trip to the lake in the SUV. This was about as simple as that. For that matter, a trip to Paris for a conference the year before had taken more planning and preparation than this little jaunt had.

Lynestra had done most of the work, of course, figuring the optimum departure time based on the interrelation of universes, and there hadn't been a whole lot to load on the ship. With next to no possessions, Matt was traveling very light, and Lynestra didn't have much more.

There had been some concern at first as to whether Element 126 produced in this universe could even be used as fuel by a ship built in the other, but test runs showed no significant difference. Perhaps there was some analogy in the fact that people from Helionn and Matt's Earth could eat the food here and still derive some nutrition, or maybe it was more that Element 126 from either universe was *so* powerful that any differences on the atomic level were trivial as far as the macroworld effect was concerned. Then, once the power cells had been infused with Glengarrium, they were as ready as they were going to be.

Just as they were finishing their lunch, the wall phone rang.

"More good news from the Foundation, no doubt..." Lynestra muttered as she stood up.

She went over to the phone and picked up the receiver, then gasped when she heard the voice on the other end. Matt felt he'd better listen in with his Astro-hearing.

"Oh, good, I'm glad I caught you at home." The voice, the cold, oily sneer, were unmistakable.

If anything was unmistakable about Lynestra's voice, it was the barely controlled hatred. "What do you want, Bolton?"

"Actually, I want to talk to your cousin. Is he there?"

"Astroman... is not available at the moment."

"Oh, really? Too bad. You'll have to do, then." Bolton's tone turned almost jaunty. "You're probably wondering how I tracked you down. It wasn't hard once I had the resources of the United States Government at my disposal. Did you and Astroman really think nobody would ever notice you two flying back and forth to your little mountain hideaway like busy little bees to your hive? You're not too far from NORAD, after all. You showed up on radar all the time, but since Astroman had done the politicians a few favors, the military was under orders to keep it a secret. Now I'm in a position to give a few orders of my own, so I got the whole scoop. It wasn't hard to figure out the general neighborhood of your clubhouse, and once I had that I could put my boys to work scouting the territory and checking the property and tax records. It didn't take long to find out about that fancy bomb shelter the Astroman Foundation bought through one of its dummy corporations. I even got the phone number and thought I'd try it... and what do you know! It worked the first time!"

Now Lynestra's voice was ice freezing on iron. "Like I said... What. Do. You. Want?"

Bolton dropped the mock-cheerful tone. "I want you to turn yourself in like you're supposed to," he snapped. "If you insist on being stubborn, we'll just to have to run you to ground some other way. But whatever you do, you can't hide out in your little play fort any more. We know where it is and we have a battalion of troops closing in to occupy it under the terms of the National Defense Security Act. You have an hour to deactivate all security devices, open any and all sealed or camouflaged entrances so the troops can enter, and leave the premises taking nothing with you. And I mean you are to leave *everything* behind. You can buy a new toothbrush somewhere. Have I made myself clear?"

Matt had a feeling of *déjà vu* from the occupation of MacTavishLab.

"What if we refuse?" Lynestra asked flatly.

"Then we will blast our way in," Bolton shot back. "I will also remind you that if you actively resist or fail to disarm any booby traps or automatic weapon systems, you will be held liable for the murder of any soldiers who die as a result. And don't think your so-called hyper-powers will protect you personally. As I'm sure you've figured out by now, I have a weapon at my disposal that will cancel your powers. Resist and you might not survive."

Lynestra nodded to herself. "I understand. How far away are the soldiers now? There's an automatic outer perimeter defense ring about five miles from the mountain that I will have to deactivate before they can cross it."

Matt looked at Lynestra in surprise. *Is she surrendering?*

Bolton chuckled. "I thought you had telescopic vision. You should know where the soldiers are already. One hour. No more." He hung up with a click.

"You're not really thinking of...?" Matt started to say.

Lynestra put the phone down, forcing herself not to slam it into its cradle, which would have shattered it.

"No, am *not* letting that louse win," she said, all but through clenched teeth. "*He killed Karsten!* He gave us an hour, so we've got to get moving!"

Lynestra led Matt to a central control room he hadn't seen before but probably should have guessed had to exist. From here, all the electrical and other systems in the Citadel were monitored and controlled, and black and white TV screens showed closed-circuit views of various locations. Lynestra manipulated some controls on an instrument console, then opened a wall panel revealing a small keypad, punched some buttons, and opened another panel with a red knifeswitch inside. She took a deep breath, as though steeling herself to do something she didn't want to do, then pulled the switch down. A sound like a ringing bell reverberated from somewhere, and every light in the Citadel flickered momentarily.

"I'm so sorry, Karsten..." she murmured, glancing off into space for a moment.

"What did you do?" Matt asked, sensing that whatever it was, it was drastic.

"What I *had* to do," she replied bleakly. "I started the self-destruct sequence. The Citadel is now set to blow itself up in just over an hour."

Matt was stunned. The Citadel's interior may have been the product of one man's obsessive attention to the details of his own life, but it was fabulous in its own way.

"Destroying the whole place seems a little... extreme," he said as he followed Lynestra out of the control room. "There are a lot of wonderful things here."

"I agree," she said, picking up her pace, "but it wasn't my idea. Karsten told me to do this if anything ever happened to him and it looked like his enemies might break in."

"The history, the Helionnian science..."

"Don't worry. I already moved copies of the really important data to a safe place. If there ever comes a time when it seems right to release it all to the world, I will. The native Helionnian artifacts like Karsten's spaceship are hyper, so they'll survive a little thing like a nuclear blast and being buried under a mountain, and can eventually be dug out. It was the personal stuff Karsten didn't want anyone finding out about. You've seen those rooms devoted to his friends."

A nuclear blast? How did he get hold of an atomic bomb, anyway? Powerful friends in high places? Oh, never mind... "How much damage will the bomb do to the surrounding terrain?" Matt asked instead as they took off flying down a long corridor. "Are the soldiers in danger?"

"Not really," she called back. "It's a small bomb, so it'll just destroy everything in the hollowed-out interior. There might be some radiation leakage, but probably not for more than a mile or two around. Nobody will be digging through the rubble for a long time, and there won't be much of anything that isn't Helionnian left to find."

Lunch was a lost cause and so was their original schedule. They had to take off immediately. They went back to the hangar and started the warm-up procedure for the *Last Hope*.

At precisely the hour mark, the telephone extension on the hangar wall rang. Lynestra answered.

"Well...?" Bolton began, not even trying to conceal the triumph he obviously felt. "The troops are ready to move in. Are you going to welcome us with your doors open or do we have to start with an artillery barrage?"

"Neither one," Lynestra said frostily. "If you have any sense, you will begin pulling your troops even further back. The Citadel will self-destruct in ten minutes."

"*What?*" Bolton shouted, rattling the diaphragm in the handset speaker. "Are you insane? I order you to stop it! You are under orders to turn over the facility completely intact to the duly constituted authorities—"

"You can't order me to do anything," Lynestra replied, cold and deadly. "Besides, I couldn't stop it now even if I wanted to. I suggest you get those soldiers out of there fast. As for you, you're welcome to come on up by yourself and watch the fireworks from ringside. Since you're a criminal, a killer, and now a would-be dictator, you'd be doing the whole country a favor—"

Bolton hung up.

"From the echo," she remarked, "it sounded like he had a speaker-phone on, so I'm sure a lot of people overheard us. I hope I caused a nice little panic. Now it's time to go. We have to get out of here before the bomb explodes."

In the cockpit, Lynestra sat at the controls while Matt took the seat next to her. It was supposed to be a co-pilot's seat, but Lynestra did everything herself and he mainly sat back and tried to relax. With a touch of a switch, the entire forward end seemingly became transparent, show-ing a projected view of the ship's surroundings, as though they were sit-ting in their seats at a console suspended in space with the interior of the hangar around them, while anyone standing outside would see the same solid, opaque hull as before.

Lynestra touched another control and the hangar doors opened in front of the ship. It was a gray, rainy day outside, the first Matt had seen on this world, with the clouds rolling just overhead and obscuring the nearer mountain peaks. She taxied the ship out of the hangar, paused for a final checkout, then started forward down the long and straight access road that doubled as a runway. Since it wasn't an airplane, the *Last Hope* didn't need the runway for takeoff, only to get clear of the hangar. Then Lynestra hit the VTOL belly thrusters and the ship lifted from the run-way. Its nose angled up and the rear thrusters kicked in, sending them into a steep climb.

Meanwhile, the clock had ticked down.

Matt watched the video screen as the rear camera caught the action. For a moment, nothing seemed to happen. Then the ground around the mountain *heaved*. The mountain's sides swelled out, then one of the cliff faces burst open in a jet of flame and a blast of dirt and rock. The moun-taintop above buckled over the side of the breakthrough, and collapsed in an avalanche. A cloud of dust and dirt rose and hid the mountain within it.

It was a funeral pyre for Karsten Thelnarr.

Being hyper, his body was probably one of the few things to have survived the explosion intact. But now it was buried under thousands of tons of radioactive rock. Lynestra wasn't sure how long a body would stay hyper, though Karsten had once estimated the probable half-life of the decreasing energy level at possibly ninety years, give or take a few. In any event, no one was likely to even approach the mountain for a long time to come, let alone dig into it.

Matt heard Lynestra choke back a sob.

Before they could gain much speed, she suddenly blurted, "They're shooting at us!"

Some forward spotter must have seen the ship emerge from the hangar and prepare for takeoff, and called it in. One of the screens showed something coming straight at them from the soldiers' lines.

Matt just had time to think, *a surface to air missile?* Then it hit just under the *Last Hope's* ascending nose. A loud blast, livid flame all around — but the ship barely trembled. The flame and smoke rapidly dissipated, and they kept on rising and accelerating as though nothing had happened. The *Last Hope* was hyper just as much as Matt and Lynestra were and even a missile had no effect on it.

Matt wanted to say something like, "Is that all you've got, Garth?" Then he remembered the green ray that had prompted this expedition in the first place and decided not to tempt Fate.

They shot through the clouds and into clear, sunlit blue sky. Onward and upward the ship went as the Earth fell away beneath them. Around them, the sky turned a deeper blue, then to indigo, then to black, and the first stars began to appear. Their speed was still increasing but the ship's artificial gravity compensated for the acceleration and Matt barely felt it.

After all the excitement leading up to takeoff, they were finally on their way. On their way into space, on their way to another star. Matt leaned back in his seat while Lynestra watched the readouts intently.

Now the Earth and its atmosphere were well behind them. His boy-hood ambition had been fulfilled and he was now in space. Even with everything that had happened and all the uncertainties that lay ahead, he could enjoy the moment for at least that much.

Just as Matt was starting to wonder if Lynestra might be in the mood for a little conversation now, she suddenly gasped.

"Look!"

"What?"

Lynestra pored over the projected screens. "There's something behind us, coming after us! I think it's catching up!"

"Did Bolton fire another missile at us?"

"I don't think so. It doesn't look like one. Let me enlarge it."

A projected screen about two feet square appeared in front of them, showing a fuzzy image from the rear scanner. The object was still too small and indistinct to make out very clearly, but some yellow gridlines superimposed on the image gave an indication of its size.

"It's about two meters long and less than one wide..." Lynestra said. "It's a human body!"

"Who could fly out here at this speed?"

"Who do you think? You fought him!"

"Berserko? But how?"

"Have you forgotten? He doesn't need to breathe. When Karsten was after him, he would often head for space because he had learned Astroman couldn't follow him there. That's probably where he went after your fight with him at the museum."

"That's right. I could only go so high when I tried to chase him and he got away. But why is he coming after us?"

Lynestra thought. "He has some of Karsten's memories that were copied into his brain when he was created, even if they are vague and confused. Maybe he recognizes this ship as Helionnian and thinks it has something to do with Astroman, and he wants to destroy it."

"If he has Astroman's memories, maybe he dimly remembers Helionn in some way and he thinks he can follow us home?"

"That would be sad."

As fast as Berserko could fly, even he must have had his limits and couldn't keep up with the steadily accelerating *Last Hope*. Eventually he was lost in the distance behind them and the ship continued onwards at an ever greater velocity.

Now that they were away from Earth and heading into deep space, the flight was more or less on programmed autopilot, and what followed was a routine of keeping an eye on the monitor screens and instrument readouts for any anomalies. Even that might not have been strictly necessary since alarms would have sounded if any trouble developed, but Lynestra wanted to have somebody continuously on watch just in case.

The trip out would take about a day and half to build up speed and reach the transition point. They ate separately in the tiny mess and took turns sleeping so one of them could be at the controls at all times. Lynestra had taught Matt the basics of flying the ship, but if anything went wrong during his shift, his most important task would be knocking on her cabin door to wake her up so she could deal with the problem. While he wished he could be a little more useful, it was her ship and her mission, and he decided not to press it. Fortunately, the Helionnians built their ships well and the flight went as smoothly as they could have asked for.

After some thirty-six hours, they had gained sufficient speed and reached the exact point in space for the transition. They both sat at the controls and waited for the countdown to reach zero. Ahead of them, who seemed to be a bright blue star rapidly increased in size and brilliance, revealing itself as a looming hole in space with livid sheets of energy seething inside.

"That's what we call the iris," Lynestra called out as the engine whine went into a shriek. "All right, here we go. Brace yourself! It's going to be rough!"

Matt thought she had to be exaggerating, until the ship plunged into the hole and everything exploded in a blast of blue lightning. He briefly wondered if something had gone horribly wrong and the ship had blown up, and this was his last second of consciousness before oblivion, but the lightning roared on and on —

Then it stopped. The only sound was the hum of the ventilators.

The lurid blue lightning had faded out. At first the 180-degree cockpit view showed only blackness, but as Matt's eyes adjusted, he saw glittering stars all around him.

Lynestra let out a long sigh. "I've been through the iris once already, and it wasn't any better the second time."

Matt felt as though his insides had been turned inside out. For a moment, he wished the sanitary cell wasn't all the way at the other end of the crew quarters, but the feeling passed and he felt normal again.

Very normal.

Matt realized that the all-pervading numbness he had felt ever since his abrupt transition from Fermilab was gone. When he looked at something across the cabin, he didn't have to control his focus so he didn't see through it or in sudden close-up. He was back in his old universe and had lost his hyperpowers. It was almost a relief in some ways.

Suddenly, he felt his socks tighten around his feet inside of his shoes, then shrivel and tear apart into fragments of the individual threads. He needed a moment to remember that while the rest of the clothes he was wearing had been hyper-energized at MacTavishLab, his socks had been one of the spare pairs he'd bought in Colorado. He had put them on without thinking about what the transition to a universe with a higher energy level would do to them.

The transition also meant that the food they'd brought along from Earth would be inedible. They'd have to fall back on the packaged rations that had been stored on the ship since it left Eristhar five years before, but Helionnian synthetic food bars had a shelf life of just about forever and would be as good as they ever were.

Lynestra felt the difference, too. "I can't believe it!" she exclaimed, glancing at Matt. "I feel… *right* again! This will take some getting used to after several years." She looked back at the control console where one of the screens showed a single large star. "That's Delta Pavonis! We made it!"

Matt was back in his own universe — and twenty light-years from home. It might have been a heady feeling to realize that no one else from his world had gone beyond Earth's moon and he had just made a journey that would have been considered impossible, but he also realized that if Lynestra's calculations had been correct, the world he knew was now ten thousand years in the past. It was further back in time than ancient Egypt had been, perhaps even more a vanished civilization buried by the millennia than Sumeria. He felt a little chilly.

From where they had emerged into this solar system, it was another day and a half to Helionn.

Matt was on duty when the planet finally loomed ahead. Shining in space through the cockpit canopy was a blue-green globe streaked with white clouds, at this distance the size of a basketball. Half of it was lit by sunlight, but the darkness of the night side was faintly lit by a glow filling out the rest of the sphere. Bioluminescent forests and seaweed, Matt remembered Lynestra telling him.

Behind Matt, Lynestra came into the cockpit, still a little sleepy and rubbing her eyes. Seeing her home planet snapped her completely awake almost instantly.

"Helionn!" she exclaimed as she settled into the seat next to Matt. "It hasn't been destroyed yet! We did it! And look over there!" She pointed to a small thin crescent off to one side. "That's Eristhar, my home — the one moon that outlived everything else." She stared at the moon for a while, then sighed. "It's hard to look at it and realize that no one I love is there yet. We're here but I still can't go home."

For the next hour as the ship approached Helionn, Lynestra watched the screens and readouts, but most of the landing sequence functions were under automatic control. Much of the time was spent decelerating. Even though the ship itself was shielded, Lynestra didn't want to hit the atmosphere at high speed. The ship might not show up on radar, but leaving a glowing trail of super-heated air hundreds of miles long would definitely attract attention.

The blue, green, and white globe of the planet bulked ever larger in front of them, until it took up their entire field of view and Matt could see details of the mountains and plains in the landscape of the continents below.

"Time to strap in," Lynestra announced and indicated the readouts. "I'm getting signs of active power sources and a huge deposit of refined metal just under the surface in the far north. That isn't something you'd expect in a nature preserve, so it has to be the Arsenal! We're almost there."

The ship plunged into denser air and the blackness of space gave way to the blue of the atmosphere. Wisps of white clouds shot past as they dove lower. Matt saw an ocean sparkling in the sunlight far below.

"The Great Northern Sea," Lynestra said. "It looks like the shield is working. I don't see any signs of anybody on our tail. If they've even noticed our vapor trail, they probably think we're a meteor, which is hardly unusual for this planet."

She brought the ship down low and they skimmed just over the whitecaps of the ocean. A coastline appeared ahead. They were steadily slowing down, and finally came almost to a stop above a dense jungle a short distance inland. After some circling, Lynestra found what she was looking for, a clearing large enough for the ship, and gently landed using the VTOL ventral thrusters. The engines faded out and the ventilators turned off. Suddenly there was only silence in the cabin.

"We're here!" Lynestra exclaimed joyfully.

They were somewhere, all right. Outside, Matt saw a thick and tangled jungle of dark green leaves. If plants here used a similar green chlorophyll for photosynthesis, it seemed to tend more towards the blue end of the blue-yellow mix than it did on Earth. The taller plants were more or less similar to trees, but he suspected that on closer examination the resemblance wouldn't hold up. Overhead, the twilight sky was mostly clear with some high scattered clouds, and it looked as though they had landed in the early evening.

Lynestra glanced at the instrument panel. "I just hope I didn't mis-figure the era. What if I got us here an hour before Helionn explodes? Easy enough to find out..."

She ran her finger along a control strip marked with numbers, prob-ably a continuum of radio frequencies. Instantly, voices in some uniden-tifiable language and snatches of unfamiliar-sounding music came out of a speaker.

"They're speaking Vensa — Modern Helionnian — on the radio, so we can't be too far off." She listened for a couple of minutes, changing from channel to channel, then turned it off. "That's a relief. I heard a date and we've arrived about twenty-four years before the end, just as Karsten calculated it. It means we have the time we need. So the next thing we should do is go outside and get our bearings, then come back and get the equipment we'll need to scout for the Arsenal. We landed on the coast of Nygotland, and the beach ought to be about half a mile from here."

Matt had always imagined that landing on another planet would be far more involved. Cameras, speeches, raising the flag. At the least, tak-ing a sample of the surrounding atmosphere to make sure it was fit to breathe. None of that was necessary here. They could step outside with-out a second thought, without even a spacesuit, just like his family get-ting out of the van when they pulled up at the lake in the north woods.

Lynestra sported something like a gray and silver track suit and boots that she had worn on her flight from Eristhar to Earth five years before since they would hold up in this universe. The suit had apparently been a little baggy on her at fifteen but she had grown into it since then. For his part, in addition to his Earthly shirt and jeans, he had put on a light tan jacket he had found in the ship's storage locker, evidently intended for a crew member who was now long past needing it. It may have been the middle of summer in Helionn's northern hemisphere, but this far north the evenings were chilly.

As Matt joined her, she touched a control on her wristband and the ship behind them shimmered and wavered, its outlines breaking up and reflecting the surrounding forest. Up close, the shielding wouldn't fool anyone into thinking there was nothing there, but from a distance, such as from aircraft passing overhead, it would look like just more clearing. The shield would also prevent the ship's metal hull and power supply from being detected by any scanning devices. The wristband was also handy in that she could use it to call the ship and it would fly to her on auto-pilot no matter where she was. If they got into a sticky situation, help could be on the way in a matter of moments — after the initial half-hour power-up, of course.

"Come on," Lynestra said, turning towards the jungle. "The beach is this way."

Helionn's gravity was actually a little less than Earth's, but Lynestra found it a burden. She had been born on the low-gravity moon Eristhar and lived there for fifteen years, then she had come to Earth where gravity was hardly a consideration for her. Now she was feeling the full effects of it for the first time in her life, and she moved slowly and stiffly, breathing hard and gasping a little, as she and Matt pushed their way through the thick and tangled foliage of the jungle. She was still holding up better than he would have thought she would, so perhaps even with hyper-powers, she had gotten at least somewhat used to quadruple the accustomed gravity during her five years on Earth.

Before long, the trees and undergrowth came to an abrupt stop and Matt and Lynestra stepped out onto the golden sands of the beach. In the west, the huge disc of Delta Pavonis, reddish in the haze, was sinking below the rim of the Great Northern Sea, painting the sky in lurid streaks of orange, red, and yellow, and reflecting on the still water. The moon Eristhar was a thin glowing crescent hanging a little above it. A few thin streaks were showing in the sky as the day faded into twilight, meteor trails from the infalling dust-sized particles that were so common in this solar system.

Nothing moved on the nearly glass-like sea, no ships, no sails. The water was beginning to glow with ghostly green light from biolumines-cent seaweed just beneath the surface. The sand of the beach also glowed, a soft, tawny, lambent radiance, giving back the light it had absorbed during the day.

Behind Matt and Lynestra, the jungle was beginning to shine in a medley of pastel colors. Each flower and fruit radiated its own distinctive hue to lure the local equivalents of pollinating insects and fruit-eating birds that on Helionn were largely nocturnal. In particular, there was a common berry that grew in clusters like grapes. Each berry in a cluster was a different color, and instead of shining steadily, the berries flashed on and off in regular patterns. It was a jungle of palely glowing Christmas lights.

Only the sea's slight waves lapping heavily on the rocks and sand, and the distant, lonely cry of some animal Matt had no name for, broke the cathedral hush as night slipped across the world.

Lynestra stood at Matt's side. "This is Helionn," she whispered, her voice thick. "My home world, the world I never knew."

Suddenly she looked up at Matt with a pathetically woebegone expression, and nothing more needed to be said.

He held her. His arms were wrapped around her back and her cheek pressed against his chest. He felt the warmth of her body against his and inhaled the fragrance of her hair. For the first time in weeks, Matt felt as though his body was working properly, with all his senses intact and functioning. The oppressive numbness was gone and he felt wonderful—

Then he heard the clank of metal, the slap of leather, and the snorts of large animals. He looked up and discovered that their path back to the jungle and their ship had been cut off by an approaching troop of about half a dozen barbarian warriors mounted on small, lean horses.

Lynestra sensed his alarm and glanced up at the same moment. "The *Skogkrigare!*" she exclaimed, shocked. "The Forest Warriors," she quickly added for Matt's benefit.

They didn't have time to do anything else. In the next moment, several of the warriors leaped off their mounts and came down on Matt, throwing him to the ground. A moment after that, he was tied with thick ropes and tossed on his stomach over the back of one of the horses, just behind the rider. Lynestra was treated more decorously, with only her hands bound behind her, and she was allowed to ride upright. That was effective enough, since it meant she couldn't work the controls on her wristband to call the *Last Hope* to their rescue.

Even though he was preoccupied by his shock at being taken prisoner on a supposedly hyper-advanced planet by barbarians nobody had told him about, Matt noticed through his distraction that the horses were somewhat different from Earthly breeds, mostly glossy black, sleeker and more streamlined, with pointed noses, like oversized racing dogs.

A hundred centuries might do that.

Their lean and sinewy riders were tanned almost brown, but their long hair and beards tended to light brunette and blond, and they wore headbands and the local version of buckskins. Their trousers and moccasins made sense in a deciduous jungle with no doubt lots of thorns and brambles in a cold climate, though that gave them the look of Vikings who had landed in North America and joined the natives. While they were armed with home-made spears, bows and arrows, and even slingshots, they certainly hadn't made their knives themselves, which looked industrially manufactured and must have been obtained from more civilized regions.

The Forest Warriors trotted down the sand. Stopping at a barely noticeable hole in the foliage fronting the beach, they drew their mounts into a single-file line and entered the jungle. Watching the dazzling display of shining fruits and berries of every imaginable color pass by might have been fascinating if Matt had been sitting upright and if the circumstances had been less strained. He preferred to hang over the horse's back and stew, though the path was narrow and he was continually brushing against bushes and branches on either side.

Matt had no chance to talk to Lynestra on the way to wherever the Forest Warriors were riding, but his mind was filled with bitter thoughts about what a fine welcome to Helionn this was.

The adventure continues in Book Two: *The Arsenal of Wonders*

Afterword

After quite a few golden years in the Chicago area, the company I worked for transferred me to Phoenix. At the time, there was little choice since it was a matter of take the transfer or be laid off, and I wasn't confident I could find a new job that was at all comparable.

So I went, but I never really felt at home in Arizona. While it was an interesting place to visit, at some point you want to go home again, and home was a place I couldn't go back to. Feeling nostalgic for Chicago, I started writing about it... and strangely enough, the result was the first half of a novel about a super-hero, set in the Windy City.

It was more than homesickness. Call it an homage, a satire, a spoof, or just straight fan fiction based on a certain comic-book character during a specific phase of his long publishing history, circa 1963 to be exact, it was my attempt to come to grips with the ideas those comics had put in my head as a child (and maybe even get them *out* of my head at long last).

I had also been playing with the idea that the character should have appeared in a science-fiction pulp magazine as a regular feature, written as prose fiction with at least some rationalization of the concept's scientific impossibilities. After all, the character had been created by someone steeped in the SF pulps of the day, and later writers and editors of the comic book were also veterans of the pulps. A couple of them had even created the pulp series *Captain Future*, which showed in a general way what could have been done with the comic-book guy. There had also been a one-shot prose novel written about the character that hinted at the possibilities as well. Since the pulp-writers didn't do it, I decided to try my hand at it, though changing the names and reworking the concepts.

What resulted, however, wasn't something that could have been a regular series, but more like the last story that tied everything up. I had also been wanting to write a rip-roaring space adventure, and a return to the home planet seemed like just the way to do it. At the same time, I

179

was taking a casual interest in learning to read Swedish, and even *that* from way out of nowhere element was added to the story.

With the demands of my regular job and building up a free-lance translating business on the side, I never seemed able to finish novels I started. This one sputtered out partway through and it ended up in my literary discard box where it languished for quite a few years. Meanwhile, I eventually moved back to Chicagoland, finally scratching that particular itch.

As time marched on, what had been one decade's discard was the next decade's asset. Having begun my own publishing program, I looked through the scrap box for something that I could finish or polish and then release to the world. The Astroman fragment turned up and I gave it some consideration. It was begun on a whim and perhaps I devoted far too much time and thought to it for any potential payoff. No serious — or at least sane — publisher would probably want to take it on. It was just too derivative of some well-known and established property. But as an homage or parody that relatively few people would likely see, it was something I could put out on my own for however small an aging audience that might get the jokes. It seemed a shame to waste the considerable amount of effort I had given it, so Astroman lived again after all those years.

In the event, finishing what I had started more than doubled the size of what had been written. It proved much too long for a single volume, or at least what was practical for me to produce and market. While many people understandably don't like continued stories or cliffhangers, splitting the novel into two parts seemed like the only option. The second and final book, *The Arsenal of Wonders*, will fortunately not be long in coming.

This first book, *The Secret Citadel*, roughly covers the portion of the novel that was originally written so long ago, though some updates and additional material have been added. That splat sound you're hearing is the author slapping his forehead as he realizes that he could have put this book out a couple of years ago since that section was largely done by then.

The title of the complete novel was originally announced as *Man and Astroman*, taking off on the title of a famous play by George Bernard Shaw. It still seems like a good title to me, but as soon as I mentioned it in public, people started pointing out that some band I had never heard of had released an album with a somewhat similar title. Since the titles weren't quite identical and books and musical productions are different products, I probably would have gone ahead with my title anyway, but after the novel was split, the title had to be changed and that was one less potential headache.

Here, then, is the first book of two. After more years than I want to count, it is now finally available to the assembled multitude. It will be interesting to see if any readers under sixty understand most of the references...

—Dwight R. Decker

Movie Note

The movie Matt sees in Colorado is a bit of wish-fulfillment on my part. Around 1961, during a period of Jules Verne-mania with a lot of movies being made based on Verne's novels, the American-International movie studio announced that it would be filming an adaptation of one of his lesser known books, *Off on a Comet*. Poverty Row publisher Charlton Comics was tied into the promotion, ballyhooing on some of its comic-book covers at the time a contest in which the winners would be whisked off to Hollywood to visit the in-production movie's set. The movie was never made, however, so what the contest winners, if there were any, got instead, is a mystery.

At about the same time, another studio made a movie called *Valley of the Dragons*, based in part on *Off on a Comet*. The two movies are occasionally confused, as though *Valley of the Dragons* was the announced *Off on a Comet* movie with its name changed, but they were unrelated projects.

Off on a Comet haunted me for years, mainly because Classics Illustrated, a line of comic books that adapted famous novels into comics-format, used a cover reproduction of its adaptation of that novel in its ad for other titles in the backlist that ran in every issue. The novel sounded interplanetary from the title and I wanted very much to read it, but I could never track it down until I was well into adulthood. (It didn't help that the original French title was the not very stirring *Hector Servadac*, the name of the lead character.) Eventually I did read the book and it turned out to be one of Verne's lesser efforts, but I still would have liked to have seen the movie.

So I indulged myself by imagining that in the other world in which this story takes place, the movie *was* made, even if Matt has some trouble watching it.

—DRD

Acknowledgements

As a parody/homage, this book owes a great deal to the creators, elaborators, and embellishers of the original concept. They put ideas in my head!

So here's to them—

Jerry Siegel
Joe Shuster
Mort Weisinger
Otto Binder
Edmond Hamilton
Julius Schwartz
Wayne Boring
Curt Swan
Al Plastino
Kurt Schaffenberger
Russell Keaton
And a special honorary mention to Gardner Fox

A further expression of gratitude is owed to Alan Fletcher Bradford for the cover and to Sam Kujava for the "Broken Symmetry" illustration.

About the Author

Dwight R. Decker was born in Ohio early one frosty January morn. After keeping one step ahead of the authorities by living variously in New York, Los Angeles, and Phoenix, he currently hangs his hat in the Chicago area. Besides earning his daily crust for quite a few years as a technical writer in the telecommunications industry, he also labored on occasion as a free-lance translator of comics and science fiction. He now has the time to devote to books like this one, with more to come.

Also Available

Novels & Short Stories

by Dwight R. Decker

Coming Soon

The Arsenal of Wonders
Book Two of the Astroman Saga.

In search of a super-weapon to fight the growing menace of a renegade master scientist, Matt Dawson and Astrogirl journey through time and space to the doomed planet of Helionn, where they find unexpected allies. Then, back on Earth, it's all-out war as the Friends of Astroman strike back to avenge him.

The Napoleon of Time
In a near-infinity of alternate worlds, two college instructors from different centuries find each other in 1912 Poughkeepsie — and in her rush to join him, she *would* have to book passage on the most famous doomed ship of all time.

Rendezvous in Sarajevo
If you found out you were destined to die in World War I, wouldn't you try to stop it before it started? Even if the Paratemporal History Institute thinks changing history corrupts the data and is out to stop *you*?

Now Available

Pleistocene Junior High
   An entire middle school full of kids winds up in the Ohio of 30,000 years in the past. Meanwhile, one boy holds the key to their return in the palm of his hand. Literally.

A Moon of Their Own
   Trapped in an orbiting theme park gone mad, 15-year-old Ronn Evans and his cousins have to find a way back to Earth before they're marooned there forever.

A Dream Flying
   An ordinary boy living in Ordinaryville, he dreamed of being able to fly like Superman. Then one day, his fantasy became his destiny, and nothing was ever very ordinary again.

Some Other Shore
   Six lighthearted short stories exploring the odder reaches of fantasy and science fiction. Hänsel and Gretel made real, pseudo-time travel, mermaids (two different kinds!), bogus UFOs and a genuine alien... and something more.

In Time for Christmas
   What was behind a basement door that had been locked for seventy years? Teenager Ryan Thayer finds out — the Christmas Spirit of Past, Present, and Future, all at the same time. With two unlikely companions from his own past and future, Ryan has to solve a few mysteries, get help from a man dead for a hundred years, and straighten out the tangle of his own life. Also included: a bonus short story continuing from the novel *A Dream Flying* as well as "Christmas Carol Critique," taking a look at Christmas song lyrics that are more rhyme than reason.

Dancing with the Squirrels: Tales from Comics Fandom and Beyond
   New and old stories featuring the misadventures of comic-book fans. The fictional locales range from a small town in Illinois to Los Angeles and even England, but the strangest story of all is set in Cincinnati... and happens to be perfectly true! (And led directly to the publication of *The Crackpot* — see next page.)

185

Collections & Translations
Edited by DRD

The Crackpot and other twisted tales of greedy fans and collectors
by John E. Stockman

Between 1962 and 1979, the reclusive Mr. Stockman wrote some of the wackiest stories ever, recounting the strange antics of deranged comic-book collectors and obsessed fans of the author Edgar Rice Burroughs.

Eight of his best stories have been rescued from the crumbling mimeographed pages of the legendary (and only too aptly named) fanzine *Tales of Torment*, including many of Stockman's own illustrations. With historical notes and commentary, published by Ramble House.

Flying Fish "Prometheus"
by Vilhelm Bergsøe

Jules Verne-style science fiction first published in Danish in 1870 and now translated into English. A journey from Denmark to Central America by airship in the far future year of 1969 goes terribly wrong. With translation notes, maps, vintage illustration, and historical background.

The Speedy Journey
by Eberhard Christian Kindermann

Published in German in 1744 and never before translated, this is the first fictional account of a trip to Mars (or at least somewhere close by). Historical and literary detective work puts together an often amusing background story that has mostly been missed until now. Was Kindermann a prophetic visionary or one of the all-time great cranks — or a little of both? With notes, new and vintage illustrations, and historical essays.

Available from the usual on-line sources, including the mail-order retailer that conducts its trade under the name of a mighty South American river. For the thrifty reader reluctant to pay for ink, glue, and paper, some of the books can be obtained in the form of their pure spiritual essence as Kindle e-book editions. Check book listings for availability.

CPSIA information can be obtained
at www.ICGtesting.com
Printed in the USA
FSHW010948190719
60188FS

9 781726 049450